DANGEROUS BLOODLINES

Sequel to Flower of Heaven

JULIEN AYOTTE

Author Photo Credit: Glenn Ruga

ISBN: 1499656092

ISBN 13: 9781499656091

To my late parents, Gaston and Idalie Ayotte, and to my brothers, Gus (deceased), Bob, Jerry, and Babe, you have all been a special part of my life, and I love you all.

CHAPTER 1

Following a successful kidney transplant in Boston, King Ahmad Maurier was healthy enough to return to his beloved Middle Eastern country of Khatamori with his wife, Queen Farah, on November 28, 1988, via a brief stop in Paris. The ordeal of the operation left the king frail, but thankful the new kidney would enable him to continue to rule his country, hopefully, for years to come. His donor had died from a fall on a construction project in Boston less than three weeks earlier, and the king had been informed he had to rush from Khatamori to Boston within two days, the limited time the kidney could be preserved until the transplant took place. The young widow of the fallen twenty-seven year-old worker had agreed to the organ donation at the request of Massachusetts General Hospital. Ahmad had been added to a list of kidney transplant recipients a year earlier, and he was not about to pass up the chance to begin a new life. Otherwise, his death from kidney failure would have been imminent.

Queen Farah, born Françoise Dupont, was a native Parisian, and these few days in Paris would be the first she had spent there since her marriage to Ahmad, thirty-three years earlier. The memories of her upbringing in the City of Light were fond ones for the most part. Although she had been just a child when World War II began, she vividly remembered the loneliness, isolation and fear the German occupation of Paris brought upon the residents of her city. When 1944 brought an end to the war, she was twelve years old and began to live normally again until she finished high school in 1948.

Flashes of these events from her earlier life in Paris went through her mind as the intercontinental flight began to land at Charles DeGaulle Airport early Sunday morning. Ahmad's entourage assisted him as he left the plane in a wheelchair. Françoise stood by his side, holding his hand, as the wheelchair was led to a waiting limousine in an isolated corner of the terminal building. The Hotel George V was a thirty minute ride away, and Ahmad was visibly pale from the long flight from Boston.

The Hotel George V was an eight story hotel set just off the Champs-Élysées on Avenue George V. It is named, like the street in which it is situated, after King George V. Kaleel, Ahmad's personal and trusted servant, had reserved both Royal Suites. Both suites had private terraces overlooking the historic art deco fountain of the Three Graces. Stuffed with magnificent French antiques, these vast suites were adorned with 18th and 19thcentury fine art, glittering crystal chandeliers, and huge vases of pale pink roses perfuming the air. During the liberation of Paris, the hotel housed Dwight D. Eisenhower. Each suite was about as close as you would get to residency in a well-appointed private home where teams of decorators have lavished vast amounts of attention and money.

As the limousine left the airport, Françoise's mind began to drift into the past, some good memories, and some she wished she could forget. Thoughts of her actions years ago, in giving up her two sons for adoption, brought back vivid images of the day she went to the Orphanage of the Sisters of Mercy in Giverny, never expecting to see her sons again.

Françoise's childhood experiences, in knowing the many sights Paris held, were evident as she gazed in awe outside the limo's window, like a child's stare when she approaches the eventual destination on a vacation trip. Ahmad, though still fragile from the transplant operation, and the recent long flight, noticed the excitement in Françoise.

"You have missed your beloved Paris for all this time, haven't you, my love?" Ahmad asked with some sadness in his weak voice.

"Not until just now, Ahmad. I remember almost everything I see," Françoise responded.

"It was wrong of me to have kept you away from here for so long, but I thought you would have wanted to forget more than to remember," Ahmad added.

"I don't think I ever really forgot Paris, Ahmad. I just never talked about it. I have been very happy in Banra all these years, but being here now is peaceful to me." Françoise's eyes lit with inspiration. "You were the bright spot which took me away to begin a new life in our enchanted country. I should like to visit the Louvre tomorrow while you rest. Hopefully, Claude is still here in Paris, and it would be nice to see him again. He was like a father to me after my sons were born and gave me my first job at the museum."

Claude Gagnon, the retired Director of the Louvre, indeed still resided in Paris, but at the age of eighty-five, he was in poor health and needed constant care from nurses at the Petites Soeurs des Pauvres Nursing Home.

Françoise rose early on Monday, bid Ahmad goodbye, and headed off in a limousine to visit Claude. As she entered his room at the nursing home, his face lit up immediately as he beamed a smile which, all too soon, turned to tears of joy as they embraced and held each other, as neither wanted to let go. The last time they had held each other this way was years before when Françoise had announced her resignation of her post at the Louvre to marry her Prince Charming, Ahmad.

Françoise whispered in his ear, "I have become someone of importance to my people in Khatamori, Claude, and it is all because of you."

"Oh, my dear sweet Françoise, you have always been someone of importance to me. I have missed you dearly all of these years. After you left that spring, it took several people to do the job you could do alone. It was never the same, and I never found a replacement that could do all of the things you never seemed to have difficulty with. You have been happy with Ahmad all these years?"

"Oh, yes, Claude. Ahmad and I still feel the same love for each other now that we did when we first met. Last week in America, Ahmad received a much-needed kidney transplant, and we stopped in Paris for him to rest before heading back to Khatamori. He was gravely ill and nearly died, Claude, I don't know what I would have done without him."

"I am pleased everything went well for Ahmad. I remember him as a very polite and intelligent young man."

"Will I ever see you again?" Claude lamented.

"If not in this life, old friend, then surely in the next. There is much to do in Khatamori, Claude, and I very seldom leave the country."

No sooner were her words uttered than she noticed Claude's eyelids droop, as if he forced himself to stay awake for as long as he could. He had waited and hoped for this meeting for a long time and he feared it would end too soon and she would be gone forever. Try as he may, he fell soundly asleep, at peace with himself. Françoise watched her friend. She held his hands as tears ran down her cheeks. After several minutes, she left. She had other things she needed to do.

"Le cimitiere de Belleville on rue du Telegraphe, veiullez," she instructed the limousine driver to take her to where her parents were buried.

Louis Dupont 1893-1965
Jacqueline Dupont 1901-1975

The headstone was well-maintained, and Françoise laid two dozen roses at the foot of her parents' graves. How proud they would be, she thought, at the wonderful life she had led. Françoise remembered their attendance at her wedding, and their stay in the royal palace. They were in wonderment at all the lavishness around them, and had difficulty understanding the enormity of such wealth, let alone the fact they had never before heard of Khatamori.

However, when her father led her down the aisle and presented her to Ahmad that glorious morning, he beamed such a smile, the whole world knew how happy he was at that moment.

Françoise touched the headstone ever so gently, and bid farewell to her parents for what she believed to be the last time. She had no plans to return to Paris. There was so much still needed to be done for the women of Khatamori.

As she left the area where her parents lay, she knew there was one more thing she needed to do. Since 1951, she had sent money to the orphanage which had taken in the twin sons she had out of wedlock. The money was to have been forwarded to the families who had adopted each son, and was to be used by the adoptive parents for the child's upbringing. It was time for Françoise to revisit this horrible reminder of what she had done in a moment of panic and anxiety. The dreadful dreams she had over the years about the orphanage, and never knowing or seeing her sons, was agonizing to her. Now that she had at least been briefly reunited with one of them, and saw how wonderful he had turned out, she wished she had acted earlier, and perhaps would have met the other son well before he had been brutally murdered at the hands of one of her kingdom's assassins.

"Shall we return to the hotel, Your Highness?" asked the driver.

"No, I have one more stop first, the Orphanage of the Sisters of Mercy in Giverny. It is not far from here, I can show you the way," Françoise answered, and then whispered, "I will never forget how to get there." The drive was only ten minutes away, but to Françoise, it was the longest ten minutes of her life.

"Hello, my child, how can I help you?" a frail voice asked from the gardens adjacent to the orphanage. The facility had not changed much since 1951. Françoise approached the nun while she eyed the orphanage at the same time.

"Are you the sister in charge here?" Françoise queried.

"Yes, Madame. What can I do for you?" she answered.

"Do you keep records of the boys and girls who have been here years ago and have since been adopted?"

"It depends, Madame, how long ago you are talking about. Before and after the war, there were many little ones who had lost their parents, the records were not kept as well as we would have liked. From 1970 to now, we have a much better system. Why do you ask, Madame? We do not give out such information, unless you were the orphan yourself, or one of the natural parents. Who are you?" Sister Marie-Louise Laliberte asked.

"I am Queen Farah of Khatamori, and I have sent money to you over the years to be used for two boys who were adopted by different families."

"Farah, as in our Farah Gardens? There have been several people asking questions over the last two weeks about two boys who were here years ago. I believe I still have those records on my desk, waiting to be placed back into our files in the basement. We are talking about the same boys here, no? The gentleman who was here earlier left a very generous donation to the orphanage."

"Yes, Sister, we are talking about two boys entrusted to you in May, 1951, one named Charles Andre and the other named Robert Conrad. The mother would have been Françoise Dupont."

"Come, let us see what we can find. You will have to be extremely careful in the basement, Queen Farah. It is very old and musty down there. We only keep old records before 1960 there, because our files in the office upstairs don't have enough room. Besides, we do not get many requests to see files that old."

Sister Marie-Louise took off her work gloves and led Françoise from the garden to the door to the basement level. As she entered and descended several stairs to the lower level of this four-story building, she flipped a switch to reveal a dimly lit hallway which led past a boiler to a separate tiny room lined with four-drawer files.

The adoption process at the orphanage in the 1950s required three copies of the same information. One copy was in alphabetical order by the children's first names and dates of birth in chronological order. Sister Marie-Louise went to this file and, under 1951, pulled the sheet for Charles Andre and the separate sheet for Robert Conrad which showed Françoise Dupont as the mother.

Next, Sister Marie-Louise went to the second file which listed the children by date of adoption and the names of the new parents. Under 1951, was the record for Robert Conrad, adopted by Carl and Jeanne Elliott, rue du Temple, Paris, France. There was no sheet for Charles Andre, so Sister Marie-Louise proceeded to the next year, 1952, and there was a sheet for Charles Andre, adopted by Vito and Camille Melucci of Orvieto, Italy. Behind this sheet was another sheet for another Charles Andre, adopted by Jean-Claude and Catherine Larouche, 23 rue Bernier, Chartres, France. Sister Marie-Louise stared at the two sheets for what seemed an eternity, and suddenly turned to Françoise in amazement. "There is something wrong here," she said, "both of these sheets say the mother was Françoise Dupont, but the new parents are different on the sheets."

"What do you mean, Sister?" Françoise asked with a surprised look on her face.

"What I mean is, this isn't right, Your Highness. How can there be two different sets of parents for the same child in the same year? Look here, the dates of adoption are even different, one in September, and one in April."

In a frenzy, Sister Marie-Louise went back to the first file, and went to 1952 and began to thumb through the sheets until she suddenly stopped. There was a sheet for a Charles Andre, born in January, 1952, mother listed as Jeanine Beauregard (deceased at childbirth, no father listed), adopted April 12, 1952 by Jean-Claude and Catherine Larouche.

The third copy in the process was filed alphabetically by the name of the natural mother. Sister Marie-Louise proceeded to the 'D' tab and hurriedly thumbed to Françoise Dupont. There were three sheets, three sheets, not two, with one for Robert Conrad and two for Charles Andre. The Mother Superior scanned down the sheets to see who the nun was who signed the admission forms. Two sheets were signed by Sister Vivian and the third by Sister Paulette. Sister Vivian was a sixty-two year old who had been a nun at the orphanage for forty years and was a very capable and meticulous worker and record keeper. Sister Paulette was ninety-two years old and not as active any longer, as her memory was no longer as sharp as it could be. She was frail but still in relatively good health. Her role at the orphanage in the 1950s was that of running the kitchen with an occasional assistance to Sister Vivian when needed in the admissions area.

Sister Marie-Louise grabbed the wall phone and frantically dialed a three-digit extension. "Sister Vivian, would you come down to the basement records room, please," she said with a serious tone in her voice.

A few minutes later, Sister Vivian appeared and was introduced to Queen Farah. Sister Vivian echoed the praises of her kindness to the orphanage as all the nuns knew the history of the naming of Farah Gardens. Sister Marie-Louise showed her the three sheets from the admissions records and said to her, "What do you make of this, Sister?"

Sister Vivian studied the sheets, then remarked, "Oh, yes, I remember these two boys, the only twins we ever had at the orphanage. One was adopted just a few months after arriving here, but the other boy was only adopted a year later. I remember talking about them with Sister Paulette and felt sad when the first parents could not adopt both boys at one time; it was too much for them. When the brother was adopted the following year, we wondered if they would ever meet one day, since the first one went to an American couple while the brother went to a nice Italian couple.

"This other Charles Andre is definitely not from Françoise Dupont." As she said this, she turned to Queen Farah and, in a subdued tone, said, "I would remember what she looks like even though it was long ago. I will never forget the sadness in her eyes the day she brought the boys here." Her voice trailed off so as not to alert Sister Marie-Louise she knew Queen Farah was indeed Françoise Dupont from years ago.

"I always thought that Mademoiselle Dupont would someday want to find out where the boys were," she stated as her glance at Françoise then shifted to Sister Marie-Louise.

"What are you saying, Sister Vivian?" Françoise asked in a frenzied tone, "Are you saying that that Charles Andre, adopted by the Larouches, is not the child of Françoise Dupont?"

"Well, yes, Madame, the second sheet in 1952 was filled out incorrectly. The other cross references verify this and, besides, I remember the young Italian couple who adopted Charles Andre in 1952. One does not forget the only twins the orphanage has ever had," asserted Sister Vivian.

"Whether you suspected or not, Sisters, I am Françoise Dupont as well as Queen Farah, and these are my sons we are talking about here. Are you absolutely certain Charles was adopted by an Italian couple, and not the Larouches?" she pleaded with both Sister Marie-Louise and Sister Vivian.

"I remember you well, Madame, you have the same agony in your eyes at this moment as you had thirty-five years ago. I could never forget that look," Sister Vivian answered. "I believe Sister Paulette, who helped me on occasions, entered the wrong name on the adoptive parents because she saw these names on the sheet just before this one. She no longer handles anything to do with the records of our children, and I had hoped that such a mistake would have never happened, but it did, Madame, and for that I am so sorry."

Françoise began to sweat profusely and found herself short of breath as she heard this news. She asked Sister Marie-Louise for copies of all the records before she hurriedly climbed the stairs and exited out the same door she had entered. The limousine driver could see her run toward him as if being chased by someone. He ran to her and she gasped, "Quickly, we must get back to the hotel immediately." The driver opened the rear passenger door to let Françoise into the limousine, shut the door, then quickly hopped into the driver's seat, and left for Paris.

For Françoise, the driver could not go fast enough. As she tried to compose herself, so many things went through her mind. First, she was elated to know her other son might indeed still be alive, although his whereabouts were still unknown to her. Secondly, and at the same time, she felt the horror of Mrs. Larouche whose only son had been murdered for no apparent reason other than mistaken identity. Charles Andre Larouche had been a successful university professor in Dijon and, at the age of thirty-five, had an equally bright future to look forward to before these events occurred.

How could Mrs. Larouche understand the death of a son because of terrible recordkeeping by an elderly nun? Françoise knew that no amount of money she could offer Mrs. Larouche would be enough to bring her son back to her, the only relative she had, and cherished. Ahmad would surely have some suggestions on what to do.

The driver finally arrived at the front entrance to the hotel and Françoise rushed inside. Why is it, she thought, that when you are waiting for an elevator, it seems to stop on every floor above yours for ever so long before finally reaching the lobby level?

To get to the eighth floor of the Hotel George V, residents on that floor were required to use a special key before the eighth-floor light on the elevator panel would work. Françoise fumbled in her shoulder bag for her key, dropped it once, and nearly a second time, as she nervously entered it in the slot of the elevator controls. The number eight finally lit up, and she pushed the button several times until the elevator doors closed and the car finally began its ascent.

As she entered the Royal Suite she and Ahmad shared, Kaleel immediately noticed the excitement in her face, and rushed her way. He quietly watched over Ahmad who rested in the nearby bedroom.

"Kaleel, is Ahmad awake," she blurted.

"No, Your Highness, he is asleep I believe," Kaleel responded. "What is wrong, Your Highness?"

"Nothing is wrong, Kaleel, yet everything is wrong," she answered. "I must wake him, I have news he must hear."

She entered the bedroom area and Ahmad's eyes were open.

"I could hear you talking to Kaleel, my love. How was your day of meeting old friends?" Ahmad asked. "Were you able to see Claude?"

"Yes, yes, Ahmad, Claude is fine, frail but fine. Then I visited my parents' grave for the last time. That was nice. But, Ahmad, I had to go once more to the orphanage of years ago. I know you understand I needed to do this one last time." Françoise spoke so quickly, Ahmad had to ask her to slow down.

"Answa's men killed the wrong man, Ahmad; my son Charles is not dead, or at least as far as I know, at least not a week ago. The nuns at the orphanage gave the address for the parents of another Charles Andre who was adopted the same year as my Charles Andre. Charles Larouche was not my son, Ahmad; my son was adopted by a young Italian couple from Orvieto, Italy. I have all the papers to prove it."

"You are telling me an innocent young man who had nothing to do with you, who was never a possible successor to my throne in Khatamori, was killed because of a nun's mistake years ago?" Ahmad asked.

"Yes, Ahmad, the mistake was made by a nun years ago, and the information was given out a few weeks ago. The nuns had no reason to think there were two Charles Andres adopted in the same year. The boy the Larouches adopted was from a woman who died at childbirth in 1952."

"You know, Françoise, Answa has three sons, and they are surely furious at his death a few days ago. My trusted cousin was not so loyal to me after all, and I am not certain this threat to kill me or your sons is over yet, and I will not know until I get a chance to meet with his sons when we return to Banra," uttered Ahmad with a worried look on his face. "In the meantime, we need to find this mysterious son of yours, wherever he may be. Perhaps your Father Merrill is needed for help again, since he is his son too," he added.

* * *

The telephone at St. Michael's in Lincoln, Rhode Island, rang at eleven o'clock in the evening, not a good sign in the rectory of a Catholic church. Usually, it ended up being a call from the local hospital to announce the need for a priest to issue the last rites to a dying patient, or where the relative of an accident victim has requested consolation if the accident was considered life-threatening. This call was different, although still considered urgent, as the operator from the Hotel George V asked to speak to Fr. Richard Merrill.

"This is Fr. Merrill," a tired and half-asleep response followed. "Who is this, please?" he asked.

"This is the operator from the Hotel George V. Father, can you hold please for Queen Farah?" the voice on the other end asked.

"Yes, of course," Fr. Merrill yelled into the phone, as if he needed to shout because the call was from so far away.

"Richard, this is Françoise, forgive me for calling you at this time. I just now realized how late it is in the United States, while it is five o'clock in the morning here. I have some news that cannot wait. While Ahmad and I stopped in Paris, for him to rest before our journey back to Khatamori, I visited the orphanage in Giverny because that is where all my trouble seemed to begin those many years ago," she said in a rush.

"Richard,' she cried, "Charles Andre was not murdered in Dijon. That person was not our son. The orphanage had made a mistake in their record. He was born from a different woman, a mother who died at childbirth in 1952. Our son, also Charles Andre, was adopted by an Italian couple, and he certainly may be very much alive today, and living somewhere in Italy. Can you help with this? I know it sounds bizarre, but it is true. Our other son may be alive, and we need to find him.

Ahmad has also told me he cannot be certain the threat on his life, or on the boys' lives, is over. Talon's sons may seek revenge for their father's death, even though he was the evil person who sought to create unrest in Khatamori."

Fr. Dick shook his head, as if trying to unravel what he heard. Was this just a bad dream, an awful prankster pulling a fast one on him at this late hour? He sat there in complete silence for nearly a minute before he was able to fathom a response.

"Françoise, are you certain of this? Are you saying that our other son was not the one murdered in Dijon?" he carefully repeated.

"Yes, Richard, our real son was adopted by Vito and Camille Melucci from Orvieto, Italy. Can you still get your people to help find him for us?" she pleaded.

"Ahmad has said we will pay whatever it costs to locate him, and make sure he is not harmed. He also asked if you would get Mr. Esten to watch Bob in Medway, just in case there are other evildoers from Answa's side still out there. There may be nothing, but Ahmad wants to talk to Answa's three sons first to know for certain they do not seek revenge for their father's death."

"Write this fax number down, four zero one, three seven five, zero two one zero, that is my fax number. Send me all the information you have. Have the hotel operator do it right away."

Fr. Merrill asked Françoise to include in the fax where she could be reached, and a number to reach her in Banra. Françoise agreed to arrange for all this information to be sent to Fr. Dick, and again apologized for calling at such a late hour.

"Are you kidding me, Françoise? Instead of mourning the death of a son I never met, I now have a chance to make things right again. I hope that Bob gives me a second chance to make things right also."

This would be a long night for Fr. Dick. He put on his bathrobe, and quietly went from his bedroom quarters to the downstairs rectory office where the fax machine was located. He did not want to wake the housekeeper, so he closed the office door as he turned on the fax machine, and waited anxiously for it to signal an incoming set of documents. The wait was torturous, as the fax machine bellowed nothing but a deafening silence. Then, suddenly, the whirring sound started, and the machine began to spit out page, after page, after page.

CHAPTER 2

Harry Esten, an FBI agent in Providence, busily attempted to complete the paperwork after the successful elimination of an assassination attempt on the lives of a foreign ruler in Boston and a son of the ruler's wife in Medway, Massachusetts. Harry, recuperating from a bullet wound in the left shoulder, found that trying to do paperwork with the use of only one hand was virtually impossible. Esten had fatally shot Answa Talon, an assassin, as Talon tried to escape pursuit by Harry and other policemen in the Massachusetts General Hospital parking garage adjacent to the hospital laundry. Harry's accurate shots pierced the side window and directly hit Talon in the shoulder, causing him to crash the confiscated laundry van into the parking garage wall, bursting it into flames upon contact. Talon was rushed into the emergency room operating area but never regained consciousness. Whether the cause of death was from Harry's gunshots or the subsequent burns to Talon's body, no one knew for certain, nor did anyone really care.

Harry had been informed by the doctors at Mass. General that he would recover completely from his flesh wounds. The Bureau had ordered him to take a few weeks off to mend his body and also to carefully document the incidences leading to the confrontation with Talon.

The case had included fake Interpol agents, disguised assailants, stolen aircraft, a murder in Dijon, France, and another attempted assassination in Medway, all related to an incident which occurred over thirty-five years earlier.

This had been the highlight in the Rhode Island FBI office, normally mired in white-collar cases in the area, or the continued pursuit of mafia criminals. Providence had been identified years earlier as the mafia capital of New England, and the local mob boss was as well-known as the governor or the ever-popular mayor of Providence.

Harry, at age forty-seven, had been married to his high school sweetheart, but she had died of complications from leukemia in 1985. They had lived in a lovely cottage along the Narragansett coast, in the southern part of Rhode Island. Harry found the loneliness here troubling, especially in these winter periods where the coastline was virtually abandoned by the summer residents who had long gone back home for the holidays. Such was the case with the neighbors on each side of Harry, whose summer homes were locked up and empty.

In late November, Harry's recuperation therapy included long walks on the beach with his faithful golden retriever, Duke. Harry would toss a rubber ball, and Duke would retrieve it each time until the game ran out its welcome after about a dozen tosses. As he petted Duke gently after his last retrieval, he bent down and whispered in his ear, "God, how I miss Lucy." For nearly twenty years, he would gladly drive the forty-five minute commute to Providence, always anxious to see Lucy's captivating smile when he walked through the door each night, except that night three years ago, when he had entered, and there was nothing but silence throughout the house. Harry's yells to Lucy were not answered. He found her unconscious on their upstairs bedroom floor, her pulse thready as she lay motionless. Once the rescue team revived her, and her vital signs were stable enough to move her, the EMTs transported her to Kent County Hospital. The emergency room doctors kept her vitals stable until Lucy's doctor, Dr. Stanley Restivo, arrived and immediately ordered all kinds of blood tests and x-rays as he was puzzled at this sudden occurrence in Lucy's health. She had experienced no symptoms of any ailment or disease in her annual physical just three months earlier.

When the diagnosis pointed clearly to a lymphoma, leukemia appeared to be the cause. The technical term was acute lymphoblastic leukemia, a rare but highly fatal disease which was treated with aggressive chemotherapy.

Exactly a year later, she died from the illness, leaving Harry in a state of confusion as to what his life had suddenly become. Lucy had been an elementary school teacher in the Wakefield Public School System for twenty years, and her funeral was a standing room only affair with all the relatives and friends saddened by her death. It took Harry several months before he was able to return to the cottage. He would find himself either working late at the Providence Bureau and checking in at a local hotel for the night, or, on many nights, he would merely sleep on the sofa in his office. The Bureau had shower facilities in the locker room for agents and Harry spent nearly his entire time living out of this office.

Finally, he decided one weekend to go back to Narragansett and attempt to begin his life again, although the memories of Lucy's smiling face were around every corner. That was when he got Duke from the local dog pound. He knew he needed someone and, for now, Duke would do.

The chill in the air, on this late November day, told Harry it was time to get back to the cottage and build a fire in the wood-burning stove. Duke had not experienced the warmth and comfort of a wood-burning stove yet, and Harry was anxious to see how he reacted.

As they climbed the dunes toward the back door of the cottage, Harry noticed movement inside the house. He quickly drew his revolver and cautiously headed toward the house, about two hundred feet ahead. The figure inside the house spotted Harry, swung the screen door open, knocked it out from its hinges, and began to fire from an automatic weapon. The bullets squirted up sand as they narrowly missed Harry. Harry retreated quickly and dove behind a nearby dune. He then crawled to the far end of the dune to get a look at the assailant from another vantage point. The screech sound of tires got Harry to his feet and running to the front of the house via the side yard, adjacent to his neighbor's vacant cottage. As the vehicle sped away, all Harry could do was glimpse at the color and make of the van, a blue Chrysler Town & Country.

Harry holstered his revolver and made his way toward the rear door of the cottage. He yelled for Duke but there was no response. Duke would always bark when called by Harry, so he ran toward the beach as he yelled out his name. Suddenly he noticed a trail of blood in the sand and he quickly followed it. Duke was lying motionless in the sand, several bullet holes in his golden fur body. Duke was dead.

Harry headed back to the house, eyes ablaze at what had just happened, and reached for a beach towel still draped over the back deck. The towel had probably been there for a month. Harry didn't remember, and he didn't care. He wrapped it around Duke with his only good arm, then carried his limp body and gently placed him on one of the recliners on the deck. Then Harry headed for the back door, his destination, the wall phone in the kitchen.

After he threw the screen door out of the way and no sooner than he turned the door handle, he heard a clicking sound above the door. Instinctively, he ran off the deck and dove into the sand. The force of the explosion nearly propelled him further. Fortunately only the screen door managed to land on him.

The house was in flames and, with the heating and cooling system being natural gas, Harry realized the cottage would not be saved. He slowly rose, still dazed and bleeding from the head, arms, and legs, and made his way to the phone in his car. He first called the fire department, then the Narragansett police before he passed out in the passenger seat of the car. This event was totally unexpected and, before losing consciousness, Harry could only wonder what had just happened.

* * *

Harry woke up in the intensive care unit at Kent County Hospital with an IV tube connected to his arm, various beeping monitors, and most of his body covered in bandages. The resident physician stood over Harry and spoke soothingly. "Welcome back, Mr. Esten, my name is Doctor Gorman. You gave us quite a scare, you know. You've been out for twenty-four hours. You were bleeding from pieces of wood embedded in your scalp, arms, and legs, but we seem to have patched you up okay, and fortunately, you have no burns anywhere. We have sutured you in a few places and your previous gunshot wound seems to be okay as well. How does your head feel?"

"Like I've just been run over by a bus. My left side is throbbing like crazy, I don't remember much of anything," Harry responded.

"The throbbing is mostly noise impact from the explosion and should go away in a day or so. We are giving you something to help that along. Are you alert enough to talk to the police? They've been waiting outside for some time now."

"Are you talking about the Narragansett police or my FBI office in Providence?" Harry asked.

"Are you sure you gave me something for this throbbing in my head?"

"We just did, Mr. Esten, I'll tell the officers to come in but only for a few minutes. What you need now is rest, not anything to further tax your mind."

"Hello, Harry, nice to see you awake again," Frank Cabral stated. Frank was the agent in charge of the Providence FBI Bureau and a close friend of Harry's for over twenty years.

"Harry, this is Chief Laplante from the Narragansett Police, and one of his detectives, Laura Broadbent."

"This note was delivered to our offices yesterday and it was addressed to you, Harry. It was left at the front desk by a thirteen year old kid who said he was given ten dollars if he just dropped it off at the front desk. The guy who paid the kid was wearing a hooded sweatshirt and sunglasses and spoke funny the kid said. He walked away once the kid entered our building."

Harry took the note out of the envelope. It said,

AN EYE FOR AN EYE,
THE WORST IS YET TO COME.

"Can you tell me anything about the explosion, Harry?"

"I remember coming back from a walk on the beach with Duke and noticed somebody in my house through the sliding doors off the kitchen. As I started to make a beeline for the house, some guy burst out my back door and opened fire toward me with an automatic rifle. I was lucky enough to duck behind a dune but Duke wasn't so lucky. After I heard the tires from his van screech out in front of the house, I chased him but only got a glimpse of his vehicle, a blue Town & Country van. So I raced back to the back door of the house to call you guys. When I turned the knob on the door, I heard a loud click. I'd know that sound anywhere from the academy training. It was the noise a detonator makes right before an explosion occurs. The last thing I remember is calling the fire department from my car."

"The fire department found parts of the detonator in the rubble, a foreign make according to your office's lab guys," Chief Laplante chimed in. "You really must have pissed off somebody, Harry, if they went to all this trouble."

"Harry, do you think this has anything to do with the Boston case you were just working on?" Cabral asked. "Maybe this Talon guy has friends out to get revenge for taking him out at Mass. General?"

"I don't know, Frank, maybe. Doesn't sound like any other case I've been working on lately, unless it's somebody I sent up some time ago and he's out of prison now."

Harry had been instrumental in the arrest of many criminals over the years, but none he could recall who would suddenly pop up with this type of vendetta. He asked Frank to have someone look at his arrest records for the last ten years to see if anything came up, a recent parolee, someone who may have threatened him harm before, anything at all.

"By the way, your buddy, Jim Howard, has been trying to reach you. He even stopped by the office yesterday and we told him you were down here at the beach," Frank added. Jim was an old Army buddy from the Vietnam days, and was recently involved with Harry on the Middle East case in Boston.

"I told him I'd pass along that he stopped by, since I didn't want to give out your phone number here to anyone."

"Hmm, I wonder what that's all about? I told him I was going to take some time off because of the shoulder wound just a few days ago," Harry wondered. "Can you give me his number, Frank? I'll call him later this week. Was there anything salvageable in the house? I had my briefcase and all my contacts back at the house, and Lucy's pictures, and....," as his mind drifted off for a moment.

"I'm afraid not, Mr. Esten," Laura Broadbent spoke up. "The house was blown to bits from the gas explosion. It's nothing but a pile of ashes right now. We'll start looking into this blue Town & Country you mentioned. Maybe somebody in your neighborhood remembers seeing it."

"While you're at it, Laura, check with the car rentals from here to Boston and to Hartford too, there can't be too many of those to rent if the van wasn't local," Harry added.

Laura was a veteran policewoman in her mid-forties. She had worked her way up the ranks in the Narragansett police, and she had recently been promoted to detective rank because of her high score on the written test given to candidates for the vacant position. She was single and the daughter of the former police chief in Newport, whose recommendation for a spot on the Narragansett force was originally seen by others as a favor between two police chiefs. Laura's performance on the job, however, proved all the critics wrong as her police record was flawless. She was intelligent but all business. Her manly tough behavior would have you believe she never got too social with any of her male partners on the force.

"Laura's my best detective, Harry, even though she's fairly new to the job," echoed Laplante, "anything she can do to help, she's at your disposal."

"Thanks, Chief. I appreciate the help. First, I've got to get out of here and find a place to stay for a while, until I decide what to do. I'm going to need some clothes too, Frank, I don't think I kept much back in my locker in Providence," Harry added.

"Um, I don't know how you'll take this, Mr. Esten, but I live on Fairway Lane in Bonnet Shores. It's not a big house, but I've got a spare bedroom and bathroom you can use for a while if you want. I'm mostly either at the station or on other cases all day long, and it's pretty quiet around there, as you know, at this time of the year. Just a thought," Laura mentioned.

"Are you serious? How do you know I'm not a serial killer or a sex fiend?" Harry was taken aback by her generous offer.

"Let's just say, I'll take my chances, Mr. Esten, based on what I've heard about you so far," she continued.

"Okay, then, it's a deal. I'll pay you whatever you feel is right. By the way, it's Harry, cut out this Mr. Esten crap, that was my father."

"Great Mr....., uh, Harry, I'll get the place in good shape. Just let me know when you'll be released here and I can pick you up. In the meantime, we'll see to it that your car is brought to my house before you get there. You won't be doing much driving for a while anyway."

"That's what you think, Laura. You'll be amazed what I can do with just one arm right now," Harry smiled at Laura.

Dr. Gorman entered the room and was about to tell everyone to leave so Harry could rest, when in came Jim Howard. The Providence Journal featured an article that morning about the explosion at Harry's home, and Jim guessed Kent County would be the logical place to find Harry.

"Glad to see you're alive, Harry, my boy. Boy do I have news for you," Jim cheerily said. Oblivious to Harry's bandaged body and head, he charged on. "You won't believe this."

Jim Howard waited for Chief Laplante, Laura, and Frank Cabral to leave Harry's hospital room before he elaborated.

When they vacated Harry's room, Jim finally spoke.

"Bob Elliott's twin brother wasn't killed in Dijon last week by Talon's people. Apparently the orphanage gave out the wrong information on the brother and another guy was killed by mistake. I got a call from Fr. Merrill and he said the real brother of Bob Elliott is some Italian guy who was adopted by a couple from Orvieto, Italy. Fr. Merrill told me that King Ahmad and Françoise would like our help in finding the guy. The king is not convinced that Talon's sons won't seek revenge for the death of their father, even though he was the aggressor in all of this. Anyway, I know this isn't an FBI case, but the king was specifically insistent on asking you to get involved in the search."

"Jim," Harry replied, "I don't think this is over by a longshot. Someone blew up my house, and this note was sent to my office yesterday."

Jim scanned the brief note and looked up at Harry in amazement. "I think you'd better lay low for a while, this sounds like more of the Talon clan at work. These guys don't quit, do they?" Jim said.

"The only way I can get involved in this is by telling my boss that I suspect the Middle East assailant has more people still in the States, and that the threat is now on me also because I was responsible for Talon's death."

"What do you want me to tell Fr. Merrill, Harry? I told him I'd get back to him to let him know what we were going to do."

"Right now I've got nothing left. My house, my dog, they're all gone. I've got nothing to lose if I decide to get involved in this. Since Lucy died, I've been living in a fog for two years. Now that the house we shared is gone, I don't even have memories to look at. Those bastards, if it's the Arabs, are going to have to kill me now to stop me from working on this. Nobody blows up my house and takes shots at me for doing my job, Jim, nobody.

Tell Fr. Merrill we'll be in touch soon. Now get out of here. I need to get some rest if I'm going to get out of here in the next couple of days. I'll be staying at Bonnet Shores. Give me the best number to reach you," Harry went on as he handed Laura Broadbent's card with her phone number and address on it. She had scribbled 56 Fairway Lane on the back of the card.

"I think I'm about to take an extended leave from the Bureau for health reasons," he added.

"You know what, Harry, I hate to see a friend of mine go it alone on this, so I'm in," Jim answered. Harry just smiled.

Harry was tired of talking and his head ached more than ever. *When is that pain killer going to kick in*, he wondered. As Jim headed for the door, Dr. Gorman reappeared. Somehow, getting more rest didn't seem to be a priority any more. He was suddenly more interested on getting out of the hospital.

Dr. Gorman agreed to release Harry the next day, so long as he had someone to care for him while he continued his recovery from all the superficial wounds and the head trauma from the explosion. Gorman obviously did not realize who he dealt with in Harry Esten. Harry had to agree to allow a visiting nurse to check in on him a few times a week to change the dressings on his cuts and bruises, if necessary, and to report back to Gorman on his progress in fourteen days. Somehow Dr. Gorman felt uneasy Harry would be satisfied with a slow but steady recovery. It would take more than a visiting nurse to hold him back from the business he needed to attend.

Dr. Gorman could see the weariness in Harry's eyes from all this traffic and ordered him to get some rest. Once Dr. Gorman had left the room, Harry could hear the deafening sound of silence. Everything that was going on, sort of hit him. As he lay on his back and looked up at the ceiling, all he could do was cry.

CHAPTER 3

Harry Esten was born in December of 1940 on Bloss Street in Rochester, New York. Harry was the third son of five boys of Arthur and Catherine Esten. His two older brothers, George and Jake, were eight and five years older than him. His younger brothers were Phil and Mike, just a year and two years younger than Harry. Their father was a public accountant, who had graduated from Northeastern University in 1932 with a law degree. Rather than take the bar exam and practice law, Arthur preferred taxes and went to work for the local IRS office in Rochester.

In 1950, after nearly eighteen years working for the government, he had decided to open up his own tax and accounting practice in the local area. Businesses were booming after the war and the demand for his services was obvious to him. With five boys to educate and feed, the IRS salary was just not enough to enable the Estens the comfort and income necessary at that time. Catherine had her hands full as a full-time mother of five super-active boys. The Esten household was never quiet! Years later, Harry could be heard telling friends at a cookout in Narragansett how his father had come home one night and told his mother that a neighbor down the street had five boys in a row too but that their sixth child had been a girl. At the time, Harry didn't understand his mother's reply to his father, "Arthur, you stay away from me!"

Harry's childhood was filled with wonderful memories, from his Little League Baseball play all the way to his Boy Scout days and his high school days at Our Lady of Mercy High School. Following graduation in 1958, he attended the University of Rochester, majored in accounting. The last three years of college were spent living in Sigma Chi Fraternity where he first met Lucy, a shy and attractive education student whose goal was to teach elementary school children. She had a flair for trivia and was the person everyone went to for answers. The two had met at a frat party, each there with someone else, and it didn't take long for the chemistry to do the rest.

Following graduation, the Army had plans of its own for Harry. He had participated in the Reserve Officers Training Corps or ROTC as it was called on campus, and once he received his commission as a second lieutenant, he needed to spend at least two years of active duty. He would be assigned for training at Ft. Belvoir in Virginia and then receive his orders for the remainder of his first two years in the military. Lucy and Harry were married early that summer in 1958 and she accompanied him to Virginia.

Once Harry had completed basic training, he received his orders of duty....Vietnam. This is when Harry met Jim Howard who served in the same unit under Major Jack Bumpus, a career soldier. While Harry came home from his tour of duty unharmed, the memories of the horrible ordeal would stay with him for life. Why he chose to apply to the FBI Academy as an agent was a puzzle that Lucy could never solve.

Harry had not seen Jim much in recent years, and their involvement in the Boston case with the Middle East ruler gave them a chance to catch up on what had transpired over the years since they both left the military, and both wished they had gotten together more often.

On Monday morning, Harry was released from Kent County Hospital and Laura Broadbent was there at curbside in her unmarked police car to transport her new houseguest to Bonnet Shores. Harry was still quite sore from the effects of the blast and some of the black and blue marks were beginning to turn yellowish, a sure sign that the wounds were healing. The stitches in his forehead and leg were to be removed by Dr. Gorman in ten days he told Laura.

As they approached 56 Fairway Lane, Harry noticed the area was as desolate as his area was just a few miles away. There is always a strange feeling about living in an area with homes just like yours and with almost all of them empty except yours, and the silence can be unbearable. For now, his head needed the peace and quiet afforded by this type of location. Laura's cottage was as she had described, nothing exquisite, just a simple-looking five-room ranch with a driveway but no garage, and a back yard abutted to someone else's back yard from the next street over. The white house with black shutters sat on nicely landscaped grounds, Harry noticed, as they headed for the kitchen door at the side of the house.

"Well, Harry, here we are, I told you it wasn't fancy, but it's clean, quiet, and a place to recuperate. The TV room is just past the kitchen on your right. Your bedroom is the next door on the same side with a connecting bathroom. My room is on the left. Towels are in this closet, and there is a shower and tub in the bathroom. I can pick up some toiletries for you on my way home tonight," Laura explained. "Coffee pot and coffee are on the kitchen counter and I've got some beer, wine, and soda in the refrigerator.

"Sounds good to me, Laura, I can't thank you enough for doing this. The thought of staying in a motel really wasn't something I was looking forward to."

"I have to get back to the station. The chief may have a lead on that van you mentioned. We're trying to track down the rental agency in Putnam. Most of their business is during the tourist season, so they're not always answering the phone at this time of year. One of your neighbors thought the van had Connecticut plates. I might need to drive out there this afternoon. How about pizza and salad tonight? I can pick one up on the way home around five o'clock."

"Mind if I use your phone to call my office later on? They'll reimburse you for any long distance charges. Oh, and can you pick up a Journal for me too, that way I can start checking out apartments in the area over the next few days?" Harry asked.

No sooner than Laura was out the door and off in her car, Harry wasn't too steady on his feet yet and decided to watch TV, maybe with a cool drink. After checking out the beer and wine, he grabbed a Diet Coke and headed for the sofa in the den. Once he turned on the set, it took him all of thirty seconds before he dozed off. At two p.m., he awoke and took a sip from the unused Diet Coke, got up and headed for the wall phone in the kitchen.

Barbara D'Angelo, Harry's assistant, answered the call and knew he would need clothes, lots of clothes. Harry's home owner's policy would pay for anything he needed, all part of his coverage for personal property. Harry rattled off shirts, pants, underwear, undershirts, sweaters, belts, shoes and Barbara stated she would deliver them all later in the afternoon at the Fairway Lane address. This is weird, Harry thought, he never realized how much he needed in basic outfits when suddenly all of his clothes and personal belongings were taken from him in one fell swoop. "I don't think I'll ever take this for granted again," he muttered to himself. There would be a new checkbook needed from the bank, replacement credit cards, licenses, medical cards, and other things he hadn't thought of yet. *One at a time, I'll replace them all in due time.*

His next call was to Jim Howard at Continental Life to find out what was happening with the news about Bob Elliott's twin brother.

"Hi, Harry, hope you're feeling better. Fr. Merrill was happy to hear that we would help him on this, but he was sorry to hear about your tragedy. When I called him, at first all he could talk about was the senseless death of Charles Larouche, a complete stranger who actually was murdered because the wrong information was given out by the orphanage."

"Makes you wonder how long any of us have on this earth, doesn't it, Jim?" Harry replied. "What's the first step, do we use your contact in Paris or do you have someone in Italy that we can use to find this kid?"

"No, Harry, Karl Pelland doesn't leave France too often, and I already talked to him yesterday after I left your hospital room. It sounded like more excitement than he wanted. He almost lost his job at the American embassy in Paris when he tracked this Larouche guy in Dijon. Are you up to flying any time soon?" Jim asked.

"Well, I do have a guy in Rome we use once in a while. I'll call him and see what he can find out. Then we can fly over there if we have to. With any luck, this Melucci guy won't be too hard to find," Harry answered.

"Let's meet first with Fr. Merrill and pick up a copy of those records faxed from the orphanage. I want to make sure we don't jeopardize another person, and that he really is Carlo Melucci. If they can screw up the first time, there's no guarantee they didn't mess it up again."

"How about I pick you up tomorrow at ten? I don't think you're in a position to drive yet, are you?" Jim chimed in.

"Do you need directions?"

"Nope, I used to go to Bonnet Shores when I was in school at URI and I know where Fairway Lane is," Jim answered.

"There's only one house on Fairway Lane with a car in the driveway, everybody else is gone for the winter," Harry replied.

Harry ended the conversation and headed back to the kitchen counter with a sudden urge for a cup of coffee. While he was making a fresh pot, he realized he still had an open can of soda on the table in the den. *I'll save the soda for the pizza when Laura comes home. Right now a hot cup of coffee is what I feel like having.*

At around four, Barbara arrived with four large shopping bags. She had shopped for three hours earlier in the day, and had every conceivable item of clothing she had seen Harry wear at one time or another. She also brought in a box with all of Harry's stuff from his locker at the office. Harry thanked her and told her that, once he checked to see what else he needed, he would call her again in a day or so.

A short while later, Laura arrived home with a pizza box and two bags, one with a large plastic container of salad and the other with a bottle of Sangiovese wine. She smiled when she spotted Harry, "So how'd your day go?"

"So far, so good. I watched some TV, made a few calls, my secretary brought over a whole new wardrobe which I put in my room, and I even made myself a cup of coffee and a couple of pieces of toast. How about you? Did you find out anything from that auto rental in Connecticut?"

"You know, Harry, I must be in the wrong business. Those people work when they feel like it at this time of year. I was scheduled to meet the dealer at eleven o'clock this morning and when I got there, the woman behind the counter was bullshitting on the phone as if I didn't even exist. I finally got her attention though."

"How did you do that?"

"I hung up the phone right in front of her. She didn't like that too much. I asked her where the owner was since I had an eleven o'clock appointment and it was already nearly eleven thirty. She said he was never on time for appointments, and sometimes never even showed up for them. I told her to get him on the phone and tell him I would have the Connecticut police issue him with an obstruction of justice charge in a criminal investigation if he didn't get his butt over there right now."

There was something infinitely appealing to Harry in how Laura could relate information. She looked very convincing in the way she handled herself in situations demanding stern measures to get what she was after. No small town auto dealer was going to treat her like some used-car vendor. She was an officer of the law and had earned the right to be respected as such. She led the charge in women police officers gaining more respect than they had been given ever before. As the daughter of a police chief herself, she knew how difficult it was for law enforcement officers to get information from citizens who seemed indifferent when asked to reveal information they had.

Laura continued relating to Harry about her episode with such an indifferent citizen. However, using her persuasive powers, Laura informed the receptionist, "If you ignore me, you will be responsible for withholding information necessary in an investigation. Why are people so reluctant to cooperate with the police, almost as if they have something to hide, some violation that may surface if they divulge too much?

"The late arrival of the auto dealer seemed to make him react that much faster when I asked him about the Town and Country van. One had been rented two days earlier, replacing a sedan that was turned in and had been from the New York location of the same dealership. The license photo with the rental agreement was of Steven Miller from New York City. The van has not been returned yet. I ran the license through the DMV in New York and noticed that no such person had been issued that license and that it was a fraud. Here's the photo."

Harry glanced at it and found nothing striking about the photo except for the small serpent's tattoo on the neck of the unknown man. Harry told Laura "I'll have the Bureau run the photo through their international data base and also the files of other foreign agencies like British Intelligence and Interpol. I'll also send an agent to the Connecticut dealer to see if there were fingerprints in the car that had been turned in for the van."

He set the photo aside. For now he was hungry and the aroma of pepperoni from the pizza easily got him to sit down at the kitchen table.

While Laura took off her coat, removed her scarf, and unbuckled her gun holster and placed it on a hallway table, Harry asked her where she kept her wine bottle opener, even though he knew that trying to open a wine bottle using only one arm was impossible. Laura quickly smiled and said that she would take care of it in a minute but first needed to freshen up before she joined him at the table.

A few minutes passed, and the smell of food drove Harry crazy. He had not realized just how hungry he was until he remembered he had eaten only two lousy pieces of toast since he was discharged from the hospital earlier that morning. He rose from the table and began to head toward Laura's bedroom to tell her to hurry up, but realized how rude and foolish this would seem. After all, this woman was giving him a place to stay and even was about to feed him. He wasn't about to overstep his welcome by doing something stupid.

As he turned to head back to the kitchen, he could see the bedroom door was only half-closed. Apparently Laura had not closed it completely after returning from the bathroom adjacent to her room. When you live alone, these things do not seem overly very important to you. When you have someone else in the house, the rules of privacy are not the same. Laura had briefly forgotten she had a guest in the house.

Harry could see Laura through the opening in the door as she combed her long brown hair, dressed only in her black bra and panties. Harry's initial reaction was to turn away, but he could not keep his eyes from returning to the view from the partially open door. Suddenly, as if by instinct, Laura turned and realized the door was partially open and she moved to close it. Harry quickly rushed around the corner of the hallway wall near the kitchen, and hoped Laura had not seen. He dashed back to his seat in the kitchen, embarrassed at his actions. A few minutes later, Laura appeared in jeans and a sweatshirt with her hair down as Harry had seen.

"Well, I see you let your hair down. Very nice. Now, excuse me for being so bold but, all of a sudden I'm starved," Harry blurted out.

"How about you nuke the pizza for about a minute or two while I open this bottle of wine and get some bowls for the salad?"

"Terrific, Laura, but I feel helpless. It's not that I haven't lived by myself for a few years too, it's just that this doggone arm is a real nuisance trying to do anything you normally do with both arms and hands."

"R and R, Harry, that's what the doctor ordered and that's what you need right now. Nothing's so important that it can't wait."

"I wish that were true all the time, Laura, but I thought I wrapped up a case a week ago and now it looks like it's far from over. I'll tell you about it over dinner."

The beep from the microwave and the pop of the wine cork occurred almost simultaneously, and they began to chat as they chowed down salad and pizza after tipping their wine glasses. Harry related the part about the wrong person being murdered in France, and that the real target was still out there somewhere. "If the FBI and the Middle Eastern royal couple knew about it, it wouldn't be a stretch to believe that others were likely aware as well. So it is indeed important to act quickly to possibly prevent another death."

Laura listened to every word that Harry spoke and the more she heard, the more she realized Harry Esten was a good person. He took his job seriously, just as she did, and was committed to seeing this case to the very end. She admired his compassion for Queen Farah whose mistake years earlier could now be forgiven if she was given a second chance to be a real mother to sons she had blindly given up. Why hadn't she ever met someone like Harry before, she thought.

"I'm taking some time off from the Bureau. I have to help this priest, the father of this guy we're looking for. He didn't even know he was a father until two weeks ago. And just when he's done mourning for a murdered son he never knew, he finds out the murdered Frenchman wasn't his son after all, and his real son may still be alive somewhere out there. It's bad enough the son he did meet in Medway won't give him the time of day. I'm not so sure that if he had known about the kids thirty-five years ago, that he would have given them up so quickly. Even the queen has suffered a lifetime of torment over her decision."

"But Harry, you're not physically well enough to do much for a while. Can't you let this Jim Howard friend of yours get on it for now?"

"No, Laura, he doesn't have the experience or the connections to do much on his own. His only contact was a guy in Paris who was able to get information in France. The last whereabouts on this Melucci guy is Italy, and rather than waste time going with outsiders, we need to use my people to work with the Italians on this. Jim's picking me up tomorrow morning, and we're going to meet Fr. Merrill in Lincoln to try to lay out a plan. After that, I don't know yet."

Laura gently reached across the table and laid her hand on Harry's arm. "Whatever I can do, I'm here," she uttered.

"I may take you up on that. I might need all the help I can get. Even with all my years with the Bureau, doing an international search isn't my strongpoint." Harry's warm smile met Laura's and their relationship appeared to suddenly take a new direction. Harry never did finish the Diet Coke in the den. He started to feel the weight of the impending ordeal he was about to undertake and felt exhausted at all the day's activities. He decided to go to bed while Laura cleaned up after the meal and mentioned that she would read the Journal to catch up on what else happened in the news. She motioned to Harry that she would leave the paper in the den for him to look through as he had requested earlier that day.

While Harry took off his shoes, slipped off his trousers and sweatshirt, and prepared himself for bed, he could hear motion in the adjacent bathroom. It sounded like the shower had just been turned on. He peeked out of his bedroom door to see if Laura's bathroom door was closed, and it was. As he went back to his bed and laid down, thoughts of Laura were now in his mind and he became aroused until he drifted off to sleep a short while later.

CHAPTER 4

Orvieto, Italy, placed in the heart of Umbria, between Lazio and Tuscany and fifty miles south of Florence, sits atop a large butte of volcanic ash. The site of the city is surrounded by cliffs, and defensive walls, built from the same volcanic ash. The city's history goes as far back as the third century B.C., ruled by the Roman Empire. Finally in the tenth century, it began to rule itself through various governors. Its relationship with past popes is intimate, and the Catholic Church did not relinquish its strong hold on Orvieto until 1860, when it was annexed to Italy.

Vito Melucci was born in Orvieto in 1923, the son of a vineyard owner whose white wine was produced in the fields below the volcanic rock. The wine from Orvieto was regularly provided to the tables of the prelates and noblemen of Rome as far back as 1450. The Melucci family had a long history of producing white wine in this region of Umbria on the shore of nearby Lake Bolsena and Vito knew the importance of the heritage he was expected to continue.

He was the only son of Vincenze and Maria Melucci and, therefore, was destined to someday take over the vineyard. His two older sisters, Lucia and Sophia, were also actively involved in the wine making operation. Lucia, at age nineteen, had expressed an interest in becoming a doctor and the nearest medical school facility was in Florence. Vincenze wasn't quite certain of her ambition as there were not too many women doctors in the early twentieth century. She, however, was extremely intelligent and had the local doctor, Dr.Giuseppe Cipolla, himself a graduate of the Florence medical school, as a sponsor. Former graduates always carried a lot of weight in their recommendations of medical school candidates.

Sophia, on the other hand, was the devout one, always reading the Bible and attending services at the Cathedral in her time away from the vineyards. She was content in spending all of her free time helping Fr. Lombardi in the church rectory and had expressed some interest in pursuing life in a convent someday. Vincenze was not too concerned at the time as Sophia was only twelve years old and would likely change her mind if she met a young man at some point whose charm would sweep her off her feet.

In 1928, when Vito was only five years old, he could already handle most of the daily chores associated with maintaining the vines and even began to learn how to properly store and bottle the aged wines in the vineyard cellars.

To Vito, as he grew up, life in Orvieto was all he knew and he hardly ever saw any place beyond the Umbrian landscape and its surrounding towns. His childhood was a very peaceful one, and the seclusion of Orvieto from many other towns meant he could spend hours and weeks in reading and painting by himself under his favorite tree overlooking the countryside. He was nearly six feet tall, quite handsome, and muscular from years of work in the vineyards, but inwards his gentleness was the characteristic which made him astutely observant of the beauty that surrounded Orvieto.

Once Vito became an accomplished reader, he would often be seen at the local store, searching for as many books to read as he could get his hands on, without paying much money for them. Through the books, he learned to paint. At first, his artwork was quite simple, a bit of landscape art, an occasional still life, and a rare portrait of a local dignitary. As time went by, the quality and depth of his work became apparent to more people in Orvieto, and he was asked to do wall paintings of patron saints in the Duomo, a majestic cathedral which contained alcoves with altars throughout. To Vito, this was all there was, and life could not be simpler. Although he had no formal training in painting and art, he was quite accomplished in his own way. He hoped one day to go to an art school to learn the finer points which would only improve his works.

The cathedral in the little town towered over every other structure. The Duomo had been built in the mid-thirteenth century. Legend has it, during a mass in a pilgrimage to Rome near Orvieto, a priest held the bread used in communion and it began to bleed, staining a linen cloth. The cloth was brought to the Pope, who was visiting Orvieto at the time. The Pope declared this to be a miracle, and to honor God, he erected this magnificent church with Italy's liveliest façade with interior gleaming mosaics, stained glass, and sculpture.

To Vito, to have some of his paintings hung in the Duomo in the same building as Signorelli's brilliantly lit frescoes was priceless since he was only seventeen years old at the time.

Inside this beautiful building in a side chapel is Luca Signorelli's "The Last Judgment," part of his End of the World cycle. Signorelli's early sixteenth century masterpiece vividly depicts demons torturing the damned with angels above standing guard.

* * *

In 1937, Japan had invaded China to initiate the war in the Pacific, and in 1939 Germany invaded Poland, unleashing the European war. In 1940, Italy entered World War II on the Axis side with Germany and Japan.

The Allied Powers, led by Great Britain, the United States, and the Soviet Union, would defeat the Axis in World War II, and Italy would be the first Axis partner to give up. Italy surrendered on September 8, 1943, six weeks after leaders of the Italian Fascist Party deposed Fascist leader and Italian dictator, Benito Mussolini.

During those four years of war, Orvieto was the target of many Allied bombing attacks which affected the surrounding towns more so than Orvieto itself, despite the city's prominence set atop its perch overlooking the Umbrian landscape. Nearby was the Airfield of Alfina which was used as a German base for bombers, making it a target for Allied aircraft. The air raids could be seen from the towers of Castel Viscardo, an important outlook point which defended Orvieto.

Vito would often hear the sirens whir from the vineyards in the valley below, which announced an air raid, and forced his parents, workers, and himself to seek shelter in the caves below the city. Orvieto had long kept the secret of its labyrinth of caves and tunnels which lied beneath the surface. Dug deep into the volcanic rock, these secret hidden tunnels would lead from the city square to emerge at a safe exit point some distance away from city walls. Throughout the war, this underground city of nearly one hundred twenty caves served as a bomb shelter for the inhabitants of Orvieto and the surrounding towns. Vito loathed the blackness of the caves, meters below the ground. The muffed sounds of explosions frightened him, and he feared the cave walls and ceiling might not hold beneath the attacks.

Orvieto's volcanic base consisted of porous stone, which is easy to cut and excavate. Many of the buildings above ground had their own caves, which are useful storerooms as well as the location for olive and wine-pressing operations. The temperature in the caves maintained a near-constant fifty eight degrees, ideal for the Melucci wines to be stored before delivery to their final destination. Although Vito knew all too well what an asset this was, his uneasiness maneuvering through these caves was obvious to his father Vincenze. Vito would sweat profusely each time he spent more than an hour inside the caves. You would have thought that because of the cool temperatures in the caves, he would not react this way, but his anxiety at being in a confined dark area for long periods was something he dreaded.

The white wine of the Orvieto district was highly prized. For centuries, Orvieto mainly produced lightly sweet wines, but as tastes drifted to dry white wine, the Melucci's vineyard wines became more popular each year. The cellar-like caves from the volcanic soil were ideal for housing wine production with a long, cool fermentation. The wine would be packed into crates and barrels, and stored in humid grottoes, carved out of the volcanic stone in the caves. Wine production was very important to the economy in the Orvieto area, and the vineyard owners did all they could to protect their output during the war period. Throughout the first few years of the war, Orvieto was untouched despite all of the bombings around the city. While residents constantly heard and saw bombings from atop their perched city, never once did Orvieto incur a single bombing. It was as if the Allies also valued the history of this hidden gem.

In June of 1944, British Major Richard Heseltine, the commander of the British Army tank squadron, approached Orvieto from Viterbo, another historic city, which unfortunately, had not been spared as the Allies drove the Germans out of Italy. The residents of Orvieto had every reason to expect the same fate for their own town. Heseltine, looked up from the turret of a tank, and could see Orvieto high up in the distance. One of his men announced a Volkswagen car was spotted with a big white flag hanging from one of its windows. Apparently, the German commander proposed to the Allied command that the city be spared because of its historic beauty and the uniqueness of its art, and any battle between the two forces be held elsewhere. Heseltine agreed, and the Germans pulled back exactly twenty kilometers before a three-day battle ensued. Orvieto was spared any damage.

Vito was in the cathedral the day Heseltine appeared outside in a jeep. Residents hid in the town until, finally, a few residents noticed the Allied uniforms. Vito, along with many others, came out from everywhere to greet them. Heseltine, an amateur painter himself, was immediately impressed by the Signorelli artwork and was reassured he had made the right decision to avoid any assault on the town. Orvieto would get a much better fate than many of its neighboring towns.

CHAPTER 5

Carlo Andrea Melucci, the only child of Vito and Camille Melucci, was born in May 1951 in Paris, France. Just like his father, Carlo was raised in Orvieto on the vineyards which had grown immensely in the years following World War II. He would often hear the war stories from his father about the sirens and bombings nearby, always in awe Orvieto and the surrounding vineyards were spared any damage whatsoever. Vito would relate the same stories over and over at night following dinner until Carlo fell asleep. Carlo loved to hear them and wondered if someday he would have such wonderful tales to relate to his own children, even though Vito's stories were not all pleasant memories.

Once Carlo went to bed, Vito would unwind from the day's activities at the vineyard by spending time in his small artist studio adjacent to their home. The Meluccis had a beautiful villa at the foot of Orvieto that had recently been remodeled to accommodate more visitors coming to the vineyards for a wine tasting or merchants interested in buying large quantities of the Melucci White Wine for sale in other large cities in Italy and France.

Camille Melucci, born Camille Denelle, had been a nurse during the war, and had been stationed near Paris, twenty minutes from her home in Giverny. She had always wanted to be a nurse and could always be seen doing good deeds in any way she could to people who were ill. She had met Vito at the Musée D'Orsay Art Gallery in Paris one Saturday on her day off from the Hopital d'instruction des armées Percy in Clamart, just outside Paris. She appreciated the beautiful paintings in the gallery, although she herself couldn't draw a straight line if she wanted. Vito had been studying art at the Paris College of Art nearby and they literally bumped into each other in one of the galleries. Vito was quite shy and seemed embarrassed at the occurrence, but Camille quickly put him at ease with her warm smile. She walked with a pronounced limp, her left leg was in a metal brace. Vito could see the pain in her eyes when she became aware he had focused on her difficulty in walking rather than on her smile.

"It is not as bad as it seems," Camille announced. "Five years ago, I was assigned to a field hospital in Vernon, and one night the Allies bombed the fields while our ambulance was heading to St. Louis Hospital a few miles away. There was shrapnel imbedded behind my knee. After they removed the shrapnel, my knee just would not work right, even with a brace. But I can get around fine, and my new assignment in Clamart will allow me to get better treatment as they find new ways to improve the knee."

"I'm sorry, Mademoiselle, I did not mean to gaze or to appear that I was having pity on you. Your warm greeting to clumsy me was lost when I thought you had hurt yourself when we bumped into each other."

Following small talk, Vito said goodbye to Camille as he needed to return to the college for another art class. As she turned to him with another smile when she was leaving, Vito could sense a future trip to the Clamart hospital would be in the cards.

Several weeks later, prior to the end of the fall term and just before the Christmas holidays, Vito rented a car and decided to visit Camille and ask her to dinner if she was free. He had a train ticket to Orvieto the following day, and his father Vincenze would be at the station to greet him.

He noticed Camille helping a recuperating soldier out of a wheel chair onto a bench near the parking lot as he approached the hospital on the sunny but brisk December day. There were never many visitors during the week at military hospitals and she could not help but notice Vito's car as it pulled into a space in the almost empty lot. As he opened the car door, she smiled to herself without acknowledging Vito, and went about her business attending to the soldier. The soldier said to her that he would be fine on the bench for about a half hour and that she should return then to help him back to the ward.

"Hello, Camille," he shouted. "I was in the area today and thought I'd stop by to see you. Is this a bad time?"

"Bonjours, Vito, I did not expect to see you again. I am quite impressed you even remember my name and where I work," Camille expressed with a slight smirk on her face. The sun on her face revealed a perfect complexion and short brown hair under her nurse's cap. Her eyes were also brown and, in spite of the brace on her left knee, her posture was quite upright. When she changed the smirk into a full-scale smile, it made Vito smile as well.

"There is a wonderful restaurant nearby called Le Coq Fin, have you ever been there?" he asked.

"Non, Monsieur, but I have heard of it. I do not go out to eat that often, I can't afford it," she replied. "I live alone in a cottage nearby that my parents left to me when they died during the war."

"Oh, I am so sorry to hear that, Camille, but surely a beautiful woman like you is married or at least with a fiancée?" he queried, hoping to get the answer he was looking for.

"Non, oh non Monsieur," she laughed. "The only things I am married to are my patients here at the hospital. Living so near to the hospital, it seems I am always filling in for someone out ill who calls out at the last minute."

"Look," he said, "it is nearly three o'clock and if you are not doing anything later on, perhaps we could try Le Coq Fin for dinner? I leave for home in Orvieto tomorrow morning for the winter holidays and I thought it would be nice to have dinner with a smiling face tonight."

"I don't know, Vito, you might be very disappointed if you took me to dinner, I may eat all the food they have. When you live alone, you either become a great cook, or you remain pretty thin because you can't cook much at all."

"You don't look too skinny to me," he blurted, almost catching himself before he spoke.

Camille blushed as she accepted his comment as a compliment rather than a shortfall in her cooking ability. "I don't end my shift until five o'clock and then I would need to go home to change. How about six o'clock? Are you sure you know what you are doing?"

"I know perfectly well what I'm doing. I'll take a ride there to make a reservation for six o'clock and I'll swing by to pick you up around quarter of six. The address?"

"I walk home from here, about one mile on rue des Espoires, number one eighty-two. Until five forty-five then."

You have never seen a more nervous person than Vito as he drove away speedily toward Le Coq Fin in Giverny, as if he was afraid the restaurant would be booked solid for six o'clock. He had no other place in mind or that he knew of in the area. He had only heard of Le Coq Fin that day from a fellow art student who had been there several times. The reservation presented no problem and, while he had some time to kill, he visited a few shops nearby and bought Camille a nice silk scarf from one of them. His artistic eye deemed the light tan color would match her hair nicely. He then visited the residence of Claude Monet and the famous lily pond, which also was nearby.

At five thirty he headed in his rental car toward rue des Espoires. Camille's cottage was fifty feet from the road, was adorned with a beautifully landscaped front with perennials, and had a stone walkway which led to the front door of the bricked façade of the house. She answered the doorbell and beamed a beautiful smile at Vito. She was dressed in an aqua buttoned down blouse, covered by a matching cardigan and wore loose-fitting black pants with a slight flare at the bottom. Her hair was flawlessly groomed and her face had rosiness to it which clearly brought out the natural attraction of her face.

She had decided not to attract attention to her knee brace by wearing a dress or knee-length skirt where the brace would show. She was conscious enough to know that her pronounced limp would be distraction enough to any onlookers at the restaurant. Perhaps more than the cost of eating out occasionally, Camille was self-conscious whenever she appeared in a public place and chose to avoid it as much as possible. Whatever the reason, it did not bother Vito from taking her by the arm and escorting her to the passenger side of his car. Camille was excited at simply being asked out by someone.

Dinner was lovely. The evening was filled with good food and wine and an even better conversation between the two. It was obvious to Camille how kind and gentle Vito was, truly a student of art. His explanation of his parents' vineyard in Orvieto gave Camille the impression that he was not your ordinary struggling art student. She had never been outside of France, not that she didn't want to travel, but simply because there had been no opportunity for her to do so during the war years. After the war, she found herself caring for recuperating soldiers who kept her close to home.

As the evening hour approached nine o'clock, Vito realized that the rental car had to be returned before the dealership closed at ten. Otherwise, he would have to return it the following day and pay for an extra day's rental. Since he had an early train to Orvieto in the morning, this was not acceptable. He led Camille to her front door, asked her politely if he could kiss her goodnight, and she willingly accepted. The moment was lost in a dream to both of them as neither was considered a social butterfly. The warmth of their connected lips ran shivers through Vito and, when he withdrew his lips from hers, Camille's eyes remained closed for some time.

"May I see you again, Camille," he said softly.

"That would be nice, Vito, that would be very nice." She stood by her doorway and waved to him as his car drove away. *Could this possibly be my knight in shining armor,* she wondered?

Both of them laid awake for hours that night thinking about the evening, the kiss, and the expectations of their next encounter.

The following morning, Vito was on a train to Orvieto for the holidays. All he could think of during the entire train ride was Camille. Hours later, when he saw his father on the station platform, he waved and greeted him with a huge smile on his face. Vito hugged his father, and grabbed his luggage as they headed for the vineyard in Vincenze's truck. No sooner was Vito seated on the passenger side of the vehicle then he started to talk about the wonderful French nurse he had met. He never mentioned a word about how his art training was going, about the art school, or anything related to art, which his father found quite odd. This would be an interesting holiday period at the Melucci's.

As the truck pulled into the villa, Vito's mother stood on the porch and waved exuberantly with a huge smile on her face. Maria Melucci cherished her only son as much as Vincenze took a greater interest in Vito's two older sisters. Lucia was expected any day now as she had nearly completed her medical training in Florence. Vincenze was amazed she was actually about to become a medical doctor, a rare feat for a woman in Italy in the 1950s. She had accomplished what she had set out to do, and was planning on opening up a practice in Orvieto. At first she would assist the local doctor, replacing him when he retired in three years. Dr. Cipolla was seventy-two years old and had delivered Lucia thirty-three years earlier. He had been the one whose recommendation to the University of Florence Medical School, his alma mater, had been instrumental in getting Lucia accepted there. She would also be qualified to do surgery and planned to do so at the Orvieto Hospital.

Sophia, the other sister, whose early plans were to enter a convent and become a nun, had not done so. She had met a classmate while in high school, fell head over heels for the guy, only to find out later in their relationship he was sleeping with several other women in Orvieto. After she dumped the loser, she became much more cautious in dating other men, and spent most of her time working at the vineyard store where she would represent the Melucci family in wine tastings and in selling wines to visitors.

Christmas at an Italian vineyard was festive. The Meluccis had always strung decorative lights in the vineyards closest to the villa and the compound reflected the joy of the season. The climate in Orvieto was always cool and brisk in December and many wine buyers would visit the Melucci Vineyards around the holidays since the coolness was quite suitable for storing white wines.

Vito jumped out of the truck as it pulled up in front of the villa, swept his mother off her feet, and hugged and kissed her.

"Mama, I met a girl in Paris, she's a nurse and I took her to dinner last night," Vito gushed.

"Well, well, my son has dated a real girl, it's about time don't you think?" Maria replied.

"Her name is Camille Denelle, and I can't wait to tell you about her."

"And the school that we are sending you to, you have some good news about that?" his mother asked.

"Oh, yes, yes, Mama, I am doing well at school too, but let me tell you about Camille!"

Vito put his arm around his mother as they entered the villa while Vincenze stood there dumfounded at being left at the door with Vito's luggage.

Vito related to his mother how Camille had been injured during the war, how her parents were killed, how she supported herself, and lived alone in the house where she was raised. Maria immediately took a liking to the girl, even though she neither knew what she looked like nor what her interests were. All she knew was Camille liked Vito, and that was enough for Maria. Vito had never dated, had always preferred the solitude that working in the vineyard presented, or painting in the small studio in the rear of the villa.

"I should like to meet this girl one day if you continue to see her when you return to Paris in January."

"We shall see, Mama, we shall see."

Three days later, Lucia arrived from Florence and the entire family gathered for their traditional wine festival in the center square in Orvieto where the year's new wine crop is offered to the local citizens first, along with pasta dishes and other Italian favorites that go with white wine. These were good times for the Melucci family and Vincenze and Maria were beaming with pride at the roles their three children all played

* * *

In Giverny, Camille was pretty much expecting to spend Christmas alone in her cottage following the holiday party at the hospital for the recuperating soldiers. As she helped out the other staff in cleaning up after the party, Camille left the lounge area with an armful of dishes and headed for the kitchen, one floor below. She entered the kitchen through the swinging doors and, before she could even react, a hand tightly covered her mouth and another one grabbed her by the waist from behind. The dishes went flying to the floor and made a loud shattering noise. Suddenly the lights went out and the figure behind her threw her onto the center island in the kitchen, splattering pots and pans to the floor. Camille was defenseless from this intruder and found that her struggles to fend off her attacker proved useless.

The attacker began to rip off her uniform and then her undergarments. He then quickly jumped on top of her in a wild and vicious rage until Camille finally bit down hard on the attacker's hand still covering her mouth. The attacker screamed and retreated from her for a brief moment allowing Camille to scream at the top of her lungs. The attacker panicked and ran out the kitchen door, pulling up his pants as he left. The open kitchen door showed the lit corridor, and Camille caught a glimpse of the attacker as he fled. She lay there on the kitchen island, grasping at her clothes to cover herself up when another nurse entered the room and saw the horror in Camille's eyes and face, and she rushed to her assistance.

Camille was in a state of shock. When asked what had occurred, she remained silent, as if still in shock over the cruel incident. But inside her mind, Camille knew who her assailant was, an orderly named Jean Matthieu, and she would deal with him in her own way.

Later the next day, Camille was released to go home but the doctors were worried she would be alone there, and pleaded with her to have someone stay with her for a few days. Camille assured the doctors that she would be fine and that her home was where she wanted to be. Dr. Dubois insisted he drive her home and would check out the house before he would leave her alone. Camille agreed to this and she asked another nurse to bring her another uniform from her locker as the other one had been turned over to the police as evidence. The police did not rule out any male in the hospital at the time of the rape and they were putting together a list of men to question.

Matthieu had been an orderly at the hospital for nearly two years and all of the nurses despised him. He had been accused of stealing items from patients' rooms, harassing nurses with lewd remarks on his masculinity, but miraculously, was vindicated each time. Camille thought to herself that this asshole was about to meet his match.

Once she changed from the hospital gowns following her final examination by a local gynecologist, she opened the hospital room door and headed for the main entrance. Doctor Dubois said he would meet her near the front door where his car was parked. As she passed the nurse's station on the first floor, she spotted Matthieu cleaning one of the hospital rooms across the hall. She stared at him until he glanced back at her. The fire in her eyes told it all. The hate and anger nearly overtook her as she did all she could to restrain herself from charging into the room and gouging his eyes out while kicking him in the groin. She knew he was fully aware she would someday seek revenge. Matthieu lowered his eyes quickly, and tried to ignore her as she passed the room. After taking a few deep breaths, Camille was out the door and on her way home.

After Dr. Dubois inspected the house, he urged Camille to keep all of the windows and doors locked and not to let anyone in unless it was the police or someone from the hospital who she knew and trusted. Camille agreed and Dr. Dubois left. It was agreed she would not return to the hospital for at least a week unless she wanted or needed to talk to a doctor beforehand for whatever reason, physical or psychological.

Camille knew Matthieu would try to get to her to quiet her from revealing his identity to the authorities. Camille had her own plans for Jean Matthieu. She knew that if she had accused him to the police at the hospital, it would have been her word against his and she was disgusted at the thought that he would get away again with his actions. Jean Matthieu would regret ever touching Camille, let alone violating her womanhood by force.

* * *

While Christmas for Vito was alive and cheerful, it certainly was not the case for Camille. She knew all too well that Jean Matthieu would appear at her door or in her house sometime soon. She just didn't know when. All she could do was prepare for his intrusion with the defensive steps she had learned while a nurse in the French military. Camille would simulate the measures several times each day as if she was preparing for the Olympic trials. Nonetheless, she would be more than ready if and when Matthieu showed his face.

Three days after the attack and a week before Christmas, Camille's phone rang and Dr. Louise Grenier, the gynecologist who had come to the hospital the night of the attack to examine Camille, called and asked if she could stop by later in the afternoon to go over the report she had prepared for the police following the examination.

At four o'clock, Dr. Grenier arrived and Camille offered her a cup of tea. Dr. Grenier politely refused and asked Camille if they could sit in the small living room to review her news.

"After reviewing the results from the tests I performed on you at the hospital following your attack, the tests show internal damage caused by the forced entry by the rapist," Dr. Grenier began. "By itself, this situation is not uncommon in cases such as this and should heal by itself over time. I can re-examine you in a few weeks to see what progress you've made."

Camille sat there looking into nowhere, as if what she had just heard was not meant for her. She was quite speechless and her silence was not unusual to Dr. Grenier who had seen similar reactions from other rape victims. She reached forward to comfort Camille by touching both of her hands, but as if from instinct, Camille quickly pulled them away as a person would do after touching a hot stove.

"I know what you must be going through right now, Camille, and I know that you probably feel like you could not ever be with a man intimately, nor ever bear a child. That's not the case. Camille, in time you will heal inside, just as I expect you to physically heal. Please don't judge all men to be the same."

"How would you know how I feel? How can you possibly know the anger and hate I have inside of me right now?" Camille blurted.

"Because I've been there, Camille, just like you. Six years ago. I was raped by a soldier in a military hospital in Paris in 1944. The soldier, it turns out, was deranged from being in battle too long and, when confronted with the charges, he didn't even remember attacking me. I wanted to kill him, Camille, I really wanted him to pay for what he did. I didn't when I realized that I had nothing to gain by killing him but a tiny amount of satisfaction that I got even. The truth is, you never get even because you still have to live with it and, sometimes, others around you do too. I was dating another doctor when this happened and he couldn't deal with it, couldn't come to grips with my pain. All he could think of was that he might marry someone who was abused, had been violated, and he left me to deal with this by myself.

"Funny thing though, Camille, I wasn't alone after all. My colleagues helped me pick up the pieces and somehow find trust in a man again. That man is my husband today and we have two beautiful children. It can happen to you, Camille, I can help you if you'll let me in," Dr. Grenier explained.

"Doctor, I very seldom date, I've got a bad limp from the war, and there aren't too many men out there chasing after me. Ironically, just a few days before this happened, I met a man I really thought might be the one, might want to be with me regardless of my bad knee, because I could still care for him and love him, and it would be enough for him. Now, I'm not so sure," Camille moaned.

"Camille, you are a very pretty and intelligent woman. If this man really cares for you, none of this will matter. He will see that and, if he doesn't, then someone else will. I can help you, Camille, I know what you are going through."

Camille just broke down crying and hugged Dr. Grenier, for ever so long. The healing was about to begin, but how she dealt with Matthieu was another story.

* * *

Christmas came and went, and the weather in Giverny turned bitter and there were days of snow flurries in the air. Camille was alone during the weeks that followed and she soon realized she could no longer stand the loneliness away from the hospital. Following her meeting with Dr. Grenier, she made arrangements to see a psychologist specializing in rape victims and began to feel confident about herself, although she still felt like there were eyes gazing at her from everywhere as she entered and left the hospital before and after each session. In early January, Camille agreed to return to her nurse's post at the hospital. The first few days she was back were the toughest. At every turn in the corridors, she was petrified at the possibility of Matthieu lurking around the corner and they would come face to face. In reality, Matthieu was nowhere to be found. He had quit his job as soon as the police had interrogated him the day following the attack. There were no witnesses and, according to Camille's report to them, the assailant could not be identified. Ironically, the police had not noticed the bruises on Matthieu's left hand when Camille had bitten him as he said to them that he had jammed his hand in a doorway a few days earlier.

Knowing Matthieu was still out there made Camille uneasy and she found herself always having a nurse colleague drive her home each night rather than walking home any longer. When she got home, all the lights on the first floor were already turned on, as well as the two outside lights on each side of the front door. Her friend would not leave until Camille had entered the house, made a walk-through, and then returned to the front door to signal that everything was fine. If someone was in the house and she was felt threatened in any way, she would give her friend the thumbs down sign, to indicate the police needed to be notified immediately.

How much longer can I live like this, she wondered. In her mind, she realized she could not continue to keep her house fully lit all day long, only turning the lights off at bedtime. No, this had to end, and the only way it would ever end is if she knew Matthieu no longer was a threat to her. She had to eliminate the possibility she would never feel safe in her own house. She had to take action against Matthieu.

During the middle of the first week back to work, Camille was gaining more and more confidence in herself. On Wednesday afternoon, as her colleague drove her home, she noticed a car parked in front of her house. As the colleague slowly approached the car, there sat Vito, all smiles and waving to Camille as he began to get out of his vehicle.

"Hi, Camille, I just returned to school earlier this week and wondered if I could take you out for a light dinner? I know that you work tomorrow, so I promise not to keep you up too late?" Vito blurted out with a childish excitement.

"Oh, Vito, I don't know, this is unexpected and I'm really not dressed for that," Camille replied with a frightened look on her face.

"I can wait if you want to change, I promise that we won't stay out late."

"Well, all right, please come in while I change." The tone in her voice was far from convincing, and Vito sensed something was not right, but he could not figure out what.

"Camille, is there something wrong, or if this is a bad time, we can do this some other time?" he queried.

"No, Vito, I'm fine, I'll just be a few minutes."

Dinner was at another local restaurant nearby and was nowhere as memorable as their dinner at Le Coq Fin in early December. Camille was very quiet for most of the meal as Vito related all the events back in Orvieto, perhaps not noticing Camille's solitude as much as he should have. Even the drive back to her house was without much conversation. As Vito pulled up in front of her house, he turned the motor off and leaned over to kiss her. She hesitated, slightly pulling her head back, and caught Vito by surprise.

"Camille, you don't have to do anything you don't want to. I won't..."

"You don't understand, Vito, I'm scared. I can't say any more about it now."

Before Vito could say anything else, Camille was out of the car and hobbling fast for the house, fumbling in her purse for her key. She opened the door, rushed in and closed it, never once looking back.

Vito returned to his apartment in Paris around eleven o'clock, thinking to himself all the way back. Had he somehow moved too fast with Camille. Perhaps he needed to get to know her more first before making any further advances toward her.

He had barely entered the apartment when the phone began to ring. Only one person had his phone number because he had just moved in the previous weekend and Camille was the only he had just given it to.

"Vito, it's me." She sounded as if she had been crying and was trying to compose herself.

"Hello, Camille. I never got the chance to tell you what a nice time I had and I'm sorry if I did something wrong."

"No, Vito, you were the perfect gentleman tonight and it's me who is sorry for having rushed off. It was not fair to you."

"Then, what's wrong, Camille, please, maybe I can help?"

"I have to tell you this by phone, Vito. I know I could never tell you this in front of you."

"What is it, Camille, can it be so bad?" Vito asked.

"Worse than you can imagine, Vito. After you left for home last month, late the next day the hospital was having its Christmas party for the patients in the main lounge on the second floor. I was helping the other nurses and workers by bringing dirty dishes back to the kitchen on the first floor when it happened."

"When what happened, Camille?" Vito became frantic.

"When a man attacked me in the kitchen and, after he put out the light, forced himself on me," Camille sobbed.

"What, what did he do to you?" Vito was now getting angry.

"He raped me, Vito, he pulled off my clothes and forced himself inside of me until I bit down hard on the hand he covered my mouth with and then he ran out as I screamed. I am so ashamed."

For a moment, there was only silence in the phone line until Vito responded in a low voice, "Oh, Camille, are you okay, are you hurt, I'm so sorry, I didn't know."

"How could you know, Vito? I'm trying to live a normal life again and I'm just having so much trouble with this right now. Maybe we shouldn't see each other for a while, maybe you meet someone else, Vito. Don't say anything, please. I'm going to hang up and go to bed right now."

There was a click in Vito's ear. She was gone. He just stood there, furious about the phone call, furious at whoever would do such a thing, and wanted to rush back to Camille's house as fast as he could. She needed some space and she needed some time. So did Vito. He undressed and went to bed, but laid awake most of the night, thinking about Camille and how someone should have been with her this night.

CHAPTER 6

Throughout the next day, Vito's mind wandered in all the art classes he was in until, finally, he just picked up his books and art supplies and left the school. Vito's parents had bought him a small Fiat so he could travel home more often on long weekends. In all the chaos that had occurred the night before, Vito hadn't even told Camille about the car, and she likely must have thought Vito had just rented another car when he stopped by to see her. He jumped into his car around five o'clock and headed for Camille's house in Giverny. Along the way, he stopped to buy a bouquet of flowers for her.

As he approached the cottage, it began to get dark. When he rang her doorbell, there were butterflies in his stomach. Camille slowly opened the door, the outside lights clearly beaming on Vito with his bouquet in one hand. Her eyes were large, very dark, and she appeared quite frightened. Vito was not certain if this was a good idea, but he just had to see her. He felt her pain as if it were his own. He feared she would not let him in and ask him to go away.

But she didn't. "Come in," she said. She felt faint and looked like she was about to collapse. Vito dropped the bouquet and reached out to grab her. She pushed herself back up, bracing herself with her uninjured leg and wrapped her arms around Vito, held on tightly and she began to cry. Vito could feel her shaking wildly and he squeezed her tightly and swayed ever so slowly while holding her in his arms, very much like lulling a baby to sleep.

After a few moments, Camille loosened her grip on Vito and began to smile, then even laughed out loud as she looked at the flowers on the floor, crushed by their feet.

"I'm scared," she said. "How can you look at me after what's happened?"

"I'm scared too," Vito admitted. "You are the first woman I have ever been with and I don't understand how someone would do this to you. What kind of a madman does this?"

Camille looked up at him and, with tears in her eyes, tried to explain. "I will be fine, Vito, I am stronger now and I am getting better every day."

When both of them had calmed down, Camille asked Vito to stay with her for a while. She prepared vegetable soup and they both sat quietly as they ate the soup with pieces of bread from a baguette. They talked calmly to each other for hours, each being careful not to say the wrong thing that might trigger a bad reaction from the other. By nine o'clock, Vito rose from the table to say goodbye for the night. Camille led him to the front door, helped him with his coat, and thanked him for coming.

"I can't tell you how much I appreciate you being here tonight."

Before she could say another word, he put his arms around her and kissed her for a long time, not wanting to stop. Camille did not push him away this time. She said goodnight to him and as he was leaving, he turned to say, "I will be back on Sunday, we can go to lunch and maybe to dinner too."

"All right, I will see you then around noon. Are you sure you know what you are doing?" she asked.

"I've never been more certain of anything in my life."

The following morning, Camille approached the personnel manager at the hospital and tried to set up a meeting with her to go over her benefits following all the time she had been home on medical leave. Camille asked to meet that day around noon but the personnel manager, after checking her calendar for the day, told Camille that she was meeting with an applicant at that time and, because of lunch, could not meet her until two o'clock. Camille agreed and left.

At eleven forty-five, Camille walked by the personnel manager's office and noticed that her door was just opening. Out came an applicant with paperwork in her hands, and the manager closed the door behind her as she headed for the hospital cafeteria. The manager had not locked the door before she left. Camille waited for the manager to get on the elevator first, and then she quickly entered her office. She had noticed in her earlier visit where the personnel files were kept and immediately headed for those files. The file drawers were also unlocked and Camille swiftly flipped from letter to letter until she reached the letter M. She thumbed through these, fumbling her way until there it was, the folder for Jean Matthieu. Camille quickly opened the file, noted the address, and grabbed a pen and paper from the manager's desk to jot the address down.

She could hear footsteps outside the doorway and hurriedly returned the folder to the file drawer as the office door opened.

"Camille, you are much too early, your appointment is at two o'clock," chimed the personnel manager as she stood there unsuspectedly with her tray of food. Apparently Camille was unaware that the manager ate her lunch in her office, even though she would buy the food from the cafeteria.

Camille apologized for the mistake and said she would return at two as she back peddled her way out the door with the address paper slightly hidden behind her back. Once out the door, she breathed a sigh of relief and placed the address in the pocket of her uniform.

The address was 1621 rue des Olives in Vernon. Camille checked the bus schedule and circled the Saturday afternoon one o'clock bus and the five o'clock return bus back to Giverny. I'm coming, Jean Matthieu, she said to herself as she pondered her next move.

On Saturday morning, Camille was busy planning her strategy if and when she confronted Matthieu that afternoon. Following an early breakfast and shower, she dressed in jeans and a sweatshirt and headed for the basement of her house. The cellar was a cement floor surrounded by stone walls and had that musty odor damp basements emit. There was a small wine cellar her father kept at one time, but now the few wine bottles still there were covered with dust. She made a mental note to one day this winter do a major cleaning job down there. She headed for an old cedar chest which had belonged to her parents and opened the chest. She removed the first layer which held old woolen sweaters and blankets and reached for a box at the bottom of the chest below more clothing.

As she slowly opened the box, there lay a German luger and a box of shells alongside the gun. Camille removed the entire box, closed the chest, and headed back upstairs. She set the box on the kitchen table and removed the gun, then reached for the cleaning oil her father had taught her how to use during the war years. *Someday you will need to protect yourself,* Camille remembered her father saying. *Someday someone will want to hurt you or your mother if I am not here to protect you myself,* he would say. *And that is you, Camille, you might need to use this someday, so I will teach you how to use it,* he would add. Late in the afternoon, when her father returned from working in the perfume factory, they would go into the field nearby, where railroad tracks ran through the property as trains passed by several times a day. When Camille's father saw a train approaching in the distance, he would set up a target of cans on tree stumps and prepare Camille to learn the art of shooting a hand gun. The sound of the passing train muffled the sound of gunfire so no one nearby would wonder about strange gunfire coming from the fields.

Camille remembered this as she began cleaning the luger and thoughts of her father brought tears to her eyes. She had been at the hospital during the war when news came that a dozen French citizens from the Giverny area had been executed by the Gestapo after they had been caught hiding members of the underground in their basement. A neighbor, fearing that the Germans would punish him for not revealing suspicious activity at the Denelle household, told a German officer there were a lot of people going in and coming out of that home, especially at night. Her parents were two of the dozen citizens shot and killed that night.

She completed cleaning the gun, reached for the box of shells, and loaded the luger. She placed it in her shoulder bag, put on her winter coat, wrapped a scarf around her neck, put on her beret, and headed for the bus stop. The trip to Vernon would take about twenty minutes. The bus stop had only a few people waiting, as weekend activity in rural areas was light. Unbeknownst to Camille, Vito had decided not only to visit her on Sunday, but he wanted to surprise her by also going there on Saturday. From a distance, Vito saw Camille boarding the bus before he could stop her. For some reason, he decided to follow the bus to see where Camille was going. He was not aware of the bus routes outside of Paris, but he thought that once she got off the bus, he would be there to offer her a ride back.

As the bus made a stop, Vito would keep his distance to see if Camille was getting off. This occurred for several stops along the way until the bus arrived in Vernon and the remainder of the passengers disembarked, including Camille.

Camille had asked the driver to drop her off as close to Rue des Olives as possible since she was not familiar with Vernon, having only been there twice in recent years. The driver told her there was an information center near the last stop and they could help her more than he could. She saw the small building and headed inside. As it turned out, Rue des Olives was two blocks away, and off she headed.

Vito's car was a short distance away and he was careful that she would not see him. If she did, it would certainly appear he had followed her and Vito did not want her to be offended at this since he meant no harm. Quite the contrary, he was more concerned with her well-being than ever.

As she approached number sixteen twenty-one, she crossed the street, and stood in the shadow of an empty storefront, and gazed at the two-story tenement. Number sixteen nineteen was on the left side, while sixteen twenty-one occupied the right half of the two-story structure, an old building that needed repainting as the white undercoating showed beneath the peeling brown color. Camille would stay until she detected anyone entering or leaving the apartment, even if it meant standing there for hours.

Vito had positioned his car so as to observe Camille, but wondered what she was doing. His curiosity got the best of him and he drove his car right up to the empty storefront and got out.

"Vito, what are you doing here, it's not Sunday? Are you following me?" she asked.

"No, no, Camille. I thought I'd surprise you by coming to see you today also. I should have called first, but I thought you'd be glad to see me. Before I got to your house, I saw you get on the bus, so I followed, hoping to offer you a ride back from wherever you were going. What are you doing here, anyway, are you waiting for someone?" Vito queried.

Before she could answer, the sound of two shots came from across the street and Vito immediately threw Camille to the ground covering her with his body as he did so. Camille looked across the street and she saw Simone Dugas hurry out of number sixteen twenty-one, and then picked up speed as she rounded the corner to another street. Camille sprang to her feet and began to hobble directly to the front door of Matthieu's apartment. Vito scrambled to catch up. He realized that Camille knew exactly where she was going. The door to the apartment was partly open and Camille pushed it open as she placed her other hand inside her shoulder bag. She carefully motioned to Vito to be quiet as she limped slowly ahead into the living room of Matthieu's apartment. There, on the living room carpet, lay Matthieu's motionless body in a pool of blood. She grabbed Vito and motioned to him to stay put.

"Vito, slowly go outside and see if anyone is around and make sure no one sees you. Then come back in and let me know," Camille shouted.

As if from instinct, Vito did exactly what she asked and returned to say that there was no one on the street at all. She led him out and they casually crossed the street to Vito's car. As they were crossing, a car came slowly from around the corner and drove by both of them. Simone Dugas noticed Camille as their eyes met, if only for a brief second, as she continued to drive away from the house. Camille climbed into the passenger seat of Vito's car and they were gone from the area in less than a minute.

After driving out of Vernon and on the way back toward Giverny, Vito pulled the car to the side of the road and stopped.

"What the hell was that, Camille, what's going on here?"

"Vito, the man's name was Jean Matthieu, he used to work at the hospital and he was the man who raped me. I was coming here to kill him, I was going to make sure he never did this to anyone again. I had no proof that the police could use and he would have just denied it anyway, Vito. But it looks like someone beat me to him."

As she continued, she pulled the luger from her shoulder bag to show Vito she was serious and she would not live in fear with this person out there somewhere. She told Vito how she had gotten his address.

"But, Vito, I know the woman who came out of his apartment after the gunshots. She is the one who found me in the kitchen after hearing my screams that night. She is a nurse in my hospital, Vito, and I know that she saw me just now. I don't know what to do, Vito," she went on.

"Perhaps, this attack on me wasn't the first time Matthieu did this. Perhaps there were other women out there who felt as I did, that he needed to pay for what he did," she added.

"Camille, we should go to the police and tell them everything," Vito said.

"And what would I say, Vito, that I was going to kill him first but someone got there before me?" she retorted. "No, it's too risky, they might accuse me of shooting Matthieu and throwing that gun away afterwards. They would never believe me if I told them Simone Dugas did it, and I have no way to be sure if that's true because we only saw her leave his apartment, not actually killing him. Maybe someone else was there too and we never saw them. No, Vito, we cannot go to the police."

As Vito started the motor again and began to drive toward Camille's house, he could sense Camille was more at ease with herself than he had seen earlier. To Camille, the thought that this monster would not be lurking around every corner made her feel like there was one less hurdle to overcome going forward. Physically, she had been declared fully healed, but psychologically, she still had issues to resolve.

In a few minutes, they arrived at Camille's and Vito was still trying to calm her down as they entered the house. She immediately went into the kitchen, reached for glasses, and pulled out a bottle of brandy from the cabinet below. She poured two glasses and gave one to Vito. Unaccustomed to drinking brandy, they both took a big gulp and both began to choke from the strength of the brandy. Unlike a glass of wine they were used to, brandy is much stronger and has more alcoholic content, not to mention that it is intended to be sipped, not gulped.

No sooner than the both of them took another sip, much smaller this time, the doorbell rang. Camille cautiously looked out the window to see who was there before she opened the door and was face to face with Simone Dugas.

"Before you say anything, Camille, I need to ask you two things," Simone stated. "Did you see me today in Vernon, and was Jean Matthieu the man who tried to rape you last month?"

Simone was not aware Vito was there since he remained in the kitchen until he realized who was at the door. He entered the living room and proceeded toward the open front door. His right hand was behind his back holding Camille's luger which he had removed from her bag as he moved closer to the door where Simone now saw him.

"Was he with you today in Vernon, Camille?" she asked.

"Leave him out of this, Simone, I think you've got some explaining to do," Camille stated.

"May I come in, please, I will try to explain what happened."

Vito cautiously back stepped into the living room, pulled out the revolver from behind his back and told Simone to hand over her handbag. Seeing the gun, Simone immediately complied. Vito grabbed the bag and began rummaging through it to see if it held a weapon. Finding none, he then told her to remove her winter coat very slowly and to lay it over the sofa nearby. He grabbed the coat, checked each pocket and again came up empty.

"Please, Camille, let me explain."

As she sat down on the sofa facing Camille who sat in a lounge chair across from her, Simone began. "Two years ago, in Chartres, my sister worked at the Hôpitaux de Chartres. Matthieu worked there at the same time. He did the same to her as he did to you, but that time he finished the job and badly damaged her. She went into traumatic shock and just couldn't cope with what happened to her, Camille. A week later, they found her body in the psychiatric ward where she was recuperating. She had hung herself in the bathroom. My sister was nineteen years old.

When I was given her personal belongings, I found a note that merely said 'Matthieu'. When I checked with the hospital, they told me that he had resigned a few days earlier to accept a position at our hospital in Giverny. I did everything I could to find out why he was not a suspect and the police said that when he was questioned about the attack, he was not on duty and not even in the hospital. This happened at night in the laundry room and no one saw anything until they found my sister unconscious on the floor the next morning. I've been watching him ever since I came to the hospital. Then, when I found you, I knew it was him again. So, after the doctors came for you, I went to the orderly's locker room area and

Matthieu was already changed into his street clothing and heading out the door."

"Camille, he wasn't going to hurt anyone again. My sister's memory deserved that much. I put a note in his mail slot the next day and told him I knew what he did. First thing I knew he was gone again, but I knew where to find him because I had followed him home one night."

"Today I went to see him and had a gun with me. I asked him to admit to what he had done to you and he just laughed at me. Then I told him about my sister and he smiled as I mentioned her. When I told him that she had hung herself because of what he did to her, he lunged at me and I fired twice, hitting him both times. I wasn't going to stay around to see if he was alive. That's when I saw you," she finished.

"Your parents, they are still alive?" Camille asked.

"My mother goes to her gravesite every day. My father can't speak about it at all. They're both retired, but now they never go out any more," Simone added.

"You are never to speak about this again, Simone," Camille said. "You must get rid of the gun where no one will ever find it. Nothing happened, do you understand me, nothing?" Camille emphasized.

Vito smiled as he heard Camille comfort Simone. There would nothing to gain by admitting her altercation with Matthieu, and the police would implicate Simone because she was holding a gun on him during the incident.

Simone rose from the sofa and hugged Camille like the sister she once had. She put on her coat and left, relieved her ordeal was over, and Camille could also begin to go on with rebuilding her life.

Camille then turned to Vito and said, "Come back tomorrow, Vito. I think that tonight I need to find out if I can be alone without all of the lights on. Tomorrow, hopefully, will be the beginning of my life again."

"I will be here by noon, Camille, just as we planned, unless you're sure you don't want me to stay here tonight?" he said.

"Perhaps tomorrow. I must be sure I'm ready for this," Camille responded.

At ten o'clock on Sunday morning, the phone rang at Vito's apartment and he quickly answered.

"Vito, you are still coming today, aren't you?"

"Yes, of course, why?"

"I went to bed last night and, before I could fall asleep, all I could think about was you, Vito. I've never had these feelings before, and I haven't ever been with a man before, if you know what I mean," she whispered.

"Camille,"

"Don't say anything, please. Just be here today. I need to be with you."

There was a click in his ear and she was gone. Vito became aroused and dressed in a hurry.

A short while later, as he rang her doorbell, he started to get butterflies in his stomach.

Camille's face was radiant and she was wearing a dress that revealed her knees. The bad knee was not in a brace, and her lips began to tremble as he entered the house.

"I'm scared, Vito, what if I'm no good at this?" she said.

"What makes you think I'm any better?" Vito had never experienced this sort of thing before, but if it was to happen now, Camille was the one he wanted to be with.

She took his hand and very slowly led him up the staircase. Once they reached the bedroom, he noticed how ordinary it was, nothing fancy, a double bed, a dresser, some artwork on the wall and a big Persian rug at the foot of the bed. Her knees started to give way, and Vito caught her. He kissed her and it was majestic. Then he backed off for a moment to look into her eyes and began to kiss her again and again.

All of a sudden, Vito's hands began to travel wildly up and down her dress and Camille began to breathe heavier after each movement. Before long, they were both ripping off each other's clothing and as their bodies met, the sensation of their interlocked bodies took over. She gasped and then lay gently on the bed to meet him. In very little time, the sounds of discovery in her voice put Vito over the edge. She buried her face into his shoulder and then finally dropped her head back on the pillow. They both lay there for a while in complete silence, neither of them quite knowing what to say. The silhouette of her body was something Vito had never seen before and he gently leaned over to her and kissed her on the cheek.

"I want to be with you, Camille, I want you to be with me, not just for now or today, I think this is getting serious."

"Oh, Vito, where have you been all my life," she moaned.

"I think it may be time for you to visit Orvieto. There is someone there you need to meet."

CHAPTER 7

Bob Elliott, the newly-found natural son of Queen Farah, was still absorbing the news that his birth mother had recently introduced herself to his family on an unexpected visit to his home in Medway, Massachusetts. Bob had successfully thwarted an assassin's attempt to kill him at his home a few weeks earlier and the major disruption to his quiet life in a small town was still something he was trying to reason.

Hearing his identical twin brother had been murdered a few weeks before, Bob could only wonder what it would have been like to meet him face to face, someone who others could easily mistake for him, if they were indeed considered identical twins. While it did not seem to matter any longer, every time Bob looked in the mirror, thoughts of his deceased twin brother ran through his mind.

His successful baseball career had just come to an end at age thirty five, the result of arm injuries dashed his hope of making a recovery and extending his playing years a bit longer. Nevertheless, Bob and his wife, Julie, a local physician, were hoping to begin a family of their own. Bob's full attention was now devoted to running his two restaurants. He was no longer faced with the extensive amount of time away from home that his baseball career demanded, and he and Julie now could spend the time that raising a family required. Hopefully, the Elliotts would be blessed with the children they wanted.

On December 5th, a FedEx delivery truck stopped in front of the Elliotts' Tiffany Lane home with a large package from Le Bien Public, Dijon, France. *Le Bien Public*, the daily newspaper in Dijon, had run several stories on Charles Larouche, the university professor brutally murdered in his apartment by an intruder. Apparently, no one who knew him could find any reason for the murder, other than perhaps Charles Larouche being in the wrong place at the wrong time.

Bob called a French teacher at Medway High School and asked if she had time after school to translate a few French newspaper articles into English for him. Eleanor Thibodeau, the department chair of the French Department at the school, gladly obliged and they agreed to meet at the high school promptly at two ten that afternoon. In the meantime, Bob started turning a few pages from the three newspapers he had received, trying to learn more about his twin brother, the main reason he ordered copies of the newspapers to begin with. Page one had the headlines and, as he scanned down the article's columns, it referred to Page six and he began flipping pages. On Page six, where the article continued, was a photo of Professor Larouche included in one of the columns. Bob gazed at this photo and tried to focus on the face. This was difficult since the photo was of a bearded man with a receding hairline. The age of the figure in the photo looked about right…thirty-five years old.

Something was strange, Bob thought. He felt very uncomfortable with the photo, not at all what he expected. He went on to the second newspaper only to find the same photo in that article. Bob cast the paper aside and picked up the third newspaper. On Page three, there was a detailed story on Charles Larouche including several photos of him with other people at groundbreaking ceremonies for the new history building at the University of Bourgogne. Bob reached into a desk drawer near the kitchen table where he was reading and took out a magnifying glass. As he placed it over the picture to enlarge it, he noticed that Charles was a very small man when compared to the others in the photos. Bob himself was six feet tall with brown hair and hazel eyes. Perhaps, he thought, we were not identical after all, just twins.

The high school was just five minutes from Tiffany Lane and Bob headed out at two o'clock. Eleanor, a frequent patron at The Lamplighter, Bob's restaurant near the edge of Medway and Bellingham, greeted him warmly when he entered the main doors of the building. They proceeded to her office, just off the library area, and sat at a conference table where Bob produced the three newspapers.

"This is interesting stuff, Bob, do I dare ask why you sent for articles from a paper in Dijon?" Eleanor asked.

"I'm doing a favor for a friend who knew this guy and wanted to know more about his recent murder," Bob answered. "My friend said he went to school with this guy in Paris years ago when he lived there himself."

"Well, let's see what we have here," she replied.

Eleanor began reading and then translating sentence by sentence of each article. Bob had his notepad out and was jotting down information that he wanted to remember, leaving out some of the nonessential bits of information that meant nothing to him. Eleanor then reached a section of the article that talked about Charles personally, and Bob paid particular attention to her translation at this point.

"Professor Larouche, a bachelor, was thirty-six years old, born on May 19, 1951 in Paris, France. He was the only son of Catherine Larouche and the late Jean-Claude Larouche and his funeral arrangements will be private at a later date."

Eleanor mentioned that the second newspaper article was pretty similar to the first one and only added that he was the adopted son of the Larouches.

Bob handed her the third newspaper and pointed to what appeared to be a sort of biography on Page three. Eleanor gazed at this article and noted that Charles was an oboe player and member of his high school orchestra in Paris. The bio went on to state that Charles was very shy and very conscious of his small stature, just slightly over five feet tall. Eleanor went on but the summary of Charles' life had little more to offer then what had earlier been written about him.

Eleanor looked at the photos included in this article and saw no striking resemblance in the photos, nor why would she? Bob thanked her and offered her a complimentary dinner the next time she was at the restaurant and headed out the door.

"Harry Esten, please," the caller asked as the receptionist in the Providence FBI office answered.

"Who may I say is calling?"

"My name is Bob Elliott from Medway, Mass. And I was recently involved in a case that Mr. Esten was working on."

The receptionist had been instructed to transfer all calls for Harry to Frank Cabral and he answered the call.

"Frank Cabral, how may I help you?" Frank inquired.

"Actually, I'm trying to speak to Harry Esten," Bob repeated.

"Yes, I know who you are, Mr. Elliott, Harry is still unavailable at the moment," Frank added. "Is there something I can help you with?"

"This may be nothing, Mr. Cabral, but has anyone seen photographs of my twin brother who was murdered in Dijon a week ago?" Bob queried.

"That's a good question, Mr. Elliott and I really can't say that I've seen any pictures at all of…Charles Larouche."

"Well, since this guy was supposed to be my twin and I never met him, I asked the Dijon newspaper to send me copies of the newspapers with articles about him after the murder. I have to tell you, Mr. Cabral, this guy was five feet tall and half bald. I'm six feet tall with a full head of hair. My hair is brown, his looks black, what little he has."

"That's very interesting, Mr. Elliott, I'm sure Harry can answer more on this than I can. Leave me your phone number and I'll try to reach Harry and he'll give you a call."

The following morning, the doorbell rang at the Elliott household in Medway. Peering through the peephole, Julie recognized Harry Esten and Jim Howard at the door and let them in.

"Good morning, gentlemen, why do I suspect that this is not a social call?" she said somewhat sarcastically.

"Sorry to be a bother, Mrs. Elliott, but your husband called my office yesterday and Jim was kind enough to chauffeur me here. I'm still not well enough to drive yet," Harry answered.

"It looks to me like the other guy won. You've got sutures all over the place, Mr. Esten, that can't all be from the incident in Boston, can it?" Julie queried.

"No, ma'am, only the arm sling has to do with the Boston issue. The rest happened after that but that's not important for now. Is Bob around?" Harry responded.

Julie led the two men into the living room and left the room. Bob was working on a second cup of coffee and the Boston Globe when the doorbell had rung. He greeted Harry and Jim and they sat down.

"Frank told me of your concern about Charles Larouche and some photos of him that you have. May I see those, please?" Harry asked.

"Sure, by the way, what happened to you?" Bob replied.

"I'll tell you that in a minute, Bob, but let me take a look at what you have here. What made you send for the newspaper articles to begin with anyway?" Harry asked.

"Well, after the news finally settled in that I had a real twin brother, even though he was dead, something inside of me said that I needed to know a little more about him. Heck, he was my brother and I never knew him."

"You know, Bob, I would have wanted to know more myself if I was in your shoes."

Bob handed the newspapers to Harry and Jim and they mainly focused on the articles with photographs in them.

They both looked at each other and Harry could only say, "so much for good police work."

"I think you should ask your wife Julie to join us for a few minutes, I think she should hear what we are about to tell you."

Bob reacted somewhat surprised at Harry's comment but left the room to find Julie. She had her topcoat on her arm as she entered the living room, about to leave for her office.

"Your birth mother, Queen Farah, or Françoise Dupont as she once was called, informed us of some news she came across while making a stop in Paris on her way home with her husband, the king of Khatamori. She had been tormented for years at having given you boys up for adoption back then, and she felt she needed to visit the orphanage in Giverny one more time. As it turns out, when she was there, she learned of an awful mistake the orphanage made in their records. Charles Larouche had been given as the other child of Françoise and that was a mistake. Charles Larouche was the child of another French woman who died giving birth to Charles and no one knew who the father was. His first and middle names, Charles Andre, were the same as your brother's, and the birth dates were not far apart. The nun who kept the records back then, did so by hand and she copied Françoise's name as the birth mother on both Charles Andres. When they crosschecked the files by the names of the adoptive parents, it seems that your twin brother was adopted by an Italian couple and may very well be alive today.

"Had we looked at these photographs you've just showed me, we would likely have come to the same conclusion you've come up with, Bob. Charles Larouche was not your brother. His death was tragic and should have been prevented. Unfortunately, it wasn't, but we now have a new challenge, to find your real brother."

"You know, Mr. Esten, something inside of me felt uneasy about this, and I've had the same feeling before in my life. Once I had this unbearable pain in my left foot for no reason. I had the foot looked at, even had x-rays taken of the foot, but they found nothing and the pain went away in a couple of days. I also suffer from migraine headaches from time to time, but the doctors have never found anything that would cause them. Maybe it's true that identical twins feel each other's pain sometimes, no matter how far apart they are."

"I don't know about that, Bob, but I think we could use your help on this. Do you have several different non-baseball pictures of yourself we could borrow and make copies of?" Harry asked.

"I want to be in on this. I'm not an investigator, but if there is any truth to these inner feelings I have at times, maybe if you get close enough to my lost brother, I'll know it. I'll get you the photos you want, but I've got to be kept in the loop on this, please. If I have a twin brother out there, I've got to help in finding him," Bob pleaded.

"Jim and I will be flying to Rome tomorrow night. We have a contact there who will take us to the last known address. This Charles Andre was adopted by a Vito and Camille Melucci of Orvieto, Italy. That's our starting point. But I promise you, Bob, I will personally keep you informed every step of the way."

Julie, who hadn't spoken a word throughout this conversation, suddenly burst out.

"That would explain those weird unexplained aches and pains you used to tell me about, Bob. Wow, is this really happening to us?" she said excitedly.

"Mr. Esten, we've discussed this new disruption in our lives in the past two weeks, and we both agree, you just can't forget that your real mother is a queen and just let it sit like that. Perhaps we need to know her more as well while you begin your search for my brother?

"Italy is not out of the question for me, Mr. Esten. If you want me there at any time, just let me know. I need to be involved here. Heck, he might just be the one to consider in this succession stuff in the queen's country. Sounds to me though like this could be a dangerous succession."

CHAPTER 8

Ahmad had rested for two days in Paris and was now well enough to fly home to Khatamori. The Mauriers' Falcon jet had been released by the FBI and Captain Kocon, Ahmad's chief pilot, had flown the plane to Paris in anticipation of the king's flight from there to Khatamori.

Françoise was anxious for news on the whereabouts of her second son in Italy. Fr. Merrill had called her the day before to let her know that Harry Esten and Jim Howard were on their way to Rome to hook up with a Harry counterpart, Mike Stewart, who worked for the FBI as a legal attaché in the American Embassy there. According to the advance fax Stewart had sent to the Providence office, the Meluccis still owned vineyards in Orvieto and the family was highly respected and one of the most prominent families in Umbria.

Mike Stewart, originally from a small town in Oregon, had been with the FBI for ten years, spoke fluent Italian, and had agreed to handle investigations in Rome for two years before deciding whether to continue there or return to the FBI headquarters in Washington, D.C. for a new assignment. Mike's wife, Anita, was born in Florence and this assignment was welcomed by her since she still had family in Italy.

Mike met Harry and Jim at the airport just outside Rome and they immediately headed for Orvieto about fifty miles away. Mike had not told anyone in the Melucci family that they were coming for fear that the family would worry that something was wrong.

The drive in Mike's car took slightly over an hour on this chilly winter day. The three men pulled into the vineyard around two o'clock and headed for the wine store on the premises. Sophia greeted the three and asked how she could help them.

"Would Vito and Camille Melucci be here today?" Mike asked in perfect Italian.

"I believe they are both in the fields today," Sophia replied. "They are my brother and his wife. Is there something I can help you with?" she continued.

"Actually, no, Signora, these gentlemen are with the government in America and have come a very long way to speak to Vito and Camille. I'm afraid that's all I can say right now. This is Mr. Esten and Mr. Howard, and I can assure you that there is nothing wrong, merely some information we need to clarify." Mike flashed his FBI badge and his American Embassy credentials which Sophia looked at and returned to him.

"I will send one of the workers to get them. May I offer you a glass of wine while you wait, or perhaps a cappuccino, something to drink?" she courteously offered.

"A cappuccino would be nice," Harry replied as Jim nodded the same.

Ten minutes later, Vito and Camille entered the store wearing jeans, warm outer clothing and work gloves. Both were in their early sixties and had ruddy complexions from having spent many days in the vineyard sunshine over the years. They approached Sophia who pointed to the three men sipping coffees and they headed for their table.

"I am Vito Melucci and this is my wife Camille, how may I help you?" Vito asked with an inquiring tone.

Mike Stewart led the conversation by asking the couple if they were the parents of a male child who had been born at the Orphanage of the Sisters of Mercy in 1951 and whom they adopted in 1952.

"Where did you get this information?" Vito asked with a surprised look on his face. He quickly turned toward Sophia who was likely not close enough to hear Mike's question. Before he continued, he asked the three to follow Camille and him to the villa where they could continue the discussion privately. Harry Esten immediately noticed this information had apparently not been shared with other members of the family, at least as far as Sophia was concerned. There was also a concern by Harry that perhaps the son himself was still unaware that he was adopted, even though he was thirty-five years old.

"Why are you bringing up my son's adoption?" asked Camille as they walked into the villa nearby.

"I'll let these two gentlemen explain this to you, Signora Melucci. This is Mr. Esten from the FBI in the United States and this is Mr. Howard, his associate in this matter," Stewart commented.

"First, I have two questions to ask of you, Mr. and Mrs. Melucci, does your son know that he is adopted and, if so, is he here at the vineyard or somewhere we can talk to him?" Harry asked.

"I will not answer any of these questions until you tell me what this is about," Vito growled.

"Were you aware when you adopted your son that he was a twin whose brother had been adopted from the orphanage a year earlier by an American couple?" Jim chimed in.

"My son was adopted by us in 1952 because his mother gave him up to the orphanage. We knew that he was a twin and that his brother had been adopted by someone else the year before. We do not know who adopted the other boy or who the mother was, and we really don't care to know," Camille said.

"But does your son know that he was adopted? It is very important for us to know," Jim continued.

"Why is it important?" Vito retorted, "this happened thirty-four years ago when the child was but a year old?"

"His real mother is a queen of a middle eastern country today. He and his twin brother may be eligible to succeed her husband when he dies. So the two of them may be in danger from certain enemies in that country who don't want this to happen and might want to harm your son and his brother in America. The small country is called Khatamori. It is very complicated, I know, but your son may be in danger if we don't get to him before others do, Mr. Melucci."

"Is your son's name Charles Andre?" asked Harry.

Vito looked at Camille and they had blank looks on their faces as Camille began to speak.

"Our son was to be raised here in Orvieto. As an Italian boy, we felt he should have an Italian name, so we changed his name to Carlo Andrea, which is the Italian name for Charles Andre."

Vito then added, "Carlo has known that he was adopted since he was eighteen years old and, although curious about who his real parents are, has never gone out of his way to find out who they are. He has too many things on his mind and not enough time to travel to the orphanage to even find out who they are. He does not live here any longer, not since he received his medical degree from the University of Florence nearly ten years ago. My sister, Lucia, herself a doctor, and Carlo's aunt, like Sophia, my other sister, have loved Carlo as if he were their own son and Lucia was the reason Carlo chose to be a doctor in the first place. Lucia is also his godmother and mentor. But Carlo has a mind of his own, that's why he is in Ethiopia today, giving his time to treat the people in the villages there who are desperately in need of medical attention. We have not seen him in almost two years, but he writes and telephones via satellite every month. We spoke to him last week by phone," Vito added.

"Carlo's birth mother is Queen Farah, originally Françoise Dupont when she lived in Paris before she gave birth to the two boys. The father of the boys is a priest in the United States named Fr. Richard Merrill who had a brief affair with Françoise Dupont thirty-six years ago and never knew about the boys until about three weeks ago. Carlo's twin brother is Robert Elliott, also from the United States," Harry began.

As he started to relate his story to Vito and Camille, he withdrew several photos of Bob Elliott from the inside pocket of his suit coat and showed them to the Meluccis. A loud gasp came out of Camille as she held her hand to her open mouth.

"This is Carlo, Mr. Esten, this is a photo of my son," Vito said in utter amazement. "Oh, my God, if this is Robert Elliott, Mr. Esten, then they surely are twins."

"We will need to get exactly where he is located in Ethiopia if we are to get information to him that he might be in danger," Harry stated.

Vito rose from his chair in the living room of the villa and slid open a drawer in the credenza near the telephone. There he pulled out a piece of paper and a pen and copied down the address for Harry.

The three men then rose and were about to leave when Harry turned to Vito and added, "Do Sofia and Lucia know that Carlo is adopted?"

"No, we never mentioned it and after we told Carlo that he was adopted long ago, he asked us not to tell them. He didn't see the point in telling them," Camille answered.

"For the time being, it would be best if this information not be discussed with anyone in case strangers start inquiring about Carlo. It's only a matter of time before that happens. You are to contact Mike Stewart in Rome immediately if anyone asks about Carlo, is that clear with the both of you?" Harry added.

Both Vito and Camille nodded their understanding of Harry's comments and both were expected to be very cautious in dealing with strangers, but Vito was concerned as to how he would pass along this information to Sophia without her asking why. Harry said that Vito should inform

Sofia that Carlo might be the victim of some scam artists seeking to steal his identity because he would not be around to stop someone from using his name. At the first mention that Carlo was in Ethiopia, the threat to his life would increase significantly. Unfortunately, as Harry explained, there shouldn't be any conversation about Carlo to anyone at all outside direct family members. Hopefully, Vito's sisters had not discussed Carlo to too many other people outside the villa, although, because they were so proud of what their nephew was doing, many in Orvieto already knew that Carlo was in Ethiopia working in a hospital there.

Harry apologized to Vito and Camille for being the bearer of this news and for disrupting their lives as a result of it. He promised to keep them informed as soon as any further news occurred. Mike handed Vito his card with all the contact information he needed.

Getting to Ethiopia in this day and age would not be an easy task.

CHAPTER 9

The flight to Banra was smooth and, as Captain Kocon prepared the Falcon jet for landing, Ahmad and Françoise both peered out the plane's windows at their beloved Khatamori.

Françoise could only think of her other son and if there was any news on his whereabouts, while Ahmad pondered his eventual meeting with Answa Talon's surviving sons. Talon's three sons were all in their twenties, with the oldest, Rafick, being the most difficult to deal with. The other two, Jamal and Nabil, were both hard-working happily married men who adored Ahmad. Ahmad's uncle, his father's brother, had passed away when the boys were very young. Ahmad, as the eventual ruler of the country, treated his cousin's sons like they were his own. Only Rafick gave Ahmad any difficulty as he believed that his father, Answa, would someday become king following Ahmad's death. Because Ahmad and Françoise had no known children, Rafick knew that if this happened to his father, he in turn would succeed Answa one day as the oldest son.

Now that Answa was dead in his failed attempt to kill Ahmad, Rafick would surely be a challenge for Ahmad. Any hint of a further uprising by Rafick would surely lead to his imprisonment or even execution by Ahmad, something he had never done or seen in all the years in the royal family. Khatamori had always been a peaceful country because the Maurier family had always shown respect for its people. Since their marriage nearly thirty-four years ago, Françoise had been the voice of women's rights and virtually all the women in the country praised her every move, from female appointments in government to high posts in the ministry of finance. Higher education for women became as available to them as it did to the men and for this, Françoise could not have been happier. Ironically, Answa had two of his five daughters, Sakinah and Najla, who were closely involved with Françoise in most of the feminist movements. Answa's three wives all had their purpose, Faridah, or Fari as Answa would call her, to bear his children, Sakara to appear with him at public places, and Nalia to maintain the household. Ahmad was aware that Answa never respected them and treated them rudely.

The royal couple was greeted at the terminal by thousands of Khatamorans as news of Ahmad's successful kidney transplant operation had been announced a week earlier, and his expected arrival had throngs of supporters amassing in or near the airport. When the Falcon jet door opened, the crowd immediately quieted down in anticipation of his appearance. Inside the plane, Ahmad insisted on being helped to his feet and guided to the open doorway which had been abutted to a ramp rather than a staircase. Françoise, although quite leery of this gesture, knew that her husband had to portray himself to his people as a sign of strength. He carefully and slowly walked to the doorway dressed in his finest regal attire and, as he emerged on the landing outside, the crowd erupted in the same way as if a new pope had appeared on the balcony in the Vatican for the first time. Ahmad limply waved to the crowd and even managed a broad smile as the cheers abounded. Shortly thereafter, he could be seen getting seated in a wheelchair with Queen Farah by his side as they were led down the ramp by Kaleel, Ahmad's loyal servant. They embarked into the king's black limousine and members of his entourage followed closely behind. As the caravan of cars left the airport, thousands more lined the streets, waving as the cars passed by.

"It is good to be home again," Ahmad said to Françoise.

"The people have missed you dearly, my love, and they show you their love the only way they can," Françoise answered.

"Kaleel, you are to assemble Answa's entire family at the palace tomorrow afternoon at two o'clock. If someone will not be there, I want to know immediately. They must hear directly from me as to what has happened over the last two weeks," Ahmad declared.

"Ahmad, are you sure that you are up to this so soon after the surgery?" Françoise asked with a worrisome tone in her voice.

"This cannot wait, especially if Rafick is involved somehow. I will be fine. There will be several security people in the room with us, men who are still loyal to me and not to Answa and his malicious band of rebels."

As the entourage reached the long entryway to the palace grounds, all of the palace's workers were lined up in single file on both sides of the road, all the way to the main steps leading into the palace.

"Kaleel, I would like you to take me to the gardens for a while, Françoise and I need to be there right now. I will have her summon you when I am ready to rest in my suite," Ahmad instructed.

"Yes, Your Highness, as you wish."

Once in their enchanted gardens, the late afternoon sunshine radiated comfortable warmth as the skyline reflected the golden rays of sun off the puffs of clouds above. Françoise sat in a chair near Ahmad's wheelchair and they did not speak for minutes. Then, as if Ahmad had suddenly regained his alertness, he spoke. "My dearest love, how many more years has this new kidney brought to me, and what is to happen to Khatamori when I am gone? You cannot know that your two sons will ever be interested in living here, learning our culture and our beliefs, and giving up everything they are accustomed to, just to succeed me. You know that I will have nothing but the highest respect for them when I eventually meet them, if they ever decide to come here one day. There is no assurance that the second son will even be found yet. And your son in America may also never be heard from again. In the meantime, there are other members of our family that I must pay attention to because one of Answa's sons may very well be the one to continue what we have built here. If Rafick is involved in this attempt by Answa, he will never rule Khatamori and I shall banish him from here forever. Tomorrow will be an interesting day with Answa's family."

"Ahmad, I have brought you a burden that you did not need at this time, but I feared that you would not survive this ordeal. The thought of Answa becoming king was very troublesome to me and I knew he would find out about my sons and try to bring harm upon them. I should never have given up my sons. Perhaps you would have still seen the sweet young French woman you met at the Louvre, even though she had two young sons to care for at the time. How I wish I could undo the foolishness of so many years ago."

"It is hard to imagine what I would have done differently, even knowing of the sons already born by another man. I only wish I had known long ago so I could have been the father they deserved, and I could have brought them up in our ways. Now, who knows who they really are and what they want in life," Ahmad replied.

"Fr. Merrill has left word Harry Esten and Jim Howard are on their way to Italy to try to locate Charles Andre. It seems that he was adopted by vineyard owners in a town called Orvieto," Françoise said.

"Orvieto, my love, is the home of wonderful dry white wine. It is truly an excellent wine which we have served at many functions at the palace over the years. If their adopted son is as fine as the wine they make, your son certainly has grown in wonderful surroundings. We will have to wait to see what happens next."

The following afternoon, as planned, Ahmad entered a large room in the palace where the Talon family was assembled. He sat in his wheelchair clad in his royal robes and surrounded by armed guards as he addressed them all.

"This is the saddest moment in my life other than when my father, your late king, died some years ago. Answa and I were very close at one time, but his rush to take my place before its time led him to do a foolish thing, and that caused him to die sooner than he should have. Those who were entrusted to protect me in America did exactly as they should, and because of them, I am here today and your husband and father is not." Ahmad was looking directly at Rafick when he made those comments and carefully went on.

"There will be no further events in this matter, or I will punish any of you who cause trouble in this family again. I mourn for your loss, and I will do all that is in my power to have you continue your lives in our kingdom as they were, but I will not allow harm or attempts to harm anyone whose position was to protect me. What Answa has done was wrong and he has paid the price. It is not something I had wished for."

"Your Highness," Rafick said with a defiant air in his voice, "was it right for your queen to deceive you all these years by not telling you of sons she had with a holy man? Sons she chose to give up because she knew she was not worthy to raise them? Sons that she is trying to place in line to succeed you when so many others have been loyal to you all these years?"

"Queen Farah has made few mistakes in all the years she has been your queen. The only mistake here is she did not tell me long ago. The two sons were unfortunate, and she did not know her lover at the time was a priest. Once she found out, she immediately ended their brief affair. Even the priest was unaware she bore two sons until a few weeks ago. The decision as to who will follow me in ruling Khatamori is mine and mine alone. If I choose to name one of her sons or one of you, it is for me to decide. Your father was not able to accept that others could be considered to succeed me. Answa believed that he had to kill me to be sure he would be the next king before I met Queen Farah's sons. To be sure they had no chance to succeed me, he even attempted to kill them as well, but failed miserably."

"My father was a direct descendant of the royal family and deserved to succeed you," Rafick retorted.

"And he most likely would have, but not by trying to remove me before my time," Ahmad responded.

Rafick rose to his feet and started to head out of the room, but several guards blocked the doorway. Rafick turned to Ahmad and demanded, "Am I to be detained or killed too, even if my only crime is that I am the oldest son of your dead cousin and the next descendant in line to succeed you?"

"You are free to go, Rafick, but hear me well, nothing is to happen to the queen's sons or you will be held accountable." The king made eye contact with each of the Talon family members. "The rest of you are not to talk about this to anyone outside this family again. Am I understood?"

The other two sons, all five daughters, and the three widows all agreed not to discuss this until Ahmad allowed it. Following this agreement, two of the daughters asked Ahmad if this also meant they could no longer work with Queen Farah in promoting more women's activities throughout the kingdom. Ahmad could sense the concern in the two young women who cherished what Queen Farah had accomplished and that the forward momentum for women would suddenly stop. They both smiled when Ahmad allowed them to continue their interaction with the queen. At this news, Ahmad ended the meeting and Answa's family left the room.

"So, Ahmad, how did it go with the family?" Françoise asked as Ahmad was wheeled into their suite.

"I fear we have not heard the last of Rafick. He will never accept anyone but himself as my successor, not even one of his own brothers if I choose one of them over him. The thought that one of your sons would be considered as king, he will never condone this. What we have here, my love, is the making of a dangerous succession."

"He is like his father, Ahmad, always believing that he is entitled to rule Khatamori, even if he has never shown any kind of leadership or loyalty to you. Answa was more interested in his own power than using his position in a responsible way. If Rafick is not involved in his father's evildoing, I would be surprised. How could Rafick know of my sons, it has never before been discussed? When I spoke to Fr. Merrill yesterday after we arrived, he told me that someone destroyed Harry Esten's home in America and left a note addressed to him that said 'An Eye for an Eye, The Worst Is Yet To Come'. Clearly someone is seeking revenge for Answa's death. Who else would do this if not his own son?" Françoise continued.

"I will ask Kaleel to find out, if he can, where Rafick has been when all of this transpired. You must tell the Americans that your Bob Elliott may still be in trouble if Rafick is up to something. We cannot allow more bloodshed to these people. They have done nothing to deserve any of this."

"I will call Fr. Merrill again and ask him to speak to Mr. Esten to make sure Robert is not harmed. But there is more, Ahmad. It seems that my other son is named Carlo Melucci and he is a doctor, a surgeon Ahmad! It seems he has that good upbringing you talked about earlier. He has given his time to help the poor in the African country of Ethiopia, and no one knows when he will return to Orvieto. Fr. Merrill said that it may take months for Mr. Esten and Mr. Howard to even get there because of all the vaccines they need and the papers they must prepare just to go there. Apparently, it is a dangerous country these days and, with the poor food conditions there, there is a great amount of unrest with the government and a great deal of risk in being there. He is in a very difficult place my Charles...err, Carlo as they had renamed him long ago. He knows he was adopted but does not know who I am. It will be some time before we can protect him, Ahmad, first we have to find him," Françoise continued.

"I will rest now, Françoise, all of this news and the confrontation with Rafick has tired me greatly. You should know though that Sakinah and Najla want to continue to work with you if you will have them. They bear no ill will toward you and believe in what you do for them and for all the women here. They are good people, Françoise," Ahmad stated, looking very frail.

"Perhaps it was too soon to talk to Answa's family?"

"Now that I have seen and spoken to Rafick, I wish it had been even sooner," Ahmad replied sorrowfully.

* * *

Rafick had very little in common with his two brothers, and they did not agree with his rebellious attitude toward Ahmad. Unlike Rafick, Jamal and Nabil were very much involved in the oil business and negotiated most of the contracts with foreign buyers. Jamal, at twenty-six, was two years older than Nabil and held a higher position than Nabil.

He worked hard to assure the country's main resource was never jeopardized as he stayed informed on the latest technologies in the oil industry. He hired experts when he had to, but always tried to employ Khatamorans when he could. Nabil was responsible for the exportation segment of the industry and the pipeline system used to transport the oil to tankers along the Mediterranean Sea.

Looking at the logistics of routing oil to the rest of the world from Khatamori and other Arab nations to the Indian Ocean and the rest of the globe, the only other option besides the Mediterranean route was to route the pipelines to different sites on the Arabian Peninsula. This route would channel the oil pipelines directly to the Red Sea. It was essential that all of the Arab oil-producing countries worked in cooperation with each other and were not enemies with each other.

Jamal maintained excellent relations with the surrounding Arab nations and Khatamori always treated its allies with much respect. They, in turn, held Jamal in high regard and he would often attend receptions at the palace for visiting dignitaries from these nations. His wife, Malika, also assisted the queen in her women's advocacy programs. She was the mother of two sons and, like Ahmad, Jamal had but one wife. In his mind, if you have a wife that you love, that has borne your children, and who is very presentable in social settings, why would you need another?

Nabil, at age twenty-four, was more the engineer of the family and would oversee the production facilities to assure the smooth flow of oil from the wells to the pipelines. Since Khatamori did not have its own refining plant, the crude oil was sent to a plant closer to the Mediterranean for processing before being loaded on tankers and shipped worldwide.

Both brothers served their roles well and Ahmad was hopeful that this would continue despite the abrupt death of their father. They had trouble understanding why Answa had revolted against Ahmad rather than waiting for normal succession after Ahmad's death. They thought news about the queen's sons did not impose a threat, and they agreed the eventual decision for succession should be Ahmad's. Being eligible to succeed the king, as opposed to being likely to succeed him, was no assurance that either Bob Elliott or Carlo Melucci would ever be seriously considered, especially until Ahmad had the opportunity to meet them and make that determination after spending an extensive period of time with them.

For now, Françoise was only interested in finding Carlo. The rest would play itself out as it occurred. Ethiopia, she thought, is so much closer to Khatamori, and if Carlo was found there alive, all she could imagine was him walking up the palace steps one day.

Ethiopia was so close, and yet so far away.

CHAPTER 10

In 1985, Dr. Carlo Melucci had agreed to spend at least two years as a surgeon at the Mekelle Hospital in Tigray, a region in northern Ethiopia which had been hit hard with famines as a result of terrible droughts twice in recent years. Trained medical personnel were in short supply in a country with over forty million people and the ratio of citizens to physicians was one of the worst in the world. Carlo had listened to a plea at the Florence Medical School from a missionary group running a medical school in Ethiopia. The existing medical personnel could not possibly handle all the people seeking medical attention. Carlo believed he was young enough to sacrifice a few years of his life to help people in need and still return afterwards to begin a practice in Italy.

Ethiopia is unique among African countries because, with the brief exception of an Italian invasion during World War II, it was never ruled by another country. It is the oldest independent country in Africa, and one of the oldest in the world. Ethiopia is a landlocked country bordered by Eritrea to the north, Djibouti and Somalia to the east, Sudan to the west, and Kenya to the south. It is the second-most populated nation on the African continent, about roughly twice the size of Texas, has around eighty ethnic groups, its own alphabet and calendar, and nearly eighty percent of its people work in agriculture. Recurring droughts hit this industry hard, leading to widespread food shortages and famine in one of the poorest countries in the world.

Carlo was single, never having had any serious relationship with the women he had dated over the years throughout medical school. Not that medical school offered much time for dating to begin with. Other than his parents who were surrounded by other family members, he was not leaving anyone behind by volunteering for this mercy mission.

He had taken a flight to Addis Ababa by way of Copenhagen and Cairo in late summer of that year. As the plane descended for the airport in Addis Ababa, all you could see at first were scattered clouds. The city looked completely sealed afterward by dense forests of eucalyptus trees. Years earlier, an old emperor in Ethiopia had imported eucalyptus from Madagascar, not for its oil, but as firewood since Addis Ababa needed it badly at the time. Eucalyptus had thrived in the Ethiopian soil, and it grew rapidly. It seems these trees were indestructible, always returning in strength wherever they were cut down, and proved ideal for framing houses.

When openings in the trees finally emerged, he could see circular, thatched-roofed houses and corrugated-tin-roofed houses, cramped together throughout. Finally, Carlo could see a glimpse of the modern city center. As the plane neared the airport, an entire hillside turned to a flaming orange from the blooming of the meskel flower which signaled the rainy season had ended. Another hillside displayed brown lean-tos and shacks of corrugated tin. The pilot made a quick pass by the runway to alert the customs agent below to get on his bicycle and shoo stray cows from the runway. He then circled and landed.

Within minutes, Carlo grabbed his luggage and headed for his connecting flight to Mekelle, Tigray where the hospital was located about three hundred miles north of Addis Ababa, Ethiopia's capital city. Mekelle would be only an hour flight away via Ethiopian Airlines.

At the Alula Aba Airport, he was greeted by Dr. Jean Gerard, a French surgeon, who was ecstatic at the sight of another surgeon. Dr. Gerard was the only surgeon at Mekelle Hospital and very badly needed assistance. He had been at the hospital for two years and had not had an entire day without having to attend to some emergency procedure. He had threatened to leave if he was not given another surgeon and that was when the plea was sent to the University of Florence Medical School, among others. Gerard hailed from a small hospital just outside Paris and had lost interest in his general practice following the death of his wife. His three sons were all grown, married and with careers of their own and, at age fifty-six, he decided to do missionary-type medical work which led him to Mekelle Hospital.

Dr. Gerard and Carlo became close friends over the next two years and shared their experiences as they often consulted with each other on many operations, even assisting each other on major surgeries. They both had needed to learn to speak English better to communicate with each other. English was the language commonly spoken in the hospital setting, although the various local dialects were always a challenge were it not for the local nurses who could translate information from the patients.

The only other person Carlo got to know quite well was Dr. Rachel Owens, a native of Johannesburg, South Africa and an AIDS specialist. The rapid onslaught of AIDS cases in the region was rampant and Owens was in the region to attempt to stem further growth of the disease. She would visit surrounding villages in the Tigray region that recently had patients diagnosed with the disease at Mekelle or other hospitals in the Tigray region. Not only was this work time-consuming, but very dangerous, as the roads in Tigray leading to many villages could often be the sight of rebel forces. The region of Tigray was not well-supported by the Ethiopian government in the late 1980s and rebel forces were formed to prevent any food crops from being removed from the region by government troops. At times, it was not uncommon for missionaries or medical personnel to either be captured or killed without warning or logical reasons. On other occasions, these people were held for ransom and the threat of being killed certainly was real. These threats didn't bother Dr. Owens as she ventured into small villages with her local guide and tended to any AIDS afflicted person there. For this service, she would always be greeted by the woman of the house with a traditional coffee.

Ethiopia is considered to be the birthplace of coffee as far back as the ninth century and the cultivation and picking of coffee was a central part of Ethiopian culture. Asking someone to stay for coffee in one of the villages literally meant a two-to three-hour ceremony as a thank you for the service provided to anyone in the household.

The coffee ceremony was considered to be the most important social occasion in the villages she visited, and was considered a sign of respect and friendship not to be taken lightly. At such ceremony, Dr. Owens would discuss topics such as politics, the local community, or just about anything she wanted to. She also had been trained beforehand to throw abundant praise to the ceremony's performer and the brew produced.

The coffee ceremony played a spiritual role in Ethiopia, one which emphasized the importance of Ethiopian coffee culture where supposedly a transformation of the spirit took place during the ceremony. Women who performed it would spread fresh, aromatic grasses and flowers across the floor. They then began by burning incense to ward off evil spirits and continued to burn incense throughout the ceremony. From filling a black-clay coffeepot with water and placing it over hot coals, to stirring and shaking coffee beans before roasting them in a pan, to grinding the beans before boiling them, the ceremony exerted the powerful aroma of the roasted coffee, considered to be an important aspect of the ceremony.

Dr. Owens would watch the hostess in one of the houses then pour the coffee in a single stream from about a foot above the ceramic cups without ever getting coffee grounds in the cups. Dr. Owens would encounter this same ceremony at least two to three times a day as the ceremony was performed in most of the villages. The courtesy that she had to extend to each hostess meant she was limited in the number of villages she could visit each day.

Dr. Owens was subsidized by the World Health Organization and other AIDS groups beginning to crop up. Her schedule was very similar to the schedules of other doctors in the local hospitals, with very little time off throughout the year. Her parents lived in Krugersdorp, South Africa, just south of Johannesburg. At thirty-seven years old, Rachel could have easily been a model or an actress, her beauty and intelligence shone through in her every action. She looked out of place in this environment afflicted with this dreaded disease. However, if you observed her in practice, you would see the tenderness and concern she conveyed to all the patients she attended. Her Christian upbringing in South Africa made this commitment to serve others all that much easier. She was more at ease wearing pants and a tee shirt while in the villages than trying to impress anyone with finer clothes. She believed she was in Ethiopia to make a difference, not an impression. She lived a simple life and had a small apartment within walking distance to Mekelle Hospital which she used as her base of operation.

When they first met in late 1985, Carlo, at first glance, thought she was too laid back about her appearance. As their relationship grew, he noticed subtle changes in her dress and grooming habits which brought out her long blonde hair and sleek long legs on her five-foot seven inch body.

Their relationship had been as friends only, even if they had dinner together with a bottle of wine with candlelight and soft music. On these occasions, because both of them were probably exhausted following a long day in surgery or out in the dusty and windy hot surroundings, they both welcomed the peace and quiet from a simple dinner at a local restaurant.

One of Rachel's only breaks from the seven day schedule she kept was the annual conference on AIDS held in different cities of the world each year. In June, 1988, the International AIDS Conference was to be held in Stockholm, Sweden, and since the World Health Organization paid for all her expenses to attend, it was something she looked forward to, and talked about it often with Carlo. He had recalled the 1987 conference in Washington, D.C. and that was when he realized how much he missed her company, even though she was gone for a week. In late 1987, when Rachel went home to South Africa for two weeks during the holidays, Carlo realized Rachel likely was becoming more than just a friend, at least in his mind. He was about to see if the feelings were mutual.

Carlo was six feet tall, light brown hair and in excellent physical condition. His daily regimen included a five-mile run, followed by a series of aerobic exercises and weight-lifting. A shower and breakfast would follow, and by seven o'clock he would then be off to the hospital. He suffered from occasional severe headaches which he attributed to his rigorous schedule, but a few aspirins usually would do the trick at getting rid of the headaches. He brushed aside any personal ailments he had for the sake of staying on schedule with surgeries at the hospital and soon realized that Dr. Gerard did the same. So, if Carlo accidentally twisted an ankle running the streets of Mekelle some mornings because of poor road conditions, he would suffer the foot pain even during surgery. Such was the life of a surgeon in a remote overpopulated location.

His two-year commitment at Mekelle Hospital was coming to an end and Carlo and Jean Gerard were now discussing Carlo's future plans almost daily. The addition of Carlo as a second surgeon eased the impossible load on Gerard to the point where he hoped Carlo would continue on at the hospital for a while longer. Carlo had not made up his mind yet, although clearly his parents in Orvieto wanted him back home to practice there, alongside his Aunt Lucia, now one of the more visible and well-respected doctors in Orvieto.

In her early sixties, the timing for Carlo to step into her practice was ideal. The facilities in Orvieto were quite modern, much more so than at Mekelle, and the compensation would be much greater, more than enough to raise a family. Not that a huge salary was essential since he would no doubt inherit most of the vineyard one day, a property and business worth millions of dollars. There was another person with whom he needed to discuss this with.

Rachel's plans for her future would directly impact Carlo's decision, and these plans would not occur overnight. If he was to test the waters on a relationship with Rachel anytime soon, it would necessitate his staying on at Mekelle for at least one more year. He pondered this on his way to pick up Rachel at the airport.

Rachel's parents owned a summer house on the coast at Richards Bay where they spent the Christmas holidays. The twenty-eight hundred mile trip from South Africa to Tigray would be very tiring, and following six hours of flight time, Carlo knew she would be exhausted and not in the mood for talking about their future relationship today. That was fine with Carlo, and it could be the subject for another day. Right now he was just anxious to see her again.

As she emerged from the small terminal and headed toward the baggage claim area, Carlo spotted her and waved eagerly as she approached. In the spur of the moment, Carlo greeted her with a huge hug and then kissed her, something he had not done before. Rachel was immediately startled by this move and withdrew from Carlo, her face flush with surprise.

"Welcome back, Rachel, it's not been the same without you around here. I've got no one else to bear my soul to, no one to listen to my moans about the crazy schedule I've got, just no one who listens like you do."

"Well, Carlo, my man, sitting on the beach with a margarita, at our summer home, was quite nice, so you'll excuse me if I tell you that Mekelle was the last thing on my mind for the last two weeks," Rachel countered.

"And me, what about me, Rachel? Did you at least miss my smiling face a little bit during that time?"

"Well, maybe during the first cocktail because I had no one to clang glasses with, but after that, it gets all blurry."

Rachel looked marvelous with her new tan and her smile brought a smile to Carlo as well. Nevertheless, Rachel still wondered about the kiss, and did not quite know how to react to it. So she said nothing further as they grabbed her luggage and headed back to her apartment in Mekelle. It was a short ride and, as he suspected, Rachel was tired from the long flight and was ready to call it a day. Carlo bid her goodnight and headed out the door after bringing in her luggage. Tomorrow would be another day.

CHAPTER 11

Harry and Jim had hit the proverbial wall in their efforts
to arrange for their trip to Ethiopia in search of Carlo
Melucci. The problem was not in properly getting all the
necessary vaccinations before being allowed to fly to Addis
Ababa. The problem stemmed from the ongoing turmoil
between the rebel forces and the Ethiopian government
troops in the Tigray section of the country. The current
administration was seen as non-supportive in assisting to
the needs of the northern residents hit hardest by droughts
and famine. On occasion, the government troops were
accused of redirecting food supplies destined for the
Tigray region. This action caused the people of that region
to form resistance units to prevent this from re-occurring.
So, Harry and Jim had difficulty in gaining visas to this area.
The Ethiopian government believed the risks of allowing

travel to this territory were too great, and no visas would be issued except for groups issuing food and medical supplies until the danger subsided.

They returned to Rhode Island and were informed that they would be notified when the visas could be issued, perhaps not for several months. Jim returned to Continental Life while Harry was reassigned to an office assignment at the Bureau pending doctor's clearance to return to field work. From the office, he called Laura at the Narragansett police station and asked if he was still welcome at her place until he found an apartment nearby. She was pleasantly surprised by the phone call and immediately agreed to let him stay as long as he needed. She was disappointed to hear the Italian trip came up empty, and now Ethiopia was the next possible location of Carlo. As a gesture of appreciation, Harry asked Laura if he could take her to dinner that night. He was getting a ride to her house and could be there around six o'clock. They could then take his car for dinner. Laura agreed and would pick the restaurant, as he requested.

At six o'clock, the car carrying Harry pulled into Laura's driveway behind Harry's car. Headlights glared into Laura's kitchen window which signaled his arrival. Laura opened the kitchen door and greeted Harry with a warm smile. Harry did a double take when he saw Laura in a beautiful red dress, her hair down, and her facial features bringing out a beauty he never expected. He was momentarily stunned, then finally managed to mutter an inarticulate "Wow."

Flustered by his reaction, Harry averted his eyes quickly and reached for his car keys on the kitchen counter. With his gunshot wound now healed and the sutures removed,

Harry had shed the arm sling. Knowing Harry had yet to begin physical therapy, Laura offered to drive, but Harry insisted that he could handle it. As they left the house, light snow began to fall.

Laura had chosen the Lobster Pot Restaurant because of its extensive menu and the closeness to her home. She had called earlier that day and made reservations.

They entered the Lobster Pot, Harry took off their coats and handed them to the coat room attendant and they were led to a table near the fireplace. The candle-light dinner was exquisite and Harry and Laura exchanged toasts before and during the meal. There was something very attractive in the way Laura looked in the red dress.

The ease of the surroundings, and the warm glow from the fireplace were affecting Laura as well, and she was finding it increasingly difficult to keep her gaze off Harry. For the week or so he had been away, she missed his company. They hardly knew each other, and yet, she felt like she had known him for years. Laura was good at assessing a situation, especially in her investigative line of work, and assessing Harry was a no-brainer. She liked what she heard, she liked what she saw, and she was not about to let it slip away.

They spent nearly three hours at the restaurant. Harry related how he and Jim had hit a snag in the next step in locating Carlo, and he likely wouldn't be able to get to Ethiopia until May or June. In the meantime, he would focus on trying to locate and identify the assailant who was responsible for razing his house. Laura again offered to help in any way she could. Having a place to stay for now was all the help Harry needed.

"Harry, there is no rush. You can stay for however long it takes. Really, it's not as if I have backed up reservations to use my spare room. And besides, even after you find a place, you'll need furniture, appliances, you name it, and that'll take some time too. So, please don't think you're putting me out, you're fine, I trust you," Laura stated.

"You have to be the most trusting soul I know, Laura, and I don't know that I deserve what you're doing for me right now. But I do enjoy your company very much and it's been quite lonely for me the last few years. I don't remember the last time I had dinner with a woman. It was with...." His mind wandered to Lucy for a moment but he quickly caught himself and went on. "I'm feeling better already."

"How can I not enjoy your company? I'm not one who's used to being taken out to dinner. Being a cop tends to scare off a lot of men these days. Most think police women are rough and tough and don't have personal lives like all other women. Tell you what, if you take me out to dinner every week, you can stay at my place forever," Laura responded with some seriousness in her voice.

Harry got the tab, paid the bill, retrieved their coats, and he and Laura headed out the door. The January air was cold in Rhode Island at night and the breeze coming off the ocean in Narragansett made it feel even colder.

"I think I'm okay to drive again, Laura, or at least I'd like to give it a try again. We're not that far from your place and there are not too many cars on the road tonight. Since I won't be heading to Ethiopia for a while, I'll probably be working out of the Providence office for a few months, and I can't expect somebody to keep giving me a ride to and from Providence, can I?" Harry said.

"If you feel up to it, Harry, go for it. I'll be close by if it doesn't feel right just yet," Laura responded.

As they left the restaurant and were about to cross the street leading to the parking lot, Harry took Laura by the hand. She did not expect this gesture from Harry, nor did she reject it. The feeling of holding hands with a man might not have been seen as a big deal by most women but, to Laura, it was not something she could remember happening in quite some time, certainly not the last few years. For Harry, this was the first time he held a woman's hand since before Lucy died nearly three years earlier.

Harry unlocked the passenger door and opened it. Laura sat down, again not remembering the last time a man held any door open for her. She smiled at Harry's simple gesture, and it made Harry more at ease as he got in on the driver's side. The short ride back to Bonnet Shores was mostly in silence, Harry and Laura, unaware of the subtle mutual advances each was making. They pulled into Laura's driveway around nine o'clock, and Harry was beginning to feel the effects of his long flight from Italy and the time change. He had been up nearly twenty hours now and started yawning as they entered the house.

"I'm sorry, Laura, I think the long day and the couple of glasses of wine at dinner are catching up to me."

"You most certainly have been busy, and a good night's sleep should hit the spot tonight," Laura answered.

He took his coat off and hung it on the nearby hallway coat rack, Laura turned to do the same with her coat. She then turned to face Harry, he put his hands around her waist and kissed her gently on the lips. Laura was at first surprised at this short kiss but then wrapped her arms around Harry and embraced him warmly. Her body in his were seamless at that moment.

"Thank you for a lovely dinner out, Laura. I needed this tonight. I've been alone for a long time, and I'm not sure if I've overstepped my welcome here."

"Harry, you stayed at my house for just a few days. Then you went off to Italy for a week and now your back. I missed you. I missed your company and I enjoyed waiting on you while you were recuperating. I don't know what's going to happen next, but right now I am enjoying what I'm feeling and those are not feelings I've had for anyone in a long, long time."

"I'd better stop here for now, Laura, I don't want to do anything foolish because I've been up for so long and, besides, I think I've been bolder tonight than I've been in quite some time. I'd better get ready for bed."

"That's fine, Harry, I understand. I think I'll take a shower before bed and I'll see you in the morning," Laura answered.

Harry grabbed his suitcase from near the kitchen table and headed for his room. Laura did a few housekeeping chores in the kitchen and turned on the hallway light leading to her room after she turned off the lights in the kitchen and the outside light.

Harry was pondering many thoughts as he began to undress and slip into his flannel pajamas. Cold winter nights in New England meant winter sleepwear as the temperature often went down into the teens or lower at night. He brushed his teeth in the bathroom and could hear the shower running in the bathroom next to his. Thoughts of Laura in the shower brought a smile to his face and he suddenly was at ease with himself despite an unsuccessful trip to Orvieto and the likelihood of delays for months in going to the next step. He turned off the bathroom light and headed for bed with the bedroom door slightly open to faintly catch the glow of the night light in the hallway.

He lay down in bed, physically drained, and fell asleep nearly as quickly as his head hit the pillow. A short while later, Laura, in her nightgown, would have been visible by Harry at his bedroom door as she stood there in silence. Unfortunately for her, Harry was sound asleep and never knew she was there. Tomorrow would be another day and she could wait. She had waited this long for something like this to happen, and she could wait a little longer.

The next morning, Harry was up by six o'clock, while Laura was still asleep. He showered, shaved and dressed while the coffee brewed. He was scrambling a few eggs when Laura entered the kitchen area in her long blue flannel robe and slippers.

"Just in time, how do you like your eggs? You're looking at the best short order breakfast chef in town. Coffee's ready."

"My, my, aren't you the chipper one in the morning. I suppose you've already been on your two-mile walk before this?" she joked with him.

"No, not yet, but I'll do that at the office gym in Providence this afternoon. What time do you leave for work today?"

"Not until about eight thirty. It's not like I have to drive thirty miles to get to the station. Did you sleep well?"

"I guess I did. I don't remember much of anything once I hit the bed last night."

They casually chatted as he prepared breakfast for her, another thing that no one had done for her since she was a child. This man is the real deal, a keeper.

"Laura, I'll follow up today on trying to identify the license photo from the Connecticut rental van that I've asked the Bureau to run through international police pictures. Hopefully, it's someone in their database. I'll be back here late in the afternoon since I do not want to get caught in the five o'clock commuter traffic, at least not until I feel more comfortable driving again."

"Is there anything I can do to help?"

"Just bring the Providence Journal home so I can check for listed apartments for rent in the South County edition."

"I'll check with other police officers at the station to see if they know of any places available to rent right now. I'll leave work to be home around five thirty."

* * *

The man on the license photo from the Connecticut car dealer was indeed in the international database. The small tattoo on his neck was a dead giveaway for Manouch Haddad, a Middle Eastern henchman for hire, who had recently been a person of interest in a bombing outside a café in Beirut, Lebanon. His latest whereabouts, according to the CIA, was in Yemen, but he had been sighted a week earlier in Montréal, Canada before he disappeared. Harry studied Haddad's file very carefully, looking for any further information that would shed light on who hired him to eliminate Harry.

Meanwhile, Laura had difficulty concentrating on police work at the Narragansett police station. Anyone passing by her desk would certainly have noticed the doodling of Harry's name all over the notepad in front of her. All at once, she realized what she was doing and quickly crumbled the top sheet on her pad and tossed it in the waste basket nearby.

Chief LaPlante stopped at her desk and asked how she was doing working with Harry now that he was back. Laura related the update of events to LaPlante who then asked if she needed more time working with Harry going forward. She told LaPlante she would be discussing any further involvement in Harry's case later that day. LaPlante, in turn, gave Laura a list of a few apartments that Harry could rent until May when owners would be returning to their vacation homes in the area. Many college students did this while attending the University of Rhode Island in nearby Kingston.

Harry took the afternoon to meet with his insurance agent at the site of his previous house, which had now been completely razed and cleared. The agent went into his car and handed Harry two boxes of memorabilia which had been collected by the cleanup crew after the explosion. Harry treasured these items and would sift through the two boxes later on at Laura's house.

"Have you considered rebuilding here, Harry? Beachfront property is not easy to get these days, and your property sits right off the beach," the agent asked.

"Haven't given it much thought yet," he replied.

"Well, Harry, the insurance settlement for the house itself, and the personal property lost, would adequately allow you to rebuild. Plus we have provided you with a rent stipend which should hold you over in the meantime."

"I'm glad I had replacement coverage for the house because Lucy and I had been here for so long that we couldn't have afforded to rebuild anything if the coverage was only for our cost years ago," Harry added.

Harry really liked the area and, the thought of putting up another house might be a consideration, although there was no rush in making a decision. He thought about this as he headed to Laura's house around three o'clock. Once inside, Harry took the time alone to go through the two boxes the agent had given him. One item was a photo of Lucy and him on the beach deck during a cookout they had held the summer before she died. That one he would treasure. Other items he remembered but none seemed to mean as much to him as that one photo, the only one he now had with Lucy. He placed the two boxes in a corner of his bedroom and put Lucy's photo on the dresser nearby. He then grabbed the bottle of Chardonnay from the refrigerator and poured a glass as he just sat there gazing nowhere, his mind in another day and time.

When Laura arrived around five thirty, she found Harry asleep on the sofa in the living room, his half-empty wineglass on the end table nearby. She quietly moved to her room and changed into her jeans and sweatshirt. When she returned to the kitchen area, Harry woke up and spoke.

"Hi, I must have been more tired than I thought. This time change and jet lag really hit me today. How was your day?"

"Uneventful, Harry, a very quiet day. We get a lot of these in the off-season, except for occasional break-ins at the vacant homes belonging to summer residents."

"We got a name for that license photo, a guy from the Middle East whose location right now is unknown. I met my insurance guy at my property today. He wanted to know what I planned on doing with it."

"What did you tell him?"

"I haven't made up my mind yet, I don't know."

Laura prepared spaghetti and meatballs for dinner and opened a bottle of Chianti. Dinner was quiet, and neither had more news to share and Laura could see that Harry was very somber throughout the meal. After dinner, Harry turned on the evening news and was as quiet and subdued as he was during the meal. Laura cleaned the dishes and the table and went on to separate the laundry she had done earlier during the week. As she brought sets of fresh towels to Harry's bathroom, she noticed the two boxes on the floor in his bedroom. She looked in and noticed the photo on top of the dresser. She understood why Harry was suddenly different than the day before. She headed back into the living room.

"Tell me about Lucy, Harry," Laura asked.

"What?" Harry said in amazement.

"You were married to her for many years. Can't you tell me just a little about her. If she was with you that long, she must've been quite special."

"Laura, I've never talked about Lucy to anyone, at least not in the years since she died," Harry began. "You saw her picture on the dresser, didn't you?"

"I didn't mean to, it was on top when I was walking by with the laundry. She was very pretty."

"Yes, she was. I had forgotten just how beautiful she really was until I saw that picture this afternoon. It's the only one I have left of Lucy. The explosion destroyed almost everything else except for those two boxes in the bedroom. I'm sorry if I'm feeling kind of down right now, Laura. Too much has happened to me lately, and I miss her a lot right now. I'll be okay. Nothing I wish for is going to bring her back, and I know that, but I'm still having trouble. You're the first one who's even mentioned Lucy in quite some time."

"I knew her, Harry. I gave a talk at her elementary school about five years ago. It was about public safety and her class was one of the ones I addressed. I didn't know her well, but she appeared to love the kids she taught and I admired that. It wasn't until I saw the picture that I associated her as the Lucy Esten from the elementary school."

"Lucy loved children so much and even more so when she realized we weren't going to have any. We tried in vitro fertilization and that didn't work. So, in her mind she adopted all the kids in her classes as her own. She often said they would be the kids I wanted to have, and she felt bad I never had the chance to even have that. I was content with just Lucy. When she died from leukemia in 1985, I couldn't go back to the beach house for months. Now, I don't even have that left to go to," Harry moaned.

"It will get better, Harry, I just know it will," Laura replied. Harry thanked her for her encouragement and hoped she was right. He held her hand in his and gripped it tightly as he rose from his chair, his watery eyes a cue for him to excuse himself. He headed for the bedroom and closed the door. He stayed there for about an hour, tears flowing down his cheek as he gazed at the photo on the dresser. Life had not been fair.

At around eight, he emerged from his room and headed back to the living room where Laura was reading the newspaper on the sofa, her shoes kicked off and her feet up on a hassock. She smiled when she saw him, "Hey." He offered a rueful grin.

"Can I get you something to drink?"

"Got anything stronger than the wine in the fridge?"

Laura pointed to the cabinet separating the living room from the kitchen.

"You should find something in there to your liking."

When Harry opened the double doors to the unit, he immediately took out the bottle of Jack Daniels and a small bottle of vermouth, the basic recipe for a Bourbon Manhattan. A couple of ice cubes and a few maraschino cherries from inside the refrigerator door and he was golden.

"Want one?"

Laura held up a snifter, "Nope, got my favorite after dinner drink right here."

"Oh, and what would that be?"

"Apricot brandy," Laura provided after she took a sip.

Harry grimaced, "A bit sweet for my taste."

As he plopped himself down on the lounge chair next to the sofa and separated from Laura only by an end table with a reading lamp, Laura noticed that Harry still had on his necktie and dress shoes.

"Relax, Harry. Get rid of that tie and kick off those shoes. This motel is not that formal," she added with a broad smile on her face.

"Well, what do you think, Laura, should I build a new house at the beach to replace the old one? I've lived in this area of Rhode Island for a long time and, although it's a bit of a commute to Providence every day, my schedule's so wacky, it's not often I'm in the area anyway.

"Because of the beach house, I get to host my three brothers and my nephews every summer when they come up to play golf for a few days, and I'd hate to give that up. We don't get to see each other too often anymore. Besides, owning a house at the beach is like owning a house with a pool. All of a sudden you have more friends than you knew you had. Trade that for a condo or an apartment, and nobody would ever come to see me."

"I would, Harry, but I don't play golf, so you'd have to entertain me some other way," Laura was quick to reply.

"There is a saying among a lot of agents in Providence that people who live in the South County area never leave the area, because they don't have to. They have good seafood restaurants, movie theaters nearby, the entire ocean at their doorstep, so why would they leave?" Harry continued.

"I can't remember the last time I had dinner in Providence. Might have been Capriccio's, that Italian place in the basement of a building right near the river. I went to Twin Oaks in Cranston once too, but that's about it. Your buddies at the office are probably right. So why would you want to leave this paradise, especially with the location like the one you've got?" Laura echoed.

"I'd probably build something nicer than what I had, but I still want a second floor for the view, maybe with sliders and a deck out back facing the water. I'll give it some thought. If I do go ahead and rebuild, the timing would be good. They could start in March and maybe finish it in July. That way I'd only need a place for five or six months. That could work."

"I told you before, Harry, you're welcome to stay here until you find a place or even until your new house is finished."

"Won't that look kind of strange with all the people you know in this area. What will they think with me staying here all this time? Are you ready for bullshit from nosy neighbors or fellow officers at the station?"

"Do I look like the type of woman who gives a damn about what other people are saying? I'm a big girl, and, if it doesn't bother me, why should you worry about it?"

At that comment, Harry picked up his glass and gently clanked against Laura's as they toasted what appeared to be Harry's decision to rebuild on the beach. Harry felt relieved and he breathed a sigh and found himself more relaxed than he had been in quite some time. Laura made him feel special and she gave him room to unwind from the ordeals he was involved in at the moment. The more he sat back in the lounger, the more he found himself ready to doze off. He nearly spilled his drink when he began drifting until Laura jumped up and grabbed the glass before it tumbled to the carpet below. This startled Harry as he opened his eyes only to come face-to-face with Laura kneeling in front of him. She placed his glass on the end table and smiled warmly at Harry. He cupped her cheek and brought her lips to his. Laura was beginning to breathe deeply as he continued and began to search her body as the kisses continued.

Suddenly, Laura pulled back, rose from the lounge chair they occupied and headed for her bedroom. When she was leaving, she turned to Harry.

"I'll just be a few minutes. I think I need to slip into something more comfortable."

Easy, Harry, he thought to himself. He was now wide awake and fully aroused. He headed for his room to finally remove his dress shirt and tie and to hang up the pants from his suit in the bedroom closet. All the clothes he had now were still new and some he hadn't even worn once yet.

As he closed the louvered doors to the closet, he turned and there was Laura, wearing a light blue sheer full-length nightgown in her bare feet. Her hair was shoulder length and Harry detected the faint aroma of lavender cologne as Laura walked closer and closer.

"Tell me to go away, Harry, and I will," she said softly. Harry stood there in nothing but his undershirt and boxers, nothing that would hide the protrusion that was obvious. He walked toward her and mumbled, "Is this the way you treat all of your tenants, Ms. Broadbent?"

She placed her index finger to his lips to hush his words and replied, "Only the ones that are recovering from bullet wounds and blown up houses."

Laura wrapped her arms around his neck and kissed him softly, and Harry's warmth immediately met hers. He began to untie her nightgown until it fell completely to the floor, as she began to remove his undershirt with one hand while the other slid down his leg until she made a discovery that drove Harry wild. Laura took Harry by both hands and led him toward the nearby bed. They experienced lovemaking as both of them had not had in some time. Their hungry passion erupted over and over again, until they both lay on their backs next to each other, gazing at the ceiling above, breathing heavily, spent. They turned to face each other, Harry just looked at her and said, "Wow."

"Wow to you too," she replied. Within minutes, they were under the covers and sound asleep.

CHAPTER 12

The months of January, February, and March 1952 were the most wonderful months ever for Camille Denelle. The horrible attack and rape by an employee at the hospital prior to Christmas was now clearly behind her and her newfound love, Vito Melucci, was a reality indeed. He had been there to console her and to comfort her throughout this stressful period, and from the moment they first made love, she knew this was who she wanted to spend the rest of her life with.

Vito felt the same way and was prepared to take the relationship to the next step. During the short break for Easter in April, he asked Camille to come with him to Orvieto for the holiday weekend. Camille was nervous. However, she was still somewhat conscious of her pronounced limp and how it would be perceived by Vito's parents and siblings, as if he could not do better than bringing home a handicapped woman. She thought about this on the drive from Paris to Orvieto. Vito had spent most of his time at her home over the last few months, and this gave them both a good feel for how compatible they really were with each other.

Vito was caring, generous, and surprisingly handy at doing household chores, which allowed them to spend more time with each other. Camille's full-time position at the hospital had previously left her with little time to do much else. Vito would even, on occasion, have dinner ready when she arrived home from the hospital. There would be a candlelit table, a bottle of wine, soft Italian music on her stereo, and Vito, sometimes looking like Chef Boyardee, as she walked through the door. On other occasions, Vito would pick her up at the hospital and take her out to dinner, or back home if Camille herself had some particular dish she wanted to prepare for them.

On the highway south toward Italy, all Camille could think about was Vito and her, nothing else. Since both of her parents had been killed during the war, she had gotten used to being alone. With Vito now by her side, she was not too thrilled at having to meet his family, others who likely would put themselves in a position to judge whether she was the right person for Vito. She knew this trip felt more like a test of her worthiness to be with Vito, and all she could think of was, what if they don't like me, what then?

The first stop was in Dijon, about two hundred miles from Paris. They pulled into a roadside cafeteria at noon for lunch and then headed out again, this time for Milan, about two and a half hours away. As they rode along, Camille began asking all kinds of questions about Vito's parents. She wanted to make a good impression and she felt the more she knew about them, the easier it would be when they finally came face-to-face. All this questioning made the time fly by as Vito gave Camille as much information as he could.

"Camille, please don't worry about my parents. They know you are coming, and I know they will like you because they know that I would never bring home someone they would dislike," Vito said as he tried to remove her anxiety at the upcoming meeting.

"Mama is wonderful, Camille, the best cook in all of Italy. She said, 'anyone who loves my Vito, I want to meet.' And my father is very quiet, works all day at the vineyard and then goes to bed early every night because he gets up at four in the morning."

At three-thirty in the afternoon, they arrived in Milan and checked in at the Hotel Spadari al Duomo on Via Spadari. The Hotel Spadari was located in the center of Milan, a few steps from the Piazza del Duomo, the fashion district, and the Teatro alla Scala.

After bringing up their luggage, Vito reached for the telephone in their room and dialed the operator. He asked for a good restaurant nearby and then called the restaurant for a seven o'clock reservation. Camille was excited when Vito said they would take a quick sightseeing tour of the city since she had never been to Milan before, nor had she ever been outside of France.

Camille did not speak Italian and thought she would have difficulty with learning the language, but Vito put her at ease and assured her she would pick it up quickly. They both had been taught to speak English during and after the war, and were quite content with that. When in Giverny,

Camille would often speak French at various places she and
Vito went to, and Vito was not intimidated at all. He had
started learning French phrases and could communicate
pretty well in his short time in France. He assured Camille,
"Italian would come easy for you as well. Besides, my whole
family speaks English in addition to Italian."

That evening, following a refreshing shower by both of
them, they headed for the restaurant. The Savini Ristorante
was located on Via Ugo Foscolo, a short walk from the hotel
and in the heart of the fashion district. The restaurant was
one of the oldest in Milan, established in 1884. Because of
its location close to the Manzoni Theatre, it was a popular
meeting place for both artists and scholars. Although its
popularity waned prior to World War II, the war years and
afterwards saw a rebirth of the establishment as well-known
celebrities frequented the restaurant. Names like Maria
Callas, Charlie Chaplin, and Prince Rainier of Monaco
with Grace Kelly, Frank Sinatra, and Henry Ford, all dined
at the Savini. The environment in the restaurant was nothing short of elegant. Camille scanned the menu written in
Italian with an English translation beneath, she noticed the
enormous prices next to each entrée. She turned to look at
Vito who stood there smiling at her surprise.

"Vito, are you insane, or is there something more I
should know about the Melucci family? How can you afford
this kind of money at a restaurant?' she almost shouted.

"Relax, Camille, how many times must I tell you not to
worry," replied Vito.

It was still the custom of many restaurants in Milan to
post their menus outside the restaurant to attract shoppers
from the fashion district. After Camille had read the menu,
she pleaded with Vito for them to go elsewhere where the

prices were not so expensive. Vito simply smiled again as he held the door open for her to enter ahead of him. Once in the foyer, Camille breathlessly gazed at the magnificence of the restaurant's dining room.

A doorman proceeded to open the inner double doors which led to the maître'd's stand.

"Signore Melucci, so nice to see you again. Will you be in Milan for long?" the excited maître'd extended his hand to Vito.

"No, Roberto, just for the evening, but we may be back next Tuesday. Roberto, may I introduce la signora Camille Denelle, from France."

"Signora Camille, whatever you wish, even if it's not on the menu, we will prepare it for you. Welcome to Savini's."

Roberto escorted the couple to a quiet corner table almost completely enclosed with a privacy partition. He held the chair for Camille as she began to sit. He offered to take hers and Vito's coats, then he informed them their waiter for the evening would be Sebastiano.

"Okay, what's going on here, Vito, who are you?"

"Camille, the Melucci Vineyards have been selling Orvieto white wine to Savini's since 1900 when my great-grandfather befriended the original owner of the restaurant, Virgilio Savini. Our wine continues to be sold here and the restaurant is one of our biggest customers. My father and I come to Milan twice a year to bring complimentary cases of our wine to Roberto who is in charge of selecting the wines for the restaurant. We produce excellent wine, Camille, and you will soon see what I mean," Vito explained.

"You may as well just put zeroes next to each entrée price, because that is what Roberto will charge me tonight.

Savini's sells over a thousand cases of our wine each year and they make a good profit from each bottle sold."

"You are just one surprise after another, aren't you?" she replied as she extended her hands into his across the table.

The restaurant turned out to be as wonderful as its reputation and they both enjoyed the food and quiet enchantment of their corner table. Camille had almost forgotten about the imminent meeting the next day with Vito's parents. She and Vito were engrossed for the moment, as if there was no one else in the restaurant. Just as Vito had stated earlier, when they got up to leave, there was no bill. They headed back to the hotel and went to bed. They were scheduled to have breakfast the next morning in the hotel around eight, check out, and expected to reach Orvieto by one-thirty in the afternoon, just in time for lunch. Since this was Good Friday, the vineyard was closed to visitors and would only reopen on the Monday following Easter from ten to three o'clock. Easter dinner, cooked by Maria, would be served around four, and there Camille would meet Vito's sisters, Lucia and Sophia.

Everything went as planned. While they passed Florence at noon, Vito promised her that they would stop there on the way back to France on Monday. Camille was not expected back at the hospital until Wednesday morning and Vito had no classes for the entire week. A little after one, Camille saw the road sign signifying their arrival in the Orvieto region. Suddenly, and without warning, the landscaped hills of Orvieto lay before Camille's eyes. The hills were splattered with vines, and sitting atop the hills on a fort like formation of stone, stood the city of Orvieto. When Vito saw the wonder in Camille's expression, he promised,

"I will take you on Saturday to see the cobblestoned streets, and the magnificent views from the towering city, and from the Cathedral."

Vito's car slowed as he turned off the highway to a dirt road set between long rows of oak trees which kept the sunlight from beaming down on the road. The road wound for about a mile, sunlight began to shine brightly in the open areas, and vineyards appeared to the right and to the left of the road. They passed the arch with the Melucci Vineyards sign near the vineyard store and continued on for another hundred yards. As they approached the villa, Camille's eyes could not believe the sights she had just seen, and the villa directly in front of her caused her mouth to open in awe. The two-story stone structure was nearly seventy feet long with a red slate roof and verandas across most of the second floor.

"This is where you live, Vito?" she asked in amazement.

"Yes, Camille, this is the Melucci Villa and those were our vineyards that we just passed. I have lived here all of my life and have loved every moment of it," he answered with a great deal of pride in his voice.

'Oh, Vito, oh my, this is so beautiful, I have never seen anything like this before. We have vineyards in France everywhere, but this, this is like a postcard."

"I'm so glad you feel that way," he said as he grabbed her hand and held it as the car approached the front of the villa's main stone entranceway.

"Now, take a deep breath and relax. We are here and there is nothing to fear," he said to her as they were about to get out of the car.

The front doors of the villa opened and there was Maria, wearing a smile that would welcome anyone.

"Vito, my son, welcome home. We have been waiting for you for lunch. And I take it this is Camille?" she asked.

"Mama, this is Camille Denelle. She lives in Giverny and has been a nurse for six years," Vito answered with a grin on his face.

"Hello, Camille, Vito has told us so much about you. Come, let's go in and meet Vito's father. He is probably opening a bottle of wine in the kitchen," Maria said as she gave Camille a warm hug.

Camille's limp became obvious when she began to walk up the front steps, and Maria could not help but mention it.

"Does it hurt much? You don't seem to be unable to climb stairs, and with your nursing position, I'm sure there is a great deal of walking involved."

"No, Madame Melucci, it is more of a nuisance than anything. I can get around fine, I just hate wearing this brace all the time, it gets in the way and isn't very attractive."

"Other than limiting your ability to dance then, the knee doesn't stop you from doing anything else, does it?"

"It is true, Madame Melucci, I should remember I am able to do anything except run."

"That damn war caused many people a lot of pain, my child, and your family more than most. Maybe Lucia can recommend someone in Orvieto who knows about such things. Vito's sister is a doctor in the city and she is up on all the latest advances in the medical world. You will meet her on Sunday when she comes to dinner on Easter."

Maria grabbed Camille by the arm as they entered the villa and headed for the kitchen area. "Oh, excuse me, you must want to freshen up before lunch, the bathroom is to the left."

Camille strolled through the main hallway of the villa, through the marble staircase which was surrounded on the upper landing with a marble railing. Before she entered the bathroom, she could not help but notice the large dining room on the left which was adjacent to an even larger family room to the rear of the first floor. The entire back wall of this area was covered with glass doors leading to a large flagstone patio. In the distance, atop what appeared to be a mountain, rested Orvieto, a short five miles away.

When she exited the bathroom, Camille was slightly puzzled as to where she should go. She found herself being drawn toward the glass wall in the family room. She gazed out the windows at the rows and rows of vines that seemed to go on forever, only to then again face Orvieto as if in the clouds above.

"Ah, there you are, come let us join the others in the kitchen," Maria said.

"This is so beautiful, Madame Melucci, how can you possibly leave this place?" Camille asked.

"We seldom do, except for trips to Orvieto or Milan. We have everything we want here, Camille."

When they entered the kitchen, Vincenze was opening two bottles of the Melucci Classico White and, when he spotted Camille, smiled and approached to greet her with a huge hug and a kiss on the cheek.

"Welcome to Orvieto, my dear, I hope your trip with Vito was pleasant enough?" he asked.

"Oh, yes, Monsieur Melucci, and you have a magnificent estate here. It is so beautiful," she praised.

"You can see why my grandfather started the vineyard over fifty years ago and my father enlarged it since then. So have my wife and I over the years. The villa was small, only about half the size it is today, and is much more charming now than before. We don't vacation much away from here, so we decided to make the villa as modern and comfortable as we needed. Vito has told us that you own a house in Giverny yourself. I would bet that lately he spends more time there than in Paris from all the messages we get on his answering machine day or night."

Camille blushed at these comments as Vincenze led her to a seat at the table next to him. Vincenze had always been more at ease with Lucia and Sophia when they were growing up, so it was no wonder he would also do the same with Camille. Their warmth and friendliness immediately put Camille at ease and her fears at having this meeting were put to rest.

Vito announced proudly that he would be graduating from the Paris Art School in May of that year and they toasted his accomplishment during lunch.

"Have you decided what's next for you, Vito, I'm not getting any younger you know?" Vincenze asked.

He looked directly at Camille as he answered.

"That all depends on a few things over the next few months, Papa. I think I know what I want to do, but I'd like to think a little longer about it before I say anything."

Camille again blushed, this time uncontrollably. When she held both of her hands to her face, Vito just smiled.

Following a delightful lunch, Maria showed Camille her room and Vincenze followed behind with her suitcase. Vito had told Camille to change into a pair of jeans because he was going to take her on a tour of the vineyards. He told her this would be done on an electric cart, so she needn't worry about walking in the fields with her bad knee. In the meantime, he walked to the vineyard store to see his sister,

Sophia. He told her of Camille, and Sophia was anxious to meet her.

"Well, well, finally at age twenty-nine my brother has a girlfriend. I was beginning to worry about you," she teased.

"Worry about yourself, sister, it's time for you to meet a nice guy for a change, you deserve it," Vito retorted.

"Where is this guy, little brother? I've been looking for him for quite a while now."

They talked for half an hour until Vito looked at his watch and realized Camille would be waiting for him at the villa. When he returned, he could see her standing on the patio against a railing which looked out at Orvieto in the distance.

"It is so very pretty here, Camille, one of my favorite places to sit late in the day with a glass of wine and cheese. Vineyards as far as the eye can see, and then to be faced with the beautiful Orvieto," he sighed, "always makes me happy. Come, let us take a ride around the vineyards."

Vito explained the position of the vineyard in the valley of Orvieto, the volcanic terrain exposed to the sun from dawn until dusk, and the special microclimate with significant thermal swings between night and day which had always been its good fortune. He further explained that most other vineyards in the area had formed a consortium to safeguard the high quality wines in Orvieto.

They next drove to the large wine cellars where the wines were stored at just the right temperature. Alongside these cellars were large and impressive caves, excavated in the lava rock, to produce and mature certain wines in special barrels. The constant temperatures and near one-hundred percent humidity were important factors in the development of top-quality wine making. While other vineyards in the area also produced some red wines, the Melucci Vineyards were exclusively producing high quality dry white wine.

Camille was fascinated by all of this and found herself asking question after question to Vito because she wanted to know more. She was very impressed at how much Vito knew about the wine making business, and no longer thought he was only interested in art and painting. She could see his paintings were a deliberate offshoot to his love for wine making and his family's vineyards. She was determined not to let him slip away.

When it was time for dinner, Sophia could not wait until Sunday dinner to meet Camille; so she invited herself after closing the vineyard store. Their meeting was like two sisters who had not seen each other for years. They became instantly attached to each other, and Sophia quickly invited Camille to visit her domain- the Melucci Vineyard Store and Tasting- on Saturday. Vito said she could do so early that morning because he had carefully planned sightseeing in Orvieto for the day, with dinner at Le Grotte del Funaro later that evening.

Following a wonderful dinner prepared by Maria, Vito and Camille excused themselves and headed to their rooms early. Saturday was going to be a busy day. Vito's bedroom was adjacent to Camille's and he tried to lure her into his room. His arms started to roam as he kissed her, and she pushed him away, ever so gently. "Stop," she chided. "We need to be on our best behavior. Now shoo, I'll see you in the morning."

* * *

On Saturday, Camille spent a delightful hour with Sophia before Vito popped up to whisk her away for their trip to Orvieto.

Vito drove toward the city and parked his car at the railway station. Camille was puzzled.

"Why are we stopping here?" Camille asked.

"Few cars drive all the way up into the city because there is only one road and it is quite narrow should your car confront an oncoming car in the opposite direction. Most tourists and residents alike take the funicular up over one-hundred-fifty yards to the city's historic center. The funicular is like an elevator using a water counterweight system that has two cars, each carrying about seventy-five passengers that allow each car to go uphill while the other goes downhill. Because the cars cannot climb straight upward, the funicular climbs along a five-hundred yard path, with the last one-hundred yards into the volcanic rock and exits at the Piazza Cahen."

Camille was like a child at an amusement park enjoying her first ride as they went up in the funicular. When she stepped out of the car, a beautiful cobblestoned square stood in front of her. From that moment, the rest of the day was like a dream. They went into quaint little shops, museums, other city squares and fountains until they came upon the Duomo, Orvieto's beautiful cathedral. Camille put on a small handkerchief on her head when they entered. She had seen beautiful churches in Paris, and at first, this one appeared to be but another one. Vito pointed out the work of Signorelli on the walls of the cathedral.

"And on these walls in the alcove, Camille, is the work of another famous artist," he whispered.

"Whose work is this, Vito, I can't read the name? It's too dark in here."

"These are the works of the famous Orvieto-born artist, Vito Melucci," he proudly announced.

She gazed at the paintings as if in disbelief, and yet, she was not surprised. It seemed Vito was full of surprises, and this one, to have your work hanging in a cathedral built by a pope, was just another in a world she barely knew. She hugged him tightly. She was so proud to be with him.

After lunch at the oldest restaurant in Orvieto, the Trattoria dell 'Orso, the rest of the afternoon was spent visiting more museums and shops in the center of the city until around six. The last stop would be for dinner at Le Grotte del Funaro inside a series of caves which had several openings in the cave walls with direct views of the Duomo. The two windows afforded a splendid view of the hilly countryside.

Once they entered the restaurant, the maître'd immediately greeted Vito like an old friend that you have not seen in a while. In fact, Emilio was an old friend, a boyhood playmate whom he had not seen in years. "Vito, you are still alive," Emilio stated with some sarcasm in his voice.

"Yes, Emilio, I am very much alive. You probably see my parents here much more than me," he answered.

"Your mama and papa are here almost every week, and I always ask them about you."

"I am finishing art school in Paris in May, Emilio, and should be around much more often after that."

"Your table is ready, old friend. And who do we have here, la signora?" he asked.

"She is my companion at the vineyard this weekend and she is from Paris, Mademoiselle Camille Denelle."

The Grotte del Funaro was well-known for its extensive wine collection, including the Melucci wines as well as other local wines. Dinner with Camille was both exquisite and romantic. The ambiance in the candlelit caves was overshadowed by the majestic views from their table near the outside windows. Darkness came quite late in this part of Italy, and catching a glimpse of hillside terrain at dusk was often breathtaking. Camille could not believe all of this was actually happening to her. She was definitely in love with Vito, and in her mind, no one could ever compete with him for her admiration and love. Vito felt the same way. They had been seeing each other now for nearly five months and it was as if they had always been together.

"Camille, you now have seen my world, my family, except for my sister Lucia whom you will meet at dinner tomorrow, and what most of my life is about. Would you be happy living in Italy away from Paris and the hospital if you were asked to?" Vito nervously spoke as he held both of her extended hands across the table. "I have never been in love before, Camille, but I can't imagine it being any better than the way I feel for you right now. I did not invite you here just to meet my parents. I brought you here for you to see the life we have here, and to find out if you could be happy here."

"Oh, Vito, you are the kindest, most generous person I have ever met. You were there for me those awful days after Christmas and have never left me alone ever since. You are who I want to wake up beside each morning and who I want to fall asleep beside each night. Orvieto is wonderful, your parents are wonderful, but could I be happy here, only for about a hundred years, Vito, is that long enough?" she replied.

"Marry me, Camille, be the mother of my children, another daughter to mama and papa, and the future wife of the Melucci's next generation."

"I love you, Vito, but I don't know if I can bear a child anymore. I could never promise you that after what's happened to me, and I want very much to be a mother to children of our own."

"We will be fine, Camille, and if God has decided that you should not have children, I'm sure there are small ones out there who would love to have you as their mother."

"That is true, Vito, there is an orphanage near my home that has many children with no parents. They would help us if I cannot have my own."

"Do I take that as a yes, Camille? Yes, you will marry me?" he asked eagerly.

"Yes, Vito, I would love to spend the rest of my life with you," she said as tears ran down her cheek.

By nine, they had left the Grotte and taken the last funicular down the city walls to the parking lot. The short drive back to the vineyard was with Camille cuddled closely to Vito in his Fiat, about as close as possible without sitting on the floor shift between them. As they entered the villa, Vincenze and Maria were sitting in the living room reading. Vito and Camille approached them with huge smiles on their faces and Maria knew, she just knew.

Vito announced they were engaged to be married and they wanted the wedding reception to be at the vineyard near the caves after the ceremony at the Cathedral. Vincenze and Maria were very pleased to hear this and embraced the couple warmly and they celebrated the upcoming union.

They talked for hours, very uncommon for Vincenze who normally would have been in bed by ten. Plans had to be made, announcements had to be sent with invitations, and Camille was still in a daze at all this attention. When she finally went up to her room, Vito stayed behind for a short while longer to be with his parents.

By midnight, he was ready to call it a day, and they all headed upstairs to bed. Vito stopped by Camille's room after his parents entered their bedroom suite and quietly opened the door, the room in total darkness. Hearing no sound, Vito was about to leave until Camille spoke.

"I am not asleep, Vito, how can I sleep? It is like I'm dreaming wide awake. I love you, Vito Melucci. I have never loved anyone more."

They made love that night as if it was their first time. They were clutched together most of the night until Vito quietly slipped out of the room and headed for his room next door. As he looked out his window at the brightening sky, he could see his father, as usual, make his six o'clock trek to the vineyards.

At two o'clock, Lucia arrived at the villa for the family's traditional Easter dinner. Vito and Camille, Vincenze and Maria, and Sophia had all attended Mass at the Cathedral earlier that morning. It took everything for Maria to pull Vincenze away from the fields so they could leave for church on time. The Mass also gave Camille a first-hand view of what her upcoming wedding in the beautiful structure would be like. They had chosen to have the wedding in June since Vito wanted to graduate first. There were many preparations that had to be done, and required at least a month before the ceremony, although the over four hundred invitations were scheduled to go out in April.

Lucia was a very busy doctor in Orvieto and her schedule did not allow her much free time, so she cherished this afternoon and early evening get-together with her family very much. She had not seen them since the Christmas holidays and even then, for just one day. Vito introduced Camille and Lucia was very pleased to meet her. She too was elated that Vito had found a woman to be with at last. Vito was not exactly known as a social butterfly. Lucia also had spoken to Maria and knew of Camille's bad knee.

"Camille, would you mind if I remove your brace and take a look at that knee?" she asked.

"No, of course not. I'll remove it myself for you."

After briefly examining the knee, Lucia said, "Would you be willing to stop by the hospital for x-rays on Monday before you and Vito head back to Paris?"

"Certainly, but I do not have much hope anything can be done to improve its condition."

"The newer technology today might be more advanced than the one at the military hospital. The x-rays will be reviewed by a colleague of mine who specializes in knee and hip surgery and an assessment will be shared with you when the diagnosis is complete. Since you are a nurse, Camille, you know and understand more than most about such things."

Following the x-rays on Monday morning, Vito and Camille bid farewell to his parents and headed back toward Paris with a deliberate stop in Florence as Vito had promised.

In Florence, they had lunch at the Café Rivoire facing the palazzo Vecchio. Because their time in the city was limited, Vito picked out a few museums of note and several cathedrals. Quick tours of the Uffizi Museum, the Duomo, and the Pitti Palace were the highlights before they left for Milan late that afternoon.

They returned to the Hotel Spadari in Milan and had a quiet dinner in the hotel restaurant.

On Tuesday, after breakfast, they drove toward Dijon and to Giverny. The conversation the entire way centered on wedding arrangements, announcing at the hospital of her intentions to leave in early June, and what to do with her house, assuming they would be moving to Orvieto.

* * *

On Wednesday, Camille returned to her position at the hospital and arranged to meet with her nursing supervisor later that day, while Vito went to Paris to prepare for his final days at school before graduation on May 6. Vito's parents would be attending his graduation.

Camille went about her duties as usual before her three o'clock meeting. At one, Dr. Marchand appeared on her ward and had news about her test results. Now that her outer wounds had healed completely, these final tests were meant to explore if there was any internal damage. The sudden appearance by Dr. Marchand for a face-to-face meeting made Camille think the worst. Her fears were not far from reality.

Dr. Marchand began, "Camille, as I had told you some time ago, the outer part of your vagina has healed nicely and having sex with other men in the future should not be a problem. However, the latest test results from the gynecologist suggest that you have small fibro tumors on the inside which have caused scarring. This may make it nearly impossible for you to conceive a child, because the fertile egg would not be able to attach to the uterine wall properly. Ironically, Camille, this was not a result of your attack, just something that you probably had before."

"Oh, my God, Doctor, I was just engaged to be married two days ago to the man I told you about, and our wedding is scheduled for this June."

"So, why would that change, Camille? Remember our discussion on the right man accepting you for who you are, whether you can have children or not? If this man really loves you, then he will accept this and move on with life. At worst, which is certainly not so bad, you can adopt children who are in need of good parents," Dr. Marchand said as she tried to reassure her.

This news did not sit well with Camille as she left the doctor's office and returned to her ward. She cancelled the meeting with the nursing supervisor and instead of finishing her shift, left the hospital early, claiming a sudden illness.

The weekend out of a fairy tale had now turned into an unwanted reality. *How can I tell Vito? How is he going to react?* she wondered as she walked home in tears on this chilly Wednesday afternoon. He had to know now, this couldn't wait. As soon as she arrived home, she called and left a message on Vito's answering machine in his apartment. She sat in a daze and pondered how she would break this news to him.

CHAPTER 13

The sound of the telephone ringing woke up Camille. She had cried herself to sleep after leaving a message on Vito's answering machine earlier.

"Vito, I cannot have children of my own. I met with Dr. Marchand today and I have small tumors inside which won't allow me to get pregnant. There may be a procedure to fix this, but it is much too dangerous right now and the gynecologist who conducted the tests won't take that kind of risk," she blurted to Vito in anguish.

"Calm down, Camille, calm down. I keep telling you not to get all worked up about this. It's not your fault. We will handle this."

"You don't understand, Vito, it's not anything to do with the attack on me, it's just something I had even before that happened."

"I don't care, Camille, it doesn't change anything. If it was meant to be that you cannot have children of your own, then it means that some other baby out there, who is seeking a family, will get an Italian couple to call their own. Let's go to this orphanage you talked about this weekend, the one near you in Giverny. They can tell us what we have to do and what children are available."

"You're not upset at this news, Vito?" she asked in a surprised manner.

"It is not good news, if that's what you mean, but it happens, Camille, and, unfortunately, it is happening to you. But it changes nothing, nothing at all."

The following Saturday morning, they drove to the orphanage and were informed by Sister Vivian of the detailed procedure to adopt a child. It seemed there was a one-year old boy who was available, but it could not happen until they were officially married and had been thoroughly screened by the orphanage. Camille and Vito were reassured the family they thought would elude them, was in fact more of a reality than ever before.

The plan was to hold the wedding in June, honeymoon in France on the Riviera, then drive to Camille's house in Giverny in July to begin the process at the orphanage. They would put together all the necessary references, proof of employment, a copy of their birth certificates and marriage license, and any other information that was required. It was expected the whole adoption process would allow the Meluccis to finalize the adoption by September, 1952. It was their plan to then move into the villa with Vito's parents until they could make arrangements for a place of their own.

When Vito's parents came to Paris in early May to attend his graduation from art school, they explained to

Vincenze and Maria the condition Camille had, and their intentions to adopt a child later that summer. Maria was angry at the continued hardship that Camille encountered and was very supportive of their plans. The thought of a grandchild, adopted or not, excited Vincenze and Maria. They all agreed there was no need to tell anyone the child was adopted. Instead, they would tell Lucia and Sophia the child had been born to Camille before they were married, and Vito and Camille had decided to marry a year later.

At Camille's request, they ate dinner after the graduation at Le Coq Fin, where Vito and she had gone to on their first date. Maria and Camille discussed wedding plans while Vito and Vincenze talked about Vito's full-time involvement at the vineyard going forward. Both Vincenze and Maria were in their mid-fifties and were looking forward to having Vito take a leadership role as early as the end of the upcoming harvest in late summer. They both insisted on Vito and Camille living in the villa until they determined where they wanted to live.

The day after the graduation, Vincenze and Maria drove to Giverny and visited Camille's home before heading back to Orvieto. Vincenze suggested that they keep the house to be used for family vacations and short business trips to the Paris area. Camille thought it was a wonderful idea. The house had been in her family for over fifty years and she had fond memories growing up there. Even though it also was her parents' death knell during the war, Camille would have hated to see the house leave her family.

* * *

The wedding date of Saturday, June 28 was nearing and a week before, Vito and Camille arrived at the villa. Maria had planned a small luncheon for Camille at the Il Guglio D'Oro Ristorante on Piazza Duomo where she expected about thirty women, most of them good friends of the Meluccis and a few of Camille's co-workers from the hospital who found time to make the trip to Orvieto. Vincenze would be the best man at the wedding, while Sophia was ecstatic at being asked to be the maid of honor. Camille had brought her mother's wedding gown which had been stored for years in an upstairs closet. Maria had arranged to take care of any alterations when she and Camille visited one of the dress shops in the city. Vito and Vincenze worked on the grand reception near the vineyard caves by tending to caterers, music, decorations, and any other last minute arrangements.

Lucia met Maria and Camille at the luncheon, and had very optimistic news for Camille. Dr. Franco Maggiacomo, the Orvieto Hospital chief surgeon, had evaluated the x-rays taken in April of Camille's knee, and found that minor surgery to repair torn cartilage in the knee, followed by extensive therapy, could likely eliminate the need for her knee brace, and could dramatically reduce or eliminate her limp.

"Are you certain, Lucia, can he really do this?" Camille asked in utter surprise.

"The x-rays showed that behind the pins that were inserted in your knee, there were two cartilages that were badly torn and probably went unnoticed in earlier x-rays. The shots we took of your knee were from four different angles, and the tears in the cartilages were very visible."

Camille hugged Lucia very tightly as tears of joy rolled down her cheeks. This news became the highlight of the day, overshadowing the many wonderful gifts she received at the luncheon. When Vito heard the news later that day, he was very pleased, yet not surprised.

"My sister has always gone out of her way to help others, even if this isn't her area of expertise. Lucia is a very special doctor, Camille. Her patients are very fortunate to have her."

* * *

On the day of the wedding, the Cathedral was filled with hundreds of well-wishers when Vito and Camille exchanged marriage vows. After a joyous reception at the vineyard, the young couple departed for their honeymoon and then back toward Giverny. There were no unwelcome surprises this time around and they finalized the adoption papers at the orphanage in late August.

When they arrived back to the villa in early September, Maria and Vincenze were very pleased to see them. Most of all, they were pleased to greet the newest Melucci to the family, one-year old Carlo Andrea. A new generation of Meluccis had just begun.

CHAPTER 14

The spring months in Khatamori were periods when Ahmad gradually accepted his new kidney and regained his strength. He had shed the use of a wheelchair, and could be seen walking vigorously everywhere he went. The more his health improved, the more he was seen throughout Khatamori. He attempted to reinforce his connections with the populace. Khatamorans responded well to his local visits and dedication ceremonies whenever a new road or bridge was built, or when he gave out awards to deserving citizens throughout the kingdom.

Kaleel had looked into the whereabouts of Rafick throughout weeks before the assassination attempt on Ahmad, and similar attempts on Françoise's two sons. It seemed Rafick was nowhere to be found for several weeks after his father's death. He claimed he had needed to be away to mourn, and had decided to isolate himself in prayer at his home outside Banra. No one had seen him for those two-weeks, and he claimed this was what he intended. No one around Rafick would either refute or confirm this tale and Kaleel's report to his king was inconclusive at best. If Rafick had been involved in the attempt on Harry Esten's life in Rhode Island, there was no evidence which placed him in the area, although he might have hired someone else to do his dirty work. If he indeed was like his father, hiring assassins would not have been out of the question.

In the meantime, Françoise had informed Ahmad that she had received a faxed photo of Manouch Haddad from Harry. Haddad was the person who had rented the van used to blow up Harry's house. When Ahmad told Kaleel about the photo, Kaleel sent Harry a request to submit other photos of Haddad with known associates in the same photo over recent months. Perhaps these photos would reveal a link to Rafick, whom the CIA would not recognize as a person of interest. Yemen was not far from Khatamori, and if Haddad had been in the country in recent months, it would have been easy for Rafick to meet him there.

Ahmad asked Kaleel to pursue the Haddad connection further and to inform him when anything further developed.

It appeared Rafick Talon was as devious as his father had been. He had prepared a likely alibi to where he was during much of the uprising, even though no one could verify the information. He believed he could pull similar plots going forward without being detected. Rafick may have been brash and outspoken, but he was a clever villain, and extremely bitter about his father's death. His devious mind could not fathom the brutal attempts by his father toward his cousin were unjustified. In his mind, any threat to succeeding Ahmad must be met by either eliminating the threat or eliminating Ahmad.

Ahmad tried to focus on the issues affecting his kingdom, but he found himself now surrounded by more security than he felt comfortable with.

"I have never felt in fear of my life as I moved about Khatamori, Françoise, and now I am shielded from getting close to my people because of a single incident which happened nearly six months ago," Ahmad told her in frustration.

"Those close to you, my husband, merely want you to be safe. In time, it will be calm again as it once was," she answered.

"And what of your other son in Ethiopia?" he asked.

"There has not been further news now for months. Harry and Jim cannot go there yet. The situation in Ethiopia is too dangerous, and they must wait to get a visa when it is safer. Carlo has been calling his Italian parents every month though by satellite telephone. So it appears he is still well at the hospital there," Françoise reported. "I know I am not allowed to leave the country without you, Ahmad, but I believe it would be easier for me to go there, Ethiopia, than to wait for the Americans to be allowed to. Who knows how long this will take."

"What makes you think you would not be in danger as well by doing that, Françoise? There is no reason to believe anyone else knows about Carlo other than the Americans right now. Be patient, my love, you have waited thirty-five years to pursue finding your sons. Waiting a little longer seems to be the wiser thing to do right now, even though I know you want this to finally happen," he answered.

"Ahmad, I am so angry with myself for having given the boys up back then. I would do anything to make this right. Whether they ever accept me or not, they must know I never stopped loving them, even though it must look that way in their eyes."

Ahmad could see the torment in Françoise, and was saddened to see this as he knew that there was little else he could do at the moment to ease her burden. Perhaps an eventual reunion would help solve the problem.

* * *

Ishraq Haddad had been a servant for Queen Farah at the palace for four years and had gained the queen's affection because of her dedication and attention to detail in the royal family's suite. She was twenty-three years old and had been recommended to the queen by no other than Answa Talon. She had previously worked for the Talon family until there was an opening for a servant in the royal household following the retirement of the queen's elderly servant.

Unfortunately, Ishraq also was the estranged daughter of Manouch Haddad, the elusive assassin for hire involved in the recent attempt on Harry's life and a person of interest in other violent crimes in Yemen. Ishraq had broken all ties with her father after hearing about his involvement in the disappearance of a high-ranking official in Yemen four years earlier. Her mother had disappeared at about the same time and was never heard from again.

She had met Talon in Yemen when he visited her father on official security business for Khatamori. Haddad had been instrumental in developing a security force for Yemen officials and Talon was looking for guidance in security procedures for Khatamori.

Françoise never made the connection between Ishraq and Manouch, even after she heard of his name and his attempted attack on Esten. Haddad was a common surname in Arab nations, and Ishraq's position in the Maurier household did not raise anyone's curiosity.

Rafick met Ishraq late one day in May, 1988 when she left the palace to visit friends in downtown Banra.

"Hello, Ishraq, how is your position going with Queen Farah?" he asked.

"Oh, Rafick, so nice to see you. I cannot thank your father enough for having given me the chance to work for the queen after my time with your family. I was sorry to hear of your father's death. He was so young and had such a position of prominence in the king's guard."

"That is why I came here to meet you today, Ishraq, I need a favor," Rafick added.

"Anything I can do to help, Rafick. I owe your family a great deal," she replied.

"The queen is always busy in the kingdom, doing wonderful things for women. At times, there are some who are not in agreement with her work, and believe the role of women should remain as it has been in Khatamori for hundreds of years. Her western ways are not accepted by everyone and we are concerned with harassing telephone calls she may get. We would like to be able to trace those calls and find these people to see if they are a threat to her highness or just a nuisance."

"I would do anything to protect the queen from these people," Ishraq answered.

"I was hoping you would help. This device can be placed inside her telephone receiver and it allows us to monitor any incoming calls to her highness. That way we can intercept bad calls and trace them back to these malicious people. I would put it in her telephone myself but the queen and I are not exactly on good speaking terms since I met Ahmad last week. Since my father did a foolish thing which got him killed, the king thinks all the Talons are to be watched carefully. However, I have taken over some of my father's security duties for now and the queen should be protected from any intruders gaining access to her telephone and leaving harassing messages."

"I do not understand, Rafick, what are you asking me to do?"

"Merely unscrew the bottom of her telephone in the royal suite and insert this small device. Then simply screw the receiver back on. That's all you need to do, Ishraq. But don't do it when she is there because it might make her nervous every time she speaks on her telephone. It is best if she does not know the device is there," Rafick insisted.

"Oh, I don't know, Rafick, this does not seem right. I wouldn't want to upset her highness if she found out I did this," Ishraq responded.

"Ishraq, we have never told her your father is a wanted criminal. What do you think this would do to your position if they knew you were the daughter of Manouch Haddad?" Rafick insinuated.

"I have nothing to do with my father, Rafick, and you know that."

"I know, Ishraq, but others who only know of his evil acts will not think the same way. Many would think you are like him and cannot be trusted."

"I will do this for you, Rafick, but if you are lying to me about any of this and the queen somehow finds out about the device, I will tell her the truth and you will have to answer to the king. Is that clear?" she emphasized.

"Yes, of course, I understand; you must trust me on this. I would never do anything to hurt the queen, never."

Ishraq took the telephone bug, and placed it in her shoulder bag, and left. Rafick watched her until she was met up with several other women for lunch in a small café. She had told Rafick she would insert the device while the family was dining that night. Ahmad was welcoming guests from a neighboring country for dinner that night, his first night of entertaining since the kidney transplant.

The following day, Rafick was in a building adjacent to the palace grounds and listening to the first recordings from the telephone tap in the royal suite. The device worked perfectly and Rafick knew any news about Françoise's son from the Americans in charge of protecting him, especially Harry Esten, whom Rafick had a score to settle with, would allow him to act quickly.

After monitoring the wiretap for several weeks, Rafick knew what he had to do next. On her way to her weekly lunch with friends in Banra, Ishraq was handed a note by a young boy in the downtown street leading to the café. The note simply said:

"Meet me at 32 Mecca Street before your lunch today. I have good news for you."

The note was signed 'R'.

Ishraq entered the building a short walk away. It was a dilapidated structure, mostly empty, and she took the stairs to the second floor and knocked on the door to room 204. No one answered and she turned the door knob and found the door to be unlocked. She entered the darkened room and groped the wall for a light switch. Two rapid shots from a silencer followed and she fell to the floor. Rafick had just eliminated the only other person who knew about the telephone tap. He could now continue to eavesdrop on the queen's conversations with no threat that Ishraq, in a moment of guilt, would tell the queen what she had done. He wrapped her small body in an old rug, and hoisted it over his shoulder. Disguised in a cap and sunglasses, he left the building and dumped her body in the back of an old van. Ishraq's body was never to be found.

The staff at the royal palace was questioned on her whereabouts after she failed to return from a scheduled luncheon with friends, who claimed that she never showed up at the café. This news was disturbing to Françoise and Ahmad, and they both were puzzled by her sudden disappearance. A loyal servant was always hard to find, and Ahmad did not rule out foul play, not with the events of the last six months. Kaleel was asked to investigate her disappearance.

CHAPTER 15

In late May, 1988, Julie Elliott had decided to attend the World Health Organization's International AIDS Conference in Stockholm, Sweden from June 12th through June 16th, and Bob had agreed to accompany her. This was their first trip abroad in quite some time. While Harry tried to discourage them from leaving the country just yet, Bob was determined not to stay in and around Medway while unknown people might or might not be watching his every move. Their plans to begin a family appeared to be successful as Julie was pregnant at age thirty-five. With no baseball season confronting him following his retirement from the Red Sox, Bob had enough help at his two restaurants to break away for a week or two.

Julie's medical practice did not deal directly with AIDS patients, but she was interested in supporting her colleague

and friend, Dr. Marjorie Smith, who was a strong advo-
cate for better AIDS education in Massachusetts. Marjorie
would attend the conference as well and return after the
four-day event, while Julie and Bob would extend their stay
three days longer to do some sightseeing in Lapland, land
of the Midnight Sun and the last European wilderness.

All three were on a direct flight from Logan Airport in
Boston to Stockholm, Sweden on June 10th.. The weather in
Stockholm was expected to be in the seventies, which made
for light packing for the trip. The flight on Scandinavian was
smooth and they arrived at the Stockholm Airport right on
time. They took a taxi to the Hotel Alvsjo, about four hundred yards from the conference center, and checked in.
Julie and Bob invited Marjorie to join them later for some
local sightseeing before an early dinner at the hotel. There
was a six hour time difference from Boston to Stockholm.
If they finished dinner by eight o'clock, it meant they likely
would have been up for over twenty-four hours without
any sleep. The conference was scheduled to begin the following morning at the Stockholm International Fairs, and
run through Thursday morning. The conference was spon-
sored by the Swedish Ministry of Health and Social Affairs,
and its opening ceremony was to feature King Carl XVI
Gustaf, of Sweden.

Rachel Owens gave a kiss to Carlo after saying goodbye
to him at the airport in Addis Ababa. He had decided to
drive her there from Mekelle rather than her risking any
delays in taking a shuttle from Mekelle to Addis Ababa. If
she missed the one flight to Dubai, she would not get to the
conference on time, and she did not want to get there late.

Rachel and Carlo's relationship over the last four
months had flourished, and Rachel, who at first merely

considered Carlo a friend and colleague, was becoming more attracted to Carlo in an intimate way. She, however, was still focused on her work with AIDS patients, and had little time left to pursue a personal relationship with Carlo, except for the occasional day off when they spent more time together. Lucia, Carlo's aunt, had written to Carlo recently to express her concern for the increasing number of AIDS cases in the surrounding area of Orvieto. Her concern was that the area did not seem to address the issue seriously enough since there were no doctors there specializing in the disease. Although the news from Lucia's letters was depressing, it was encouraging to Carlo. He could envision Rachel having such a practice in Orvieto if he had his way by the end of his term at Mekelle.

Rachel's flight from Addis Ababa to Dubai, via Ethiopian Airlines, went well and she had an overnight stop-over there until her connecting flight to Stockholm the following morning. Upon arrival in Stockholm, she checked into the Colonial Hotel, about one half mile from the conference center. Her allowed budget by the World Health Organization for the conference meant she had to be very selective of the restaurants she chose, since the organization always scrutinized her expense reports. This also meant her hotel was further away than she liked from the conference location, the further away from the conference center, the cheaper the hotel.

While she sat at a table near the window of the Abyssinia Restaurant, she ordered a vodka martini, her drink of choice since she had been introduced to them by her father. At six o'clock in this southern suburb of Stockholm, the hotels and downtown areas were bustling with people, some heading home after work, and many still shopping or coming out for dinner at some local spot. As she gazed idly at the passersby while she casually enjoyed her drink, Bob and Julie Elliott and Marjorie Smith passed by on their way back to their hotel for dinner. Rachel paid no attention to this at first, since many people were shuffling back and forth each way in continual foot traffic.

Suddenly, she jumped up, raced to the restaurant door and onto the sidewalk staring from side to side, after she realized what she had just seen, or thought she had seen. She spotted no one at this time and returned to the restaurant, shook her head and wondered if her eyes had just played tricks on her. *Carlo must be on my mind*, she thought. She immediately ordered a light dinner, and within thirty minutes, headed back to her hotel. She retired to bed early to be fresh for the opening of the conference on Sunday morning.

Nearly seventy-five hundred people were expected at the worldwide event. The onslaught of HIV/AIDS in the world had escalated to major numbers and no one knew how to stem the growth of this disease which often proved fatal to its victims. The conference had hundreds of side sessions which participants could choose from. These sessions lasted usually for an hour and were scheduled before and after major speaking events in the Grand Hall. Rachel had carefully selected the sessions she was interested in, and always attempted to squeeze in as many of these as possible during the four-day period.

While attending a general session in the Grand Hall on the third day of the conference, Rachel was about one-hundred fifty feet from the stage and podium. She had deliberately entered the main hall early to try to get a seat as close to the front as possible. When she sat down, glanced down at her program, and then lifted her head toward the stage, the Elliotts walked by her in the aisle to her right, and headed for their seats several rows behind her. Rachel merely caught a glimpse of them as they walked by, and again, paid no immediate attention to them as they disappeared in the crowd behind her. Once again, in a sudden reaction, she rose from her seat and started scanning the aisles behind her.

What's wrong with me? she wondered. *Am I seeing things or is Carlo flashing before my eyes for some reason?* Then, suddenly, she spotted the Elliotts, and couldn't believe her eyes. She was staring at Carlo, several rows behind and Bob Elliott could sense her eyes on him from where he was sitting.

"Why is that woman staring at me, Julie?" Bob asked.

"It must be the natural charm and attractiveness women see in you, Bob, but maybe she's not looking at you but at someone around you or behind you," Julie answered.

"I've got to hit the men's room, Julie, do me a favor. Just watch her to see if she follows my moves out of the hall," Bob stated.

"What are you, paranoid or something? What's the problem?"

"I don't know. I just sense this woman is staring this way too long."

As Bob exited the row he was in and walked toward the back of the hall, Julie noticed Rachel's eyes never left his sight. Bob was right. She was focusing on him the entire time until he was out of sight. For the next few minutes, Julie noticed that Rachel kept glancing back to their seats, obviously looking for Bob to return. When he did return, she again stared his way until the master of ceremonies began speaking to welcome all attendees to the final conference session prior to the closing ceremony by the king on Thursday.

Following the brief speech, the assembly was dispersed for participants to attend their last side sessions in various adjacent rooms throughout the two-story conference center. While Julie had agreed to attend a session with Marjorie which was scheduled for fifteen minutes later, Bob decided he would head for the coffee shop on the second floor to read the USA Today he had picked up at the hotel earlier. They agreed to meet there after the session to decide what to do for lunch.

Rachel lost sight of Bob as the crowd made its way for the exits of the Grand Hall, and she hurried into the hallways trying to catch a glimpse of him again. She had scheduled herself to attend a session, but this interruption was troubling her. *Who is this man? Does he realize how much he looks like Carlo,* she wondered.

She scoured the hallways where thousands were walking in both directions until she spotted him riding the escalator toward the second level. She headed quickly his way, and in her mind, the escalator was not moving fast enough, nor could she pass people in front of her. Finally reaching the second floor, she had no clue in which direction he had gone. She headed to the left, and started looking into each small conference room, scanning the rooms to see if he was there. Once she was convinced he was not in the area, she quickly headed back toward the escalator to do the same search of conference rooms at the other end. About half way down on this side was an open-area coffee shop behind a glass entrance. As she looked in through the glass windows, she spotted him standing at the counter inside. She waited until he found a table and sat down with his newspaper under his arm.

She felt uneasy to approach him, since she did not know him. He looked strikingly like Carlo, and she knew it couldn't be him simply by the way he dressed. The facial features, the color of his hair, the physique, they were identical to Carlo. She hesitated to move forward, but finally did.

Bob noticed her coming and immediately put his newspaper down on the table and rose.

"Ah, the woman in the Grand Hall. I see. Was I dreaming or were you staring at me from your seat a few rows ahead of my wife and me?" Bob asked.

"Was I so obvious? I'm terribly sorry for doing that, but you look so much like a friend of mine, it's unbelievable," she blurted.

"Well, I can honestly say I don't know who you are and I know we have never met," Bob added.

"Forgive me, my name is Dr. Rachel Owens and I am from South Africa," Rachel stated.

"Hi, my name is Bob Elliott and I am from the United States. I am attending the conference with my wife and her colleague, both of whom are also doctors."

"May I join you for a moment?" Rachel asked.

"Be my guest. Would you like a cup of coffee or tea?"

He went back to the counter for another coffee. He was not certain if this resemblance she talked about was just a come on, or if she was legitimately convinced he looked like someone else. He handed her the coffee and sat down facing her.

"This friend you say I remind you of, is he from South Africa too?" Bob asked.

"No, he is from Italy. We are working together at the same hospital. He is a doctor also, a surgeon."

"What is a doctor from Italy doing in South Africa?" Bob asked.

"I'm sorry. I didn't explain myself too well. We are not practicing in South Africa, Mr. Elliott. We are on a mission at a hospital in Ethiopia. He is a surgeon and I am an AIDS specialist for the people in the villages of Tigray in northern Ethiopia," Rachel added.

Bob's mouth gaped open for just a moment as the word Ethiopia came out. He had been told months before by Harry Esten his twin brother was a doctor currently working in Ethiopia, and this was more than a coincidence.

"This doctor friend of yours who looks like me, can you tell me his name?" asked Bob cautiously.

"Dr. Carlo Melucci, from Orvieto, Italy."

"Is this some kind of a joke? You work in Ethiopia with Carlo Melucci?"

"Oh, no, Mr. Elliott, let me show you a picture of him I have in my wallet. See, this is us at Mekelle Hospital with other staff members at the Christmas party last year. It's not a great picture, but you can certainly see Carlo right here," she pointed to the photo in front of Bob.

Bob gazed at the photo for minutes and was literally speechless during that time.

"Are you okay, Mr. Elliott, you look like you've just seen a ghost?" she asked.

"Dr. Owens, exactly how well do you know this Carlo person?" he queried.

"We've been at Mekelle now for over two years, and I guess you would say maybe now we are more than just friends. Oh, my God, you've even got the same color eyes as Carlo."

"Can you tell me what his family does in Italy? Has he ever talked about them to you? I'm just curious," he continued the questioning.

"They own a vineyard in Orvieto," she answered.

The time flew by, and the conversation between Rachel and Bob had gone on for nearly an hour, until Julie and Marjorie appeared to meet Bob.

"Ladies, this is Dr. Rachel Owens, and I've asked her to join us for lunch." Julie was surprised to hear this as she looked at Bob in a puzzled way.

"Oh, I wish I could join you, but I'm scheduled to attend a buffet luncheon of other U.S. doctors in a separate room at the conference center," Marjorie replied. "I'll meet you back at the hotel later this afternoon for a drink and to discuss dinner plans. Nice to have met you, Rachel."

"Julie, Dr. Owens works at a hospital in Ethiopia and thought I looked very much like one of her colleagues and a close friend of hers," cited Bob as he handed Julie the photo.

"Oh, Bob, is this?" she stopped.

"His name is Carlo Melucci, Julie, Dr. Carlo Melucci, from Orvieto, Italy."

The look on Julie's face gave it away. Rachel knew there was something more here, something she wasn't aware of.

"There is something about Carlo you are not telling me, isn't there?" Rachel asked the both of them.

"How much do you know about Carlo, his background, his family? Has he ever mentioned anything to you?" asked Bob very seriously.

"No, not really, we first met at Mekelle. I didn't know him before. He has shown me pictures of his parents and his aunts, and a few pictures from their home in Orvieto, quite nice, I thought. What is it I should know, Mr. Elliott, you're freaking me out right about now?"

"Wow, where do I begin? This is something my wife and I found out about six months ago. When I was born on May 9, 1951 in Paris, France, I was given up for adoption by my mother who was young, single, and had no money. Lucky for me, I was adopted right away by an American couple. When I was twenty, my parents told me about the adoption, but it really didn't bother me at the time. Six months ago, I met my birth mother for the first time. She's now a queen in a Middle East country and this brief affair she had, happened long before she even met her husband."

"What does this have to do with Carlo?" asked Rachel.

"My natural mother had identical twins, Rachel, and my twin brother was adopted from the same orphanage, but a year later. Do you know if Carlo was adopted?"

"Of course not, how in the world would I know that?"

"Do you know the names of his parents?" Bob asked.

"Oh, he did mention their names to me a few times."

"Vito and Camille Melucci?" Bob asked.

"Yes, yes, that's their names. What are you saying?"

"Look at me, Dr. Owens, look at me and look at this picture you have. Do we look like identical twins to you? I believe that Carlo is my brother," Bob added with a sense of relief in saying it.

"My God, he has never mentioned any of this to me. Does he even know that he was adopted and has a brother?" she asked.

"I do know from others he was told when he was eighteen that he was adopted in 1952 at one year old, but I don't think his parents knew anything about a brother out there. It took me a while to accept I was adopted and I never did anything about it. Later, when I met my birth mother and found that I had a twin brother, it kind of hit me one morning when I looked in the mirror after shaving. The reflection in the mirror reminded me I had a twin brother somewhere and I had to find him. Our investigators found his family in Orvieto and he was a doctor serving at a hospital in Ethiopia. This was in January, Dr. Owens, but because of the rebels and fighting in that area, they haven't been able to get a visa to go there and talk to him."

Rachel just sat there speechless as she listened to this entire story and had trouble accepting it. She didn't know these people, yet how could anyone concoct such a story out of nowhere? No, she thought, it sounded very realistic, even though she felt defenseless at how to react to the news.

Bob suggested they find a quiet café nearby. He needed a drink and Rachel was eager to accommodate them. Julie assured her she had been as surprised when Bob and she had heard the news, and actually met his real mother right after Thanksgiving.

Rachel had so many questions to ask about all of this and Julie smiled at her as she nodded. These were the same questions she had asked. They found a small lounge in their hotel nearby and stayed there for several hours, munching snacks instead of lunch, and sipping martinis.

"Rachel, please do not discuss any of this with anyone until you see Carlo when you return to Ethiopia, because there is some danger if others know this information. Also, do not speak to Carlo about this by telephone or by fax, just to be on the safe side. The danger involves problems in the country where our birth mother is from, and until these are resolved, it is best not to discuss our birth mother to anyone else."

Bob wrote down his address in Medway along with his telephone number. He asked Rachel for the address at the Mekelle Hospital and a telephone number where Carlo could be reached at the hospital. As they exchanged information, they could only guess what their return flights would be like. They rose from their seats in the lounge, and Bob reached into his sport jacket's inside pocket and pulled out a photo of himself with Julie. He handed it to Rachel and simply said,

"Give this to Carlo for me, please. If he was born on May 9, 1951, tell him his brother says 'Hi'. He knows where to reach me and it might be harder for me to call him in Ethiopia."

She hugged him tightly and also hugged Julie when she left the hotel and headed back to hers. She would be flying out the next morning, while Bob and Julie would begin their three-day extended vacation. Somehow, the next three days in Lapland would be meaningless to the Elliotts, while Rachel's anxiety at sharing the news with Carlo was building the closer her flight neared Ethiopia.

CHAPTER 16

Bob could not wait to call Harry about the events in Stockholm. Ironically, Harry and Jim had just received word their visas to Ethiopia had finally been approved.

Carlo met Rachel at the Addis Ababa airport on Friday afternoon, and they planned to spend the night there before driving back to Mekelle on Saturday. Rachel was not comfortable bringing up Bob Elliott, since Carlo had never mentioned his being adopted in the two and a half years they had known each other. Perhaps Carlo had not found it necessary to do so, as he never pursued digging into who his birth parents were. Nevertheless, she had to discuss this with him.

"Let's check in to the hotel and then go down to the lounge for a drink. I have so much to tell you, I can't wait," Rachel said to Carlo excitedly.

"Well, aren't we the perky one after such a long flight."

"There'll be plenty of time to sleep later tonight, but for now, I think you'll want to hear what I have to say."

"Then tell me now," Carlo answered.

"No, Carlo, I think you'll want more than a glass of wine with what I'm about to tell you," she replied.

No sooner than her luggage hit the floor in her room and Carlo had dropped off his overnighter, they were headed for the hotel lounge on the main floor. Rachel ordered a martini and told Carlo that he should order the same for himself.

Following their usual toast to each other with the clang of glasses, they sipped their drinks until Rachel began.

"You've often told me about your parents and the vineyard they own in Orvieto, and about your two aunts, but you've never mentioned any brothers or sisters."

"That's because I don't have any, I'm an only child."

"Have you ever wondered why your parents never had other children?" she asked.

"Yes, of course. Mama was hurt during the war, and she could not have other children, my father once told me."

"But she had you. Isn't that strange that she had you but could not have others?" Rachel inquired.

"No, Rachel, Mama did not have me, I was adopted when I was about a year old. They told me this years ago and it's never bothered me at all. Why are you asking about this anyway?"

"Aren't you the least bit interested to know who your real mother and father are?" she went on.

"It was just after the war, Rachel, and for all I know they're not even alive, it was thirty-five years ago," Carlo answered.

"But suppose, just suppose, that she is still alive and your real father too. Wouldn't you at least want to know that?" she continued.

"I've thought about it from time to time, but I've never had that much time to find out. I know I came from an orphanage in Giverny, France, but that's about all I know."

"All these years since you've known, you've never once wanted to find out more about them?" she prodded.

"Rachel, what is this all about? You come back from an AIDS conference in Stockholm, and all you do is bring up something I hardly talk about," Carlo snapped.

"Suppose I told you that you were an identical twin to another boy from the same orphanage, born on the same day as you, May 9, 1951? What would you say then?" she asked as she became quite serious.

"I would say that you should lighten up on these martinis. What the hell are you saying?"

She leaned down at her pocketbook on the floor near her lounge chair, reached in and pulled out a photo, and gave it to Carlo.

He gazed at the photo and could not take his eyes off of it. As he continued to stare at the picture, Rachel continued. "His name is Bob Elliott, and he's from the United States. He was born on May 9, 1951 in Paris, France, was given up for adoption shortly after by his mother. Her name was Françoise Dupont, but she is now the queen of a Middle Eastern country called Khatamori. The father's name is Fr. Richard Merrill, also from the United States, who didn't know that the French woman was pregnant after they had a brief affair. Françoise Dupont had another child that same day in May, Carlo, and he was an identical twin to Bob Elliott. She named him Charles Andre, but your parents changed it to Carlo Andrea after they adopted you in September, 1952 when you were one-year old. Both of your real parents are still alive, Carlo."

"Where in the world did you get this information, Rachel," Carlo's head began to spin from all he had just heard.

"That photo was given to me by Bob Elliott in Stockholm. He was attending the conference with his wife who is a doctor in Medway, Massachusetts where they live. Bob owns restaurants there and used to be a professional athlete. I showed him a picture of you we took at the Christmas party, and even his wife was shocked at the resemblance. When I told him we were practicing in Ethiopia, he knew you were his brother. He knew all about Vito and Camille, the vineyard, and you being in Ethiopia. Even your parents knew he must be your brother, Carlo. Some Americans were trying to contact you here at Mekelle but haven't been able to get a visa yet."

There was no way Carlo could digest all of this news so quickly. He sat there staring at Rachel, his face in disbelief at what she had just told him. Rachel was right, he needed another martini and she motioned to the bartender for two more. Rachel reached into her purse again for Bob's address and telephone number. She told Carlo that she had given Elliott his address at Mekelle. There was no mistake here, Carlo and Bob were brothers, and no denial from either of them would change that.

"I have a twin brother. Are you certain of this?" he asked even though he really knew the answer to his own question.

"Yes, Carlo, now do you believe I had news that could not wait?"

* * *

The telephone in the royal suite rang and a servant answered.

"It's a Fr. Merrill for you, Your Highness."

"Richard, how are you? Do you have news?" Françoise asked.

Fr. Dick related the news about Bob and the meeting with another woman doctor who worked with Carlo in Ethiopia at Mekelle Hospital. He gave her all of the details as they had been related to him by Harry. He also mentioned that Harry and Jim would be flying to Ethiopia within the week to arrange to meet Carlo. He told Françoise that the female doctor who worked with Carlo would tell him about them and about his twin brother so their arrival in Ethiopia would not be as dramatic as they thought it would be. But Harry and Jim still needed to brief Carlo on the imminent danger brought about by the threats from people in Khatamori on their sons' lives since they were possible successors to the throne.

Françoise was very pleased at finally receiving good news about Carlo and Bob. She told Fr. Dick she would pass along the good news to Ahmad.

Meanwhile, across the other side of the palace grounds, Rafick was replaying the most recent tape of conversations the queen had been in on. The following day, he listened to the call from Fr. Merrill. This was the call he had been waiting for. Now it was payback time for his precious queen, time to eliminate unworthy heirs to his rightful claim to the crown, and time to repay Harry Esten for what he had done to his father.

He called a private number in Yemen and spoke but a few words, "the time is near for us to meet, tomorrow night at nine."

Following the call, he jumped into his Jeep and began his drive to Salalah, the second largest city in Oman, about one-hundred fifty miles south of Banra. He would meet with Manouch Haddad at their usual meeting place, the Al Jabal Hotel. They had a lot to discuss.

* * *

Back at the palace, Kaleel entered the study where Ahmad was reading and addressed his king.

"Your Highness, I have news about Ishraq Haddad.

"I have checked with the Talon family, where she had worked before coming to the palace. After interviewing members of the Talon family, Ishraq came from Yemen and was hired by Answa as a favor to a Yemeni friend. The friend was Manouch Haddad, Ishraq's father."

Ahmad was very upset at hearing this and immediately became suspicious about her duties in the palace attending to Françoise.

"I want you to conduct a thorough search of our suite. I fear Ishraq may have been spying on us even when Answa was alive."

The search uncovered the listening device in the telephone, but Ahmad told Kaleel not to remove it yet. Perhaps, he thought, they could lure the listeners into a trap if false information was given and the intruders acted on the information. Ahmad told Françoise to not accept further calls from America on her line, but to return them using another line elsewhere in the palace that was not bugged.

In the meantime, Kaleel called Harry in the States, and told him someone else now knew of Carlo's whereabouts, and that he and Jim needed to hurry to Ethiopia to prevent anything from happening to Carlo. Harry quickly moved the date of their intended departure from the following Friday to Monday. He then faxed a message to Carlo showing their arrival date and to beware of being in public over the weekend because of dangerous assailants who might be in the area. He ended the fax with the words, "your parents have sent us to you. This is not a joke." He signed it Harry Esten, FBI, United States.

* * *

Rafick's Jeep pulled into the Al Jabal Hotel in Salalah, Oman at five-thirty in the afternoon. He checked in, and sat at the bar in the lounge, and plotted his next move in Ethiopia with Haddad. No one at Mekelle Hospital would know him, so he felt there was no need for a disguise to get close to Carlo Melucci. Rafick would not make the same mistake as his father. Haddad would be given specific directions on what to do.

At precisely nine o'clock, Haddad entered the lounge from a rear door as he always did, and was flanked by armed men. He greeted Rafick and offered his condolences on hearing about his father's death six months earlier. Most of Haddad's work had been done under Answa's orders, and he enjoyed the relationship because Answa paid well for his services. Rafick had accompanied Answa the last time he was hired for the job in Dijon, and in his mind, Haddad had carried out that assignment exactly as he had been instructed. He, unfortunately, had been instructed to kill the wrong man. Rafick assured him this time, Carlo Melucci was the right target for Haddad. Haddad collected his fee up front, as he always did. "I'll be in Ethiopia by next Tuesday, and I'll report back to you by Thursday."

"There'll be a generous bonus if you also take care of an FBI agent named Harry Esten who's expected to be in Ethiopia to protect Carlo later in the week."

"Tell my daughter, Ishraq, that her father says hello and that he still loves her very much, even if she does not approve of what I do for a living. Her mother, were she still alive, would be proud of how she has turned out. Tell her for me, Rafick, the next time you see her."

CHAPTER 17

The letter began,

My Dear Carlo,

When my wife, Julie, and I met your friend and colleague, Dr. Rachel Owens, at the World AIDS Conference in Stockholm last week, I was finally certain that you and I were identical twins, separated at birth and adopted by different parents, mine in the United States, yours in Italy.

Dr. Owens has told us that you speak and read English, which is why I am writing to you. She had also given us your telephone number in Ethiopia, but we were told that making such a call requires satellite telephones and those are hard to get. I am hoping Dr. Owens has told you the details of our meeting and how she was positive we were identical twins. Our birth mother is now a queen in some Middle East country and wants us to visit her there, but first I would very much like to meet you. Since you

are under obligations in a hospital there in Ethiopia, and Dr.
Owens has told us that you are committed to be there until the
end of 1988, it looks like I should come to you, if you allow me to
visit you in Ethiopia.

There are two other Americans who are going to Ethiopia to
speak to you, because it seems that our lives are still in danger from
enemies in our mother's country who believe we might be eligible
to succeed her husband when he dies. I don't understand much
of this, but I will likely try to fly to Addis Ababa with them on
Monday, June 20, arriving in Mekelle the next day.

I am very anxious to meet you.

Your brother,

Bob Elliott

The letter was mailed on Friday, June 17, by Federal
Express overnight mail and Bob was assured the letter
would reach Mekelle no later than Monday, June 20.

Harry, at first, thought there was not enough time
for Bob to secure a visa, buy airline tickets, and clear all
the red tape necessary to make the trip to Ethiopia with
them, but using his FBI clout to circumvent some technical issues, he was able to pull it off. Julie, however, would
have to wait for another time. There was only so much
influence Harry had, and after explaining the situation
to the State Department, the Ethiopian government hesitated to issue another visa. Ethiopia was still under rebel
exposure, especially the northern part of the country in
the Tigray region where Mekelle Hospital was situated.
Bob had just used his passport for the Stockholm conference, so it was in order.

The three men met at Logan Airport in Boston at four-
thirty on Monday morning as Julie drove Bob to the airport
and bid him goodbye as he grabbed his luggage.

"This is something, deep down, you have been hoping for, Bob, now you know it's real. I hope it all goes well for you and Carlo. Try to be calm. Whatever happens, honey, is going to happen for the best. Tell him for me I can't wait to meet him. Be safe, Bob, above all be safe, and listen to what Harry tells you. I love you and this little guy in my stomach right now needs to have his father back home as soon as possible."

"I'm okay, Julie, I'm okay. I had a whole speech ready to say when I meet him, and for the life of me, I can't remember a word. I don't know what's going to happen when I meet him, we'll see." Bob kissed her goodbye.

The flight to Washington, D.C. would take less than two hours, but the connecting flight from D.C. to Addis Ababa, a seventy-five hundred mile trek, had them arriving in Addis Ababa at eight o'clock on Tuesday morning, Ethiopian time. Once in Addis Ababa, a member of the American embassy would accompany them by helicopter to Mekelle Hospital in Tigray. The helicopter would then return on Thursday morning to bring them back to the Ethiopian capital for their scheduled return flight to the States. Accommodations had been made at the Abreha Castle Hotel. The three men would be sharing a large suite.

The Abreha Castle Hotel was a nineteenth century stone castle originally, which in recent years had been converted into a hotel. It was located on a hill overlooking the town of Mekelle, and was walking distance to the hospital. They arrived at the hotel just after noon and while Jim and Bob headed down to the restaurant on the main level, Harry decided to go directly to Mekelle Hospital, hoping to meet Carlo and to find out when he would be free to meet with them.

Carlo was having lunch in his office, the letter from Bob laying on his desk when Harry knocked on the open door.

"Yes, may I help you?" he greeted in English.

"Dr. Melucci, my name is Harry Esten from the FBI in the United States. I believe you were made aware I would be here to speak with you," Harry answered.

"Yes, yes, I did receive the telegram from your embassy in Addis Ababa, I thought there were others with you?" he asked.

"We just arrived and checked in at the Abreha Castle. The others went down for lunch first. I know you are very busy here, so I wanted to find out when it would be best to get together."

"Well, I have two operations this afternoon, and I need to do the rounds on my other patients. So I won't be free until around five o'clock. Perhaps I could meet you for dinner at the hotel restaurant at six? I would bring Rachel, Dr. Owens, with me if you don't mind. She seems to know as much about this as I do," Carlo answered.

"Oh, great, that would be excellent. We'll see you then."

"Mr. Esten, please tell Roberto that his brother says hello and that I am anxious to see him. I am assuming he is with you."

"He is also anxious to meet you, Dr. Melucci."

Bob and Carlo were thirty-five year old men with the exact genes, as they shared the same egg in their mother's womb, and that is as close as it can get. What would be the reaction from each of them when they finally met for the first time? They, of course, were strangers. They knew nothing about each other except for the little they had just learned in the previous week. One good fortune for

Bob was that Carlo spoke English as well as Italian, while Bob could only boast of his high school French class as another language he understood. There was so much to learn about each other and they probably had very little in common since they were brought up in different environments. From everything Bob had read over the last few months, especially an article written in 1979 about the "Minnesota Twins Study," identical twins separated at birth were known to have incredible similarities. He hoped this was true for Carlo and him, but it would take time to discover how much they had in common after having lived apart for all these years.

Carlo tried not to think about this because his full attention needed to be on the two patients he was operating on before dinner that evening. Bob, on the other hand, was extremely nervous, paced the floor in their suite, adjusted the furniture in the room several times, and his actions were obviously noticeable by both Harry and Jim. They said nothing at first, but then Jim asked.

"How do you want to meet Carlo, in the suite first, alone, or with the rest of us present?"

Bob didn't know what to say. He genuinely was not sure how this meeting should take place.

"I think I prefer to meet Carlo in the hotel lounge first, with Rachel there, because I know her and feel comfortable with her being there."

"We understand and we'll meet you in the lounge at six-thirty and we'll move to a private section of the dining room Jim has reserved for us."

At five, Bob was ready to head downstairs to the hotel lounge. He was wearing an open white shirt with a pair of chinos and loafers with no socks. The weather in Ethiopia was always hot and the weather in June was in the nineties. The air conditioning in the hotel was inadequate, but was supplemented by ceiling fans everywhere.

"Wish me luck, guys, and don't be late. I don't know how this will go off. It could be awkward," Bob lamented.

As he stepped out of the elevator and turned to head for the lounge, there stood Carlo and Rachel looking his way. His heart started beating rapidly as, for a moment, he stood facing them about twenty feet away. All Carlo and Bob could do was gaze at each other. Then slowly, they each moved toward each other, tears flowed down their cheeks as each tried to smile at the other. But the smiles quickly turned to more tears as they hugged each other tightly as they both cried uncontrollably. Rachel held her hand to her mouth and, she too was crying. She could not believe this moment. Two brothers, who had never met, somehow knew each other, and conveyed the same emotions at the same time.

It was uncanny. Carlo was wearing a white shirt with chinos and loafers, and you couldn't tell one apart from the other. The hair, the eyes, the facial expressions and their physiques were identical. The hotel manager noticed other people in the lobby gazing at them and he approached quickly.

"This is your first meeting, Dr. Carlo? You are twins, no doubt. Please, come with me, I will place you in a more private area. You don't need all these eyes on you right now."

"Thank you, Daniel," answered Rachel, "that would be nice."

Carlo and Rachel had dined often in the Abreha Castle's restaurant and Daniel had the highest respect for the doctors from Mekelle Hospital who volunteered to help the sick people from the Tigray region. He often gave them complimentary cocktails before dinner and the hotel had recently hosted the hospital staff Christmas party.

Bob and Carlo had not yet spoken a word to each other. Rachel grabbed the two by an arm, and led them to an area Daniel had selected in a far corner of the lounge.

"Dinner will be at seven for five of you, I believe?"

"Yes, there will be two more gentlemen joining us shortly," Bob answered.

The bartender came forward as they sat down in three soft chairs with a round table in front of them.

"Samuel, I will have a vodka martini with extra olives, please, and you two?" Rachel asked.

Carlo ordered the same as their attention turned to Bob. Not wanting to be different, but also realizing this was his drink of choice anyway, he ordered a martini as well.

For the next hour, they exchanged tales about their upbringing in totally different environments, exchanged photos of their adoptive parents, and Bob flashed a photo of his wife, Julie. When Carlo heard from Bob that he owned two restaurants, he asked if one of them was Italian.

"You may not believe this, Carlo, but I have two restaurants, one called the Lamplighter, and my newest one that I opened last year is called the Villa, serving mostly all Italian food. Who would have guessed?"

"I will tell my father to send you a case of our Orvieto classic white wine, Bob. It will be wine you will not want to be without. Over here, the wine is not so good. That is why Rachel has me drinking martinis," Carlo joked.

Rachel could not believe how similar they were. They had excelled in sports as youths, had trouble with math, and had tendencies to fall asleep in front of the television.

"Last year, Carlo, did you hurt your foot in any way?" asked Bob.

"Yes, how did you know? I twisted my ankle jogging one morning and I remember having to do surgeries that day with my foot throbbing with pain," Carlo answered.

"I haven't had much of anything up to then though, except a few years ago my shoulder would ache on and off for about a month and then it just went away," Carlo continued.

"Would that have been about a year ago in April or so?" Bob asked.

"Well, yes, that's about right, how do you know this?" Carlo asked.

"I broke my collarbone in spring training with the Red Sox at that time, Carlo, and I missed the rest of the year because of the injury."

"I guess it is true what they say about identical twins. They can feel each other's pain even if they are thousands of miles apart," Bob added.

"Sometimes I get such bad headaches, I can't stand it," Carlo said. "Rachel thinks it's from all the time under pressure at the hospital."

"I get them too, Carlo."

Harry and Jim appeared right on time and were pleased to see the reunion going so well. They ordered a cocktail, and after some small talk, all headed for their private dining area in the hotel restaurant. As the conversation continued throughout dinner, it was obvious to all that the twins even liked the same food. Toward the end of the meal, Harry felt it was time to begin talking about Françoise and Ahmad, and Khatamori. Since Bob had already met his birth mother, he took the lead in the conversation by explaining to Carlo how nice a woman Françoise was, and the adoption was something she truly regretted. Bob went on to tell Carlo, under the circumstances, she had no way to raise them at the time. As for their father, Bob said he had met him and was less than cordial with him at the time. After reflecting on the meeting later on, he told Carlo he realized their adoption had little to do with him since he never even knew their mother was pregnant. He said he would reach out to him again to see if they could get to know each other more.

"Your mother's telephone has been recently bugged and someone else outside the family probably knows of our coming here to meet Carlo, and might attempt to harm him and Bob," Harry said.

"You should avoid being in public without either me or Jim with you as a precaution for the next few days. Carlo, if you can get some time off from the hospital, even three or four days, I can probably arrange for the both of you to fly directly to Khatamori from Ethiopia. It's much closer than trying to arrange visits later on from the U.S. and Italy."

"I'll check with Dr. Girard to see if this is possible," Carlo stated, while Bob was willing to leave in a moment's notice.

At nine, the restaurant on a weekday was pretty empty except for three businessmen at a table across the room from their table. The three men rose to leave without turning Harry's way and began to head for the lobby of the hotel. At first, Harry paid little attention to them as they headed out. Suddenly, Harry recognized the small tattoo on one of the men's neck.

Quickly he scanned the room and noticed a briefcase under the men's table.

"Everybody down, now," he screamed as he turned their table over, facing the other table, and attempted to use it as a shield. Suddenly, a loud explosion splattered furniture and dishes everywhere, leaving the room in shambles.

Harry quickly looked at everyone at his side to see if they were unharmed and they appeared to be shaken up by the blast but, other than a few scratches from flying debris, they were all alert except Jim Howard. He lay face down on the floor, bleeding profusely from his head and chest. Harry rushed to him at the same time as Carlo and Rachel. Carlo had seen this before as innocent Ethiopians were often rushed to Mekelle with wounds suffered from landmines that had been placed along dirt roads on the outskirts of town. They quickly applied pressure to his head and chest wounds, while Harry rushed to the lobby and yelled for the desk clerk to call for an ambulance right away.

Jim was unconscious, his pulse weak, and the loss of blood was great. Carlo worked frantically to put pressure on the bleeding areas, but without the necessary tools, he and Rachel looked desperate in doing so.

Within minutes, an ambulance arrived and two attendants brought medical supplies and life-saving equipment to the scene. Jim was stabilized and placed in the ambulance with Carlo and Rachel jumping in as well. Harry stood there in a daze. He ran to the lobby to see if anyone had seen the three men leave the hotel and where they headed. Harry had drawn his revolver, and as he started running for the main door of the hotel, he was met by several local policemen with their guns drawn and aimed at him. He immediately stopped in his tracks, fell to his knees, and dropped his gun.

Two hours later, he was released by the police when they realized his credentials were genuine and the embassy in Addis Ababa had vouched for him. The hotel manager had told the police they were guests at the hotel, and acquaintances of Dr. Carlo Melucci, whom he praised endlessly. Harry asked the police to take him to the hospital. It was now midnight and the hospital was fairly quiet as he made his way to the front desk. He pleaded with the nurse on duty to tell him where the ambulance patient with Dr. Melucci had been taken. She pointed to the last door at the end of the corridor and Harry ran down the hallway as fast as he could.

Before he reached the last doorway, Carlo and Rachel appeared wearing operating room scrubs, their attire full of blood stains and their faces drained. They spotted Harry and held him back from entering the adjacent room.

"There was nothing we could do to save him, Harry. He had lost so much blood, and by the time we were able to stop the bleeding, he went into cardiac arrest. He's gone, Harry, he didn't make it," lamented Carlo as he held Harry with both arms.

"This is my fault. I never should have let him come here. He wasn't trained to do this, what was I thinking?" Harry murmured.

Carlo and Rachel led him to a lounge area and sat with him for some time trying to get him to agree to a mild sedative to calm him down.

"Who would do such a thing?" Rachel asked. "We do not get explosions here in town. I can't remember the last time, at least not since I have been here," she continued.

"I recognized the tattoo on one of the men's neck, the same tattoo of the person who blew up my house and tried to kill me several months ago in the States. That is the danger I was trying to tell you about earlier tonight. His name is Manouch Haddad and he is an assassin for hire from Yemen. The danger is far from over if he is still around here, and my guess is he won't leave until he has finished the job." Harry's eyes darted around the room.

"Where's Bob?"

"I don't know, Mr. Esten, we left with the ambulance and haven't seen him since the explosion," Rachel answered.

Harry jumped to his feet and headed back to the hotel. The dining area affected by the blast had been closed off by the police and the lobby area was fairly quiet at this hour. He rushed up the stairs to their second floor suite, fumbled for his door key, and finally entered the room. He turned on the light and started shouting.

"Bob, Bob, where are you?"

No answer. He started searching the area, going from one bedroom to the next, looking under the beds, inside the closets, everywhere. Nothing. Not until he tried to enter the bathroom door Bob was using. The door was locked and even as he started shouting Bob's name again, nothing happened. He backed away from the door enough to bring his foot up and kicked the door as hard as he could until it finally opened. He flipped on the light switch and pulled the shower curtain back. There, in the tub was Bob, curled up in a fetal position, shaking uncontrollably. Harry gently touched him on the shoulder until Bob looked up at Harry.

"Are you okay?"

The blast from the explosion had left Bob temporarily deaf and he tried to read Harry's lips when he spoke.

"Can you hear me, Bob?"

Bob started to get up from the bathtub and pointed to his ears with a shrug. Harry helped him out and they sat down on the sofa in the living room of the suite as Harry picked up the telephone and called the hotel operator. He asked her to contact Dr. Melucci at Mekelle Hospital and for him to come to Room 214 right away. He told the clerk to call him back if she couldn't locate him at the hospital.

Within minutes, Carlo and Rachel knocked at his door. When he answered, he pointed to Bob and quickly told Carlo, "Bob can't hear anything."

Carlo had seen this before and confronted Bob by writing on hotel stationery. He told him he was suffering from a temporary loss of hearing from the explosion, and his hearing would likely return in a day or so, if not sooner.

Bob was relieved to hear the news. "Jim, where's Jim?" he asked.

Carlo just shook his head. Bob looked over at Harry. Harry was seated in a chair, his face in his hands as he wept, and Bob realized Jim was dead.

After a few minutes, Harry regained his control, and suggested Carlo and Rachel stay in the suite until morning. The police were still all over the hotel grounds and two uniformed officers would be placed outside their suite for the night. Harry asked the hotel manager for a bottle of vodka and some extra glasses to be brought to the room. Harry had to decide what the next move would be now that further trouble was likely. Carlo and Rachel each headed to separate bathrooms to shower the blood off their bodies. The manager brought up several additional towels and robes for them to wear while he would attend to having their soiled scrubs cleaned and returned by morning.

After his shower, Carlo poured himself a glass of vodka with ice and did the same for Bob. Bob looked at him and smiled a very weak smile, but one of appreciation nevertheless.

Harry was on the phone to the embassy in Addis Ababa, and in spite of the hour of night, managed to convey they needed assistance in Mekelle by morning. The embassy assured them a helicopter would be there with military personnel on board. Harry informed the local police the helicopter would be landing nearby early the next morning.

"Tomorrow morning, a helicopter from the American embassy will be taking Bob and both of you to Addis Ababa for safekeeping until I can find these animals," Harry began. "They will also be taking Jim's body back with them for transport back to Rhode Island later this week."

"We're not going anywhere, Mr. Esten. This is where we belong right now and the hospital can't function without two of its doctors. Besides, even if we were to go with you to Addis Ababa, what's to stop these madmen from coming back when we return later on?" Carlo answered.

"It's much too dangerous for you at the hospital, Dr. Melucci, and I don't have the manpower to protect you in such a large facility. These guys could get into the hospital from a dozen different ways and we wouldn't even know it," Harry pleaded with Carlo.

"Rachel won't go either, Mr. Esten, she's driven through rebel territory, mine fields and machine gun fire out in the villages and this episode won't stop her from continuing her work," Carlo added.

"If that's how you both feel, I can't stop you. I just don't think you'll be safe there. But maybe we can be ready for them when they do show up. How well do you know the people in the hospital, Dr. Melucci?" Harry asked.

"Strangers in the hospital would attract someone's attention. If we keep most of the outside doors locked, they'll have to come in through common entrances and there are only four of those on the first floor. We should get to the hospital early in the morning and you can show these to me, Carlo. The key is not to allow anyone not with the hospital to enter the premises, unless they are here to visit a relative, and you can certainly screen these before they are allowed entrance. I'll get the embassy's military do this," Harry explained.

Harry kept thinking about Jim. Carlo and Rachel were concerned at the disruption at the hospital. Bob was worried about the deafening silence all around him. There would be very little sleep in Room 214 that night.

CHAPTER 18

At six o'clock on Wednesday morning, Carlo was already dressed in the clean scrubs that the hotel had just delivered. Rachel's set was placed in the bathroom near her bedroom in the suite.

Harry was still dressed in the same clothes he had on the night before, an evening that had started out so joyously and had ended so tragically. Harry tried to shake this from his mind as he pondered his next moves for the day. The knock on the door of the suite was met with close scrutiny. Local police scanned the food cart being brought to their room as well as the waiter delivering the cart.

"They're taking nothing for granted. This is not the time to be careless," Harry explained when Carlo appeared taken aback by the policeman's action.

Bob entered the living room area shortly after Carlo, and said, "I can hear some sounds faintly but not enough to make them out." Carlo again wrote down that his hearing would gradually return, perhaps even to one ear first over the other one.

The sound of a helicopter flying over the hotel signaled the arrival of embassy officials and military personnel. The helicopter landed in the rear of the hotel, far enough away in an empty lot to not disturb the entire area at the early morning hour. John Froment, the attaché from the embassy, who had earlier handled bringing the group to Mekelle, was accompanied by Lt. Terry Schmidt and six soldiers under his command at the embassy. The group had been cleared by Ethiopian authorities to protect persons under fire following the blast from the previous night.

Harry met Froment and Lt. Schmitt in the hotel lobby while the six soldiers established positions at all main entrances. John Froment looked at the rubble that used to be the private dining area of the hotel and shook his head.

"Wow, somebody didn't want anybody leaving this room in one piece," he stated.

"The man's name is Manouch Haddad, John, here's what he looks like," as Harry handed him a recent photo of Haddad.

"He was hired by somebody in Khatamori who wants these two brothers killed and probably still wants me killed too. I shot a cousin of the king of this country when he was in Boston. The cousin was after the king who was having a kidney transplant and he also went after one of the two brothers, the one who lives in Massachusetts. The cousin did not know about the other brother, the one who lives in Italy but is a surgeon at Mekelle."

"Well, Harry, it looks like this surgeon may have just ended his stint in Ethiopia. We can't have things like this happening under my watch, you know. It doesn't look good when Americans get involved in stuff like this. The Ethiopians have enough problems of their own without worrying about explosions that have nothing to do with these people."

"He won't leave, John, and we don't have any authority over him, he's from Italy. We can pull out the Massachusetts guy, Bob Elliott, but that's about it. But before you stomp off and just whisk this guy out of here, there may be a way to catch these guys at their own game," Harry offered.

"I don't get where you're going with this, Harry. The FBI has zero jurisdiction here, and as a matter of fact, you could be considered unwelcome, if you get my drift," Froment cautioned.

"Hear me out first. How long can your men stay here in this location before they attract too much attention?" Harry went on.

"We've had situations where we work with the local police for a few days, not much more than that. Why?" Froment asked.

"I contacted the head of the police investigating the blast from last night and they seem very interested in finding these guys before more violence happens in town. They are staying somewhere in the area, and they have to eat and sleep like the rest of us. If we get the local police to circulate Haddad's picture throughout town and places nearby, somebody has to have seen them. If we locate them, the cop I talked to has told his men to phone in any information and not to try anything alone. I'm asking for your guys, Lt. Schmidt, to just cover the hospital for a few days. If we can't flush them out by then, I'll back off."

"Two days, Harry, that's all I can stay here before somebody at the embassy starts wondering what's taking so long getting out of here. Now, let's go meet these brothers who are causing all this trouble."

Lt. Schmitt assembled his men and they were ready to walk over to the hospital. Harry informed him one of the doctors from the hospital would go with them to point out what entrances were the most vulnerable. He had asked the hotel manager to photocopy two hundred copies of Haddad's picture, some of which he would ask the soldiers to distribute to hospital staff when they went there.

Harry then led Froment to the second floor suite where the others were. As he entered the suite, he was greeted by Carlo and Rachel in their scrubs. Following his introduction by Harry, Bob appeared from his bedroom.

"What the hell? Holy shit, Harry, you didn't tell me these guys were twins. What's going on here?"

"They tried to kill Bob last November and failed, and now they just tried to get rid of Carlo here and botched that up too. I don't want to give them another chance to do the job."

"Harry, for the most part, local police in Ethiopia are quite corrupt, but throw some money their way and they'll do just about anything for you. Their idea of following the laws is superseded by their own interpretation of those laws," Froment mentioned. "They often violate human rights by beating prisoners, having others disappear, or they simply sell their services to the highest bidder. If you really want to catch these hoods, you need to go to the highest police official in town and personally offer him a large financial reward for their capture or death. This will definitely get the official's attention and the area will soon be blanketed with subordinates knocking on quite a few doors with Haddad's picture in hand.

"Offer an additional cash reward to the individual coming forward with information which leads to their capture or death. Any person taking it upon himself to attempt to apprehend Haddad and his two associates on his own gets nothing."

Harry remembered what Fr. Merrill had told Jim and him about Françoise willing to pay whatever it cost to find her son. He assumed this also included funds required to keep him alive, so he asked Froment what would be an appropriate amount to entice the police official to begin the manhunt immediately.

"Harry, you offer them $1,000 in American money now, and another $1,000 after they're caught or killed, and they'll jump at the offer. Do you know what that kind of money means to them?"

"Set it up, John. Do it right now and let's get this over with. This has to end. I want to get these boys home safe and sound. After they meet their natural mother in Khatamori, I'm done. This is the second time in seven months that I'm in the middle of an explosion, and I don't want to be a part of any more of these."

Knowing how bribes and payoffs were a way of life in the region, Froment always had several thousand dollars in American money in his briefcase, just in case. Within an hour, he returned to the hotel with the news that his police contact had disseminated several hundred photos of Haddad throughout the town with the telephone number to call and the reward amount splattered across the photo.

Several other officers were driving to surrounding towns to post more flyers there.

In the meantime, Carlo and Rachel had led the military team to Mekelle Hospital and showed Lt. Schmidt the entrances and exits on the main floor. Lt. Schmidt posted his people inside each entrance or exit, but out of direct vision to any person entering or leaving. Hospital personnel were instructed to only use the main entrance to the hospital when they left. No exit doors were to be used to leave the premises. If anyone attempted to enter the hospital through any of these, they would be greeted by an American embassy soldier, complete with an automatic weapon in his hands.

Once the soldiers were in position, Carlo and Rachel walked up the staircase to their second floor offices to change their clothes out of the operating room scrubs they were still wearing.

"Meeting my twin brother has been quite a bit more than I expected, Rachel," Carlo moaned.

"I don't think it's your brother, Carlo. It sounds to me like it's your mother and her position in this country of hers that's the problem. I guess when you marry a king, you get the good with the bad from people living there," Rachel answered.

Fortunately for Carlo, he had only one surgery scheduled, and it was at ten o'clock, a few hours away. This gave him time to change clothing, shave, and nurse another cup of coffee before scrubbing up for the upcoming procedure on an infected leg. Rachel, on the other hand, would not risk going out on this day, worried more about Carlo's safety than her own. Instead she would remain close by, and keep a watchful eye on Carlo in the operating room.

At nine-thirty, John Froment received a call in Harry's suite from his police contact. Haddad had been seen in the market square by a street vendor selling fresh coffee beans. It seemed Haddad had been spotted with two others entering the square which was filled with kiosks for nearly a hundred yards. The area was so congested with people that no vehicles were allowed during daylight hours until four o'clock in the afternoon when vendors would pack up their wares to close shop.

The police were assigned to carefully search the market area from each end, working their way toward the center. The uniformed men walked in pairs, no officers on their own. Harry jumped into an old car which was driven by one of the policemen and headed for the market square only a mile away.

Froment grabbed his military phone, called Lt. Schmidt at the hospital and told him to be on alert in case the three assailants were not found at the square. Schmidt notified all the men by using the hospital's intercom system, and then went back to his position near the main entrance. One soldier was assigned specifically to guard Carlo, and to follow his every move other than entering the sanitized operating room itself.

* * *

Haddad and his two men could see policemen approach from each direction. They immediately rose from the outside café table where they sat at, and headed inside to look for a rear entrance. As they exited the back door into an alleyway, a policeman, who had just flashed Haddad's photo to the café waiter, blew his whistle and he and his partner drew their pistols and headed into the café. The clerk at the register pointed to the back door and they rushed out the door where they were met with a volley of gunshots, wounding one officer and forcing the other to immediately drop his weapon and fall to his knees.

Haddad told the unwounded policeman to take off his uniform. Once the officer was in just his briefs, one of Haddad's men fired individual shots into both their heads and they left the area.

Upon hearing the gunfire, more policemen arrived as Harry got to the scene. After seeing the two dead officers, Harry quickly grabbed the military phone that Froment had given him and called Lt. Schmidt at the hospital.

"Lieutenant, be very careful, they may be coming your way. One of them might be dressed like a policeman, so don't be fooled by any of them. I'm on my way."

Harry jumped back into the car and sped toward the hospital. Traveling a mere one mile seemed like a short distance, but he could not get there soon enough.

Meanwhile, Haddad changed into the police uniform and the three proceeded to finish their assignment. They neared the main entrance to the hospital, and in the parking lot in the front area, they placed a detonation device in a car parked there. Within seconds, the car exploded and attracted two of the soldiers at the main entrance. They rushed toward the engulfed vehicle with their automatic weapons in hand. Other soldiers heard the blast and rushed toward the lobby, which left several other entrances unprotected. The two thugs hid behind other parked vehicles and opened fire on the approaching soldiers. Although the soldiers wore protective vests, they dove for cover behind pillars near the entranceway.

The distraction worked. Haddad found a side entrance unlocked and unguarded. Once inside, he strode past the lobby like just another policeman and was able to reach the staircase.

Lt. Schmidt caught a glimpse of him entering the stairwell and gave chase. He heard the door slam on the floor above and raced up the staircase. As he entered the floor, he noticed the soldier guarding the doorway to the operating room.

"Where did the uniformed policeman go?"

"No one's entered the floor from the stairwell and I have not seen any local policeman on the floor, Lieutenant."

Lt. Schmidt realized the slamming door was a diversion and the policeman had continued to the third floor and would likely return to the second floor using the stairwell on the other side, nearer to the operating room.

"Stay put and do not allow any policeman to come near your post, at all costs," Lt. Schmidt yelled.

Lt. Schmidt then rushed to the far side staircase and looked upward toward the third floor. In a single motion, Haddad had a gun to Schmitt's head.

"Drop your weapon or I'll shoot." Lt. Schmidt handily complied and Haddad started walking toward the other soldier, using Lt. Schmidt as a shield. The soldier immediately entered the operating room and blocked the door by sliding an instrument tray across both inside door handles. As he saw that the operating team was still working on a patient, he screamed to them.

"Get that table away from the doorway now. There's a gunman out there. Do it now, now."

* * *

The two gunmen out front had served their purpose and began to retreat from the area as Harry's car approached. He saw the two men and had the driver go to the next street to cut them off.

"Stop," he yelled as he pointed his revolver at both of them once his car faced the oncoming hired guns. One of them began shooting at Harry and he returned the volley and struck the shooter in the leg. The other assailant dropped his gun and stopped running as he raised his hands.

"If he so much as moves, shoot him," he told the driver.

Harry rushed toward the hospital and was met by onrushing soldiers in pursuit of the two gunmen.

"You two, go help them. The rest of you, come with me." They rushed up the staircase and, through the glass opening in the doorway, Harry could see Haddad in a police uniform holding a gun to the head of Lt. Schmidt.

Harry motioned to the other soldier behind him to climb to the third floor and quietly come down the far stairway and to stay there.

"Hello, Haddad," he yelled as he entered the second floor hallway.

"Do not come any closer or I will kill him," Haddad replied.

"No you won't, Haddad, if you shoot him, you're as good as dead. You should have finished the job back in Rhode Island last year. But I'm still here, you slime ball, what do you think your daughter would think of you now when she hears what you did?"

"My daughter, leave Ishraq out of this. I am paid to do a job and I get it done. My daughter wants no part of me and she is better off without me. She is doing well in Khatamori."

"Is she, Haddad, is she really? She has disappeared from the palace after they found the queen's telephone with a bug in it. It doesn't sound like she's better off right now, does it?"

"Back away, and tell the other soldier in the stairwell to back away also, or I swear I will shoot this man."

"Don't do anything foolish, Haddad. Who hired you, Haddad? Who wants all these people to die? Who is paying you to do this? If you don't tell me, your two men will. They were captured out front. How long do you think it'll take for them to tell us, especially if we offer them a deal they can't refuse?"

"My men are loyal to me, they will not tell you anything."

Haddad backed up against the wall and slid toward the staircase door. He yelled at the soldier in the stairwell to move up the stairway, but to stay in plain view. He then pushed the door open and backed into the stairwell as he looked up the staircase. The soldier stood there with his gun pointed at the two of them. He told the soldier to move around the corner out of sight or he would fire.

No sooner was the soldier out of sight then Haddad whacked his gun across the back of Lt. Schmidt's neck and he fell to the floor. Haddad hurried down the stairwell. He bolted out of the hospital in seconds and quickly out of sight.

Harry raced to the stairwell, found Lt. Schmidt groggy, but alive, and told the soldier to take care of him as he ran down the stairwell. He bolted out the side entrance nearest the staircase, but no one was in sight. He moved quickly back inside and rushed toward the main entrance where the other two assailants were being restrained.

Harry grabbed the unwounded assailant and held him up against the wall as he pointed his gun to his head.

"Who hired you to do this? Tell me the right answer and you might live. Tell me nothing and you'll die right here."

There was fury in Harry's eyes and the rage he had was something he couldn't contain. He had never experienced such rage before and the thought of actually pulling the trigger on this slime actually felt satisfying to him. He had been pushed to the limit and had had enough.

"A young man from Khatamori always would meet us in Salalah, Oman at the Al Jabal Hotel. Talon, his name is Talon. Manouch called him Ray, that's all I know."

"How did you leave it with him? Were you going to tell him the job was done in the same place, by telephone, or what?" Harry pursued.

"He always comes on a Thursday to Salalah, if not this week, then the next, but always on the same day of the week. The bartender at the hotel then calls Manouch to let him know when he is there."

Harry cocked his gun. "That's all I know," the assailant said as the sobbing man fell to the ground.

Harry had some calls to make.

CHAPTER 19

While the murder of Jim Howard occurred in Ethiopia, the death of an American on foreign soil allowed the American embassy to have the the assailants extradited to the U.S. for prosecution in a Federal court. In this case, since the crime did not involve an Ethiopian, the government chose to allow it. Besides, the Ethiopian government would be spared the cost of prosecution in Addis Ababa. If it had been left to local police officials, both of the men would have been shot and killed immediately, no questions asked.

Jim Howard's body was flown back to Rhode Island for burial with a full military ceremony. His only living relative was a sister who lived in Warwick. She had been told the government would pay for all funeral expenses. Harry had hoped to be back to attend the ceremony which was scheduled for June 30th at St. Matthew's in Lincoln. Fr. Merrill would be saying the Mass. Fr. Merrill had taken the news of Jim's death badly, and wondered how long this one mistake he had made so many years ago would continue to torment him.

For Harry, there was still a lot of work yet to be done. He had called Françoise in Banra, but used a different name. To Françoise, whose telephone still had the bugging device, this meant she should return the call immediately from a different phone line.

Harry informed her, "Your Highness, Jim Howard was killed protecting Carlo, but his death was not in vain. I hope to finally end this soon and will arrange for your two sons to reunite with you."

"Oh, I am so sorry, Mr. Esten. This is all my fault. I never thought it would be so difficult to get to know my sons," Françoise confessed.

When he heard the news, Ahmad was pleased but all the more curious as to whom in Khatamori had caused all this grief. Harry had not divulged the name of Rafick Talon in his conversation with Françoise, and this was deliberate. He had his own plan on how to handle this situation, and the fewer people who knew, the better.

His flight to Oman from Ethiopia would take six hours and would involve one connection in Muscat. He arrived in Salalah, Oman late Wednesday morning and rented a car at the airport. He drove to the port city of Salalah and registered at the Al Jabal Hotel under his code name, Brian McCann, a supposed shipping executive working for Maersk Ltd.

Harry walked into the lounge at the hotel with a record-ing machine hidden in a briefcase. He tested the device by sitting in different areas of the lounge to be sure it clearly picked up conversations. The machine was placed on a stool at the bar and went undetected by anyone there. It looked like anyone's briefcase placed beside him while ordering a drink.

Harry planned to record the conversation between Manouch Haddad and Rafick Talon whenever they met. He hoped it would happen this week, but the thought of having to wait for a subsequent Thursday, if no one showed up, was agonizing.

On Wednesday night, when he returned to his room, Harry played back the tape and could easily detect clear conversations from different locations in the lounge. The following morning, before the lounge was open for business and no bartender was on duty yet, Harry quietly positioned the recorder under a seat of a table near the back door. The recorder was capable of picking up a conversation from across a large room, and the lounge at the hotel was well within the range.

At two o'clock that afternoon, Rafick entered the lounge from the hotel lobby and ordered a drink from the bar. He sat down at a table nearby and waited. As if on cue, the bartender picked up the telephone located behind the bar and made an outgoing call. Within minutes, Haddad entered through a rear entrance with two bodyguards. It had not taken him long to replace the two that were left behind in Ethiopia.

"Ray, I have some news that will make you very happy. Those two sons are dead and so is Harry Esten. I didn't know those two guys were twins. Everything went as planned and we had no trouble. I believe I have a bonus coming for the FBI guy, as we agreed."

"That's great news, Manouch. Get me a copy of the news article in Ethiopia if you can. I want to be sure there are no slipups this time."

"No problem, Ray, I'll mail those to you in Banra as soon as I get a copy. How's Ishraq, Ray? Is she still happy working in Banra for the queen?"

"I saw her yesterday, Manouch, and she is very happy there."

"Those telephone devices I gave you about a month ago, was she the one who got to put them in the queen's telephone?"

"If it wasn't for her, Manouch, I wouldn't have had the information about Ethiopia."

"So you saw her yesterday?"

"Yes, yes, why?"

"Because I know you're lying to me, you little shit. You didn't see her yesterday because she's not been seen by anyone for over a week now. I heard they found the wiretap and she hasn't been seen since. If anything's happened to her, Ray, you're a dead man. I'm coming to Banra tomorrow, and I expect to see her, even if it's only from a distance. You'd better not be lying to me."

"I swear to you, Manouch, she is fine. What time will you be in Banra and I'll bring her to you?" Rafick inquired.

"Be on Al Hilal Street near the Yahala Restaurant around one o'clock. After I see her, you won't hear from me again, Ray, as long as Ishraq isn't harmed. I have people watching out for her. Are we clear on that?"

"We'll be there, not to worry," Rafick answered.

Following the brief meeting, Rafick jumped into his Jeep and headed back toward Banra, not exactly certain yet how he would handle Haddad the following day. Haddad had to be eliminated since he now was the only link between the recent killings and himself. Once Haddad was out of the way and the two sons were no longer a threat, so he thought, he could work on getting back on good terms with Ahmad. Rafick started to believe again that the eventual throne might be his after all. But first things first.

Not soon after Rafick left the hotel in Salalah, Harry retrieved the hidden briefcase and went straight back to his room to replay the tape. Everything he wanted to hear was loud and clear. He called Françoise, and following their telephone routine, she called him back immediately.

"I have positive proof with me of who is behind all these attempts and I'll be at the palace late tonight. Please tell Ahmad the news, and I hope we can meet immediately when I get there."

"We will be waiting for you, Mr. Esten."

Harry checked out of the hotel at four o'clock and headed south toward Khatamori, a three-hour drive away. He arrived in Banra, got directions from a local citizen on getting to the palace, and his car approached the guarded gates shortly thereafter. Harry flashed his FBI credentials which had his photo on them and was escorted by two guards to a private entrance in the palace. Once inside, he was greeted by Kaleel.

"Mr. Esten, I cannot tell you how good it is to see you again. After the episode in Boston last year, the king is truly indebted to you. We were sorry to learn of the explosion that destroyed your home in America, and of the recent killing of your friend, Mr. Howard. Ahmad still cannot believe all this violence has occurred. The queen and Ahmad are waiting for you in the gardens."

Harry was carrying his briefcase as Kaleel led him through a maze of corridors and rooms leading eventually to the exit to the gardens at the rear of the palace. Harry definitely was in awe at the opulence displayed throughout the palace.

Ahmad and Françoise were admiring the setting sun from two arm chairs, each nursing a glass of red wine. It was peaceful and Ahmad's favorite place to be after dinner each night. His kidney transplant had been well-received, and other than anti-rejection medication, his kidneys were functioning quite well. Still, at age seventy-one, he often tired quickly and was not making as many public appearances as he normally would. Françoise, at fifty-six years old, could see their age difference beginning to show.

Harry approached the royal pair and was presented to them by Kaleel who sang the highest praises about him.

"Ah, Mr. Esten, we are so pleased to welcome you to our home and to Khatamori," Ahmad said as he extended both hands in friendship. Françoise smiled broadly as she too was quite pleased to see Harry again.

"Was your flight from Ethiopia comfortable?" Ahmad asked.

"I didn't come directly from Ethiopia, Your Highness. I drove from Oman this afternoon. There was much news I couldn't tell you about on the telephone, just to be sure. My sources led me to Oman, where Manouch Haddad was going to from Ethiopia after he escaped from us yesterday. I was told he always met his contact from Banra in Salalah on a Thursday, and that is today. But first, I must tell you, your sons are safe and are both anxious to come here to meet both of you. It might be beneficial if somehow Fr. Merrill were here too when that happens, because Carlo will either be in Italy or still in Ethiopia for a while, and will unlikely be able to meet Fr. Merrill otherwise. If all goes well in the next few days, this mess may finally be over with and the meeting with your sons could happen in a week or so, if this is acceptable to you," Harry explained.

"Did you say that Robert was with Carlo in Ethiopia?" Françoise asked.

"Yes, they have met and seemed to hit it off very nicely until the attempt to kill them in Mekelle."

"I am deeply troubled by your loss of Mr. Howard, Mr. Esten. I cannot express how sorry I am for having caused all this trouble," Françoise's voice shook and her eyes welled up with tears.

Ahmad reached over to her and gently placed his arm on hers as he spoke. "I cannot speak for my wife, Mr. Esten. She has always had a mind of her own, as far back as when we first met in 1956 in Paris. I can tell you though, there is nothing more I wish for than to see the pain lifted from her heart once and for all, for something that happened so long ago. We cannot undo what happened, but we can now at least try to make peace with these boys for however much time we have left on this earth," Ahmad said.

"Now, Mr. Esten, your news?" Françoise asked excitedly.

Harry picked up his briefcase, pulled out a portable recorder, and placed it on the table near their wine glasses.

"This is the meeting I taped today at the Al Jabal Hotel in Salalah. Tell me if you recognize who one of these men is?"

Harry pressed the play key on the recorder and the recorded message came through loud and clear. Ahmad and Françoise merely shook their heads as they had Harry replay the message over and over.

"It is no use, Mr. Esten, as much as I would like to say I do not recognize whose voice this is, it would not be true. To know Rafick is involved in treachery and murder is very disappointing to anyone in the royal family. He shall stand before me in the morning," Ahmad stated with a look never before seen by Françoise. There was so much hatred and sorrow in his eyes. She was afraid that he would become ill over this news.

"Hold off on that for now, Your Highness, because I believe Haddad will also be here tomorrow. Haddad has heard of Ishraq's disappearance. It seems he has people keeping an eye out for her here in Banra. They must report back to him from time to time on how she is. Rafick, or Ray as Haddad calls him, told Haddad he had seen Ishraq yesterday, and this is unlikely unless he is hiding her. Either way, if she is still alive and Rafick brings her to the Yahala Restaurant tomorrow afternoon, we might be able to get all three of them at once. In the meantime, I would make sure someone is watching Rafick at all times. He might be getting ready to leave Khatamori quickly rather than getting caught by Haddad and his men."

"Kaleel has had two security officers watching him day and night since he was suspected of being involved in the explosion of your home late last year." Ahmad called over to Kaleel who was standing away from the conversation but was familiar with the king's sign to come forward.

"Kaleel, what is the latest information you have on Rafick?" Ahmad asked.

"He is still at his home at the moment, Your Highness. He returned from a trip to Salalah at about five o'clock today. While he was there, he met with a man in the lounge of the Al Jabal Hotel and they left. We have a photo of the men he met, taken outside the hotel as the men were leaving. We are now trying to find out who these men are."

"Do you have that photo available?" Harry asked.

Kaleel left the gardens for just a short time, then returned with a folder which contained several photos of Haddad, some with the two associates captured in Ethiopia and the more recent ones with two other associates.

"Your Highness, this is the assassin, Manouch Haddad. This is the man Rafick is talking to on the tape and the one responsible for all these acts of violence."

"Kaleel, have several more men watch Rafick tonight. Be sure they are not seen. If his father before him had an escape route from his home, it would not surprise me if Rafick also will try to sneak away in the night."

Kaleel left immediately to carry out Ahmad's instructions.

* * *

Ishraq had been a petite woman, no more than five feet tall and very thin. As custom would have it, many women in Khatamori still covered their head and face when walking in public places. They would remove the front veil if they entered a restaurant or met others in a more private setting. Revealing the head and face was no longer considered a crime, one of the more modern rules that Françoise had pushed for several years earlier. While many men considered this practice sacrilegious, they nevertheless accepted the change because it came from the queen.

Rafick summoned one of his house servants who was about the same stature as Ishraq, and he asked her to accompany him on some business the next day in the center of Banra. Since he did not want others spreading rumors about him with a woman, he asked the servant to cover her head and face before they left. The innocent servant gladly agreed to do so. He next called three of his security guards and told them of his meeting on Friday with Haddad, who likely would not be alone. Rafick alerted his men that Haddad and his associates would definitely be armed and within sight of Haddad at all times. He told them that if Haddad so much as stepped toward the restaurant he was entering with the servant, they should open fire on him and his men. They understood clearly and would position themselves in the area long before the anticipated meeting at one o'clock.

Françoise insisted Harry stay at the palace that night, and after hinting that he had not eaten anything since noon in Oman, was brought enough food in his room to feed a whole family. After nibbling at some of what was offered, Harry was content to relax with a few glasses of the red wine which accompanied the food. He sat on the bed to take off his clothes, but he quickly fell asleep, still fully dressed. Tomorrow would be a busy day and their plan of action had been decided on.

CHAPTER 20

Harry was dressed in a long white robe and wore a turban around his head. His revolver was tucked underneath the robe, out of sight. At noon, he sat at a table, outside at a café, across the street from the Yahala Restaurant. He was accompanied by two of Ahmad's security officers dressed in robes like him. They ordered coffees and a light lunch. It was not their intention to attract anyone's attention. Several other tables were occupied by shoppers and workers from the area who sat for lunch as well.

In the alley behind the Yahala were two more of Ahmad's men, dressed with white aprons and smoking cigarettes, posing as workers on a break from the restaurant. Further down the street, at yet another café, were two more of Ahmad's men serving as waiters at tables. The area crawled with Ahmad's men to ensure no one escaped.

Rafick's men were seen by the guard who sat sitting with Harry, and he casually told Harry of their location. The bulge under their robes clearly indicated they were armed, likely with automatic weapons.

At ten minutes before one, Harry spotted Haddad, with his two associates, standing in front of a shop, right next door to where he and Ahmad's men were sitting. Harry quickly lowered his head and turned slightly away from Haddad and his men, and motioned to the guards to let him know the moment Haddad headed toward the restaurant.

Rafick entered the square with the veiled servant and headed directly toward the Yahala Restaurant. Harry was told of Haddad's movement when he started to cross the street toward the restaurant. Ahmad's two security guards and Harry immediately rose and casually started walking toward the shop next door. In seconds, they had guns pointed at Haddad's two men. They were ordered to fall to their knees, and the guards disarmed them.

The commotion caused a mild panic among the bystanders. As Haddad crossed the street, he realized what had just occurred, and knew at once he had been set up. He rushed into the restaurant, right on the heels of Rafick and the female servant.

Rafick's men saw Haddad run into the restaurant, but also saw his associates on the ground. Ahmad's men removed their robes to reveal their uniforms. The crowd quieted down once they realized they were Banra security. Rafick's men were confused as to what to do next, so they headed for the restaurant to protect Rafick. They were immediately confronted by several more of Ahmad's men coming from all directions, with guns pointing at them. One of Rafick's men began to run toward the entrance of the restaurant in spite of the shouts for him to stop. The security force opened fire on him, and he fell to the ground motionless. The other Rafick guard dropped his weapon and raised his hands.

Harry had made his way to the restaurant, where Haddad could be seen through the glass window holding a gun pointed toward the rear of the restaurant. Other patrons began to run out of the restaurant, screaming as they fled.

Rafick stood behind the servant, and held a gun to her head as he faced Haddad.

"You can't get rid of me that easy, can you, Ray?" Haddad said as he slowly began to approach them.

"I kept my word, Manouch. Your daughter is here. What more do you want from me?" Rafick sneered.

"You may have my men, Ray, but if you want to live, you'll show me my daughter and remove the veil."

"Please do not shoot me, I am not your daughter, just a poor servant following his orders," the servant pleaded as she ripped the veil off her face.

"Hiding behind her won't help you now will it, Ray?" Haddad said as he aimed his gun right at them.

Suddenly, two shots were fired through the glass window and Haddad fell to the floor without firing a shot. Harry entered the doorway to the restaurant, his gun still drawn, as he faced Rafick.

"Let her go, Rafick, it's me you want. I'm Harry Esten. I'm the guy who shot your chicken-shit father last year. I'm the one you want to kill, not her," Harry said as he quickly hid from behind the tipped restaurant table he used for a shield.

Rafick opened fire on Harry while still hiding behind the servant.

"Ahmad's men are all around the restaurant, Rafick. There's nowhere to go. And unless you've got more weapons on you, they'll just wait until you're out of bullets."

Rafick was confused and began to panic. He looked out the restaurant and all he could see were security people with guns drawn. For an instant, he lost his grip on the servant's arm and she fell to the floor. As Rafick turned to grab the servant, Harry shot once and hit Rafick in the shoulder. When Rafick and his gun hit the floor, Harry quickly moved forward, kicked the gun away, and pointed his revolver directly at Rafick's face.

"This is for Jim Howard," he said as he cocked the firing pin and aimed right at Rafick's head.

For the longest time, he stood there, ready to fire, but unable to pull the trigger.

"He is not worth it, Mr. Esten," Kaleel said as he entered behind Harry. "He will not harm anyone any longer, I can promise you that. Let us deal with him now."

Never before had Harry wanted to kill someone as he did now. The thought of letting Rafick live, even for now, never entered his mind. Then logic set in. Harry lowered his gun and collapsed into a chair nearby as a swarm of officers grabbed Rafick, attended to the bleeding from his shoulder, and led him out to a waiting ambulance.

"Thank you, sir, for saving my life," the servant cried as she approached Harry with tears in her eyes.

"You're welcome," Harry responded with tears in his own eyes. She was escorted out of the restaurant, and would be questioned to be certain that she was an innocent servant just accompanying Rafick that day.

Kaleel put his hand on Harry's shoulder to comfort him. "Come, my friend, it is over, it is time to go home."

CHAPTER 21

The headline on the article on page three of the July 5 New York Times read:

Traitor to Royal Family Executed

At noon on July 5, Rafick Talon was executed before a firing squad in Banra, Khatamori, the oil-rich Middle Eastern country, north of Saudi Arabia. King Ahmad Maurier ordered the execution of Talon after he was unanimously found guilty by a tribunal for assassination attempts against members of the royal family, and for the brutal murders of two civilians in their nation. The royal family members involved were not disclosed. Talon was the son of Answa Talon, a cousin of the king and head of the Khatamori security forces, who died last year in the line of duty.

Bob and Carlo were still in Ethiopia on that day in early July, but were preparing to fly to Khatamori for the meeting with their birth mother. Françoise had pleaded with Harry to remain at the palace in Banra until the sons arrived. She knew all too well this meeting would never have been possible were it not for Harry. After continuous prodding from both Françoise and Ahmad, Harry reluctantly agreed, but stated he would schedule himself on a flight to Paris the day after the twins arrived. He was exhausted from this ordeal. It had taken its toll on him. He kept thinking about Jim Howard, and how he should have been at his funeral the week before.

The twins were expected on July 7th, and Françoise was a bundle of nerves anticipating their arrival. Ahmad noticed the change in her behavior immediately following Harry's announcement of the arrangements for them to be transported to Banra after having called John Froment at the embassy in Addis Ababa. Françoise sensed she might finally begin the reconciliation with her two sons, however long it took. She sent Fr. Merrill plane tickets to Khatamori through a travel agency in Rhode Island. The return flight was not until a week later, but Françoise had not received word from him as to whether he would be on the booked flight. She had earlier sent him a fax notifying him of the reunion in Banra. She was still uneasy calling him by phone to make such a request. It would be unfamiliar ground for him, and she was not quite sure how he would react to the invitation.

Harry had given the royal couple the most recent picture of the sons, taken together in Mekelle by Rachel before the explosion occurred. Fortunately, her camera was in her purse behind her chair that night, and the camera survived the blast. Ahmad and Françoise could not tell one from the other, nor could Harry.

The seventh of July finally arrived, and Françoise was up by five o'clock that morning, having tossed and turned in bed the whole night long. She was so nervous, all she could eat at breakfast was a small piece of pita bread with a cup of tea.

The 9:00 a.m. flight from Ethiopia to Banra, by way of Dubai, would take nearly six hours in all, and Françoise would be there to welcome them. She would greet them outside the terminal as they debarked from the plane's staircase. She did not want to bring attention to the twins by appearing in the terminal where curious onlookers would surely gather to see who the queen was greeting. By two o'clock, she was ready to go. Ahmad was there to try to calm her, and even offered to go with her if she wanted him to. She knew all too well Ahmad's appearance at the airport would immediately draw the attention of everyone there, precisely what she was trying to avoid.

"Wish me well, Ahmad, I am heading on the longest journey of my life right now. I want them to be a part of our lives, something they should have been long ago. Perhaps God has forgiven me, Ahmad, we shall see."

"You are a good woman, Françoise, you have changed the way all women in Khatamori are treated and respected, something which has not been done since my father used to tell me of what my mother wanted to do so long ago. That is why my father liked you so much, because you reminded him of my mother. This is why I love you even more now than ever. You are trying to make things right."

They hugged each other so tenderly that Françoise almost forgot she had to leave.

At three o'clock, the Emirates Airlines connector from Dubai landed at the Banra Airport. Since it was a small jet, the debarkation was made by using a rolling staircase and the passengers would walk a short distance outside to a lower terminal door.

The royal family's limousine was parked to the side of this entrance, and barely visible to anyone looking out the glass terminal windows on the upper level. Françoise stood inconspicuously behind the limousine until she caught a glimpse of Robert and Carlo, each walking with a small carry-on shoulder bag. She gasped, held her hand to her mouth, and motioned to Kaleel.

He too was surprised by what he saw. He began walking toward them.

"You are Robert and Carlo from the United States and Italy?" he asked.

"Yes, we are, so happy to meet you," Carlo answered.

Bob's hearing was almost completely restored, but he still occasionally had a ringing sensation in his left ear. Consequently, he did not initiate too many conversations.

"Please, would you follow me, the queen is waiting for you," Kaleel added.

As if suddenly making a cameo appearance on stage, Françoise emerged from the shadow of the limousine as her two sons approached.

"Hello, Robert, so very pleased to see you again," she said as she instinctively looked directly at Bob.

She then looked directly at Carlo, smiled faintly as she approached him and said.

"You then must be Carlo, who I had named Charles Andre when you were born. I am your natural mother,

Françoise Dupont, and now Queen Farah of Khatamori. I am so pleased to meet you at last."

"Hello, I am happy to meet you as well. This is all so unbelievable to me that I'm afraid I still don't understand it much," Carlo replied.

"Come, let us leave for our home in Banra. We can talk much more on the way. Then you shall meet my husband, Ahmad, who is the king here, and a wonderful man. Kaleel will see to any other luggage you have and bring it later," Françoise said.

They all entered the limousine, which was escorted out of the airport by two other vehicles with security guards. When the limousine approached the main gate to the palace grounds, each of the sons looked out the car windows at the huge stone structure. They were in awe at the massiveness of the palace. Françoise had briefly reviewed what had happened years ago, and how she struggled to survive on her own after their birth. She had regretted giving them up for adoption, but now wanted to make things right again. She mentioned she in no way was ever going to replace the love and care their parents had given them.

As they exited the limousine, Françoise had one of the servants lead them to their rooms. A half hour later, they would be escorted to the palace gardens to meet her husband.

Bob and Carlo settled into their rooms, and shortly after their arrival, their luggage was brought to them. Bob and Carlo each walked outside to their separate terraces to the rear of their rooms. They gazed out at the manicured grounds below. In the distance, they could see a figure walking slowly in the gardens. Then they saw Françoise approach this individual, kiss him gently and take his arm as they walked together.

Exactly thirty minutes later, there was a knock on each bedroom door, and the twins followed Kaleel to the gardens. Françoise saw them and approached them first. She turned to Ahmad and introduced them.

"So, these are your sons from long ago. I must say this has been quite a journey to find you. I am happy to see you have met each other before today, and hope you can get to know each other much more now that you know you are brothers. How I wish I had had a brother."

A few minutes later, Harry Esten appeared in the garden, and was warmly greeted by everyone there. Harry finally had something to smile about as he truly enjoyed this moment. He felt complete in what he had been able to accomplish. He now realized his work here was done, and he could return home with a sense of relief. He told all of them it was time for him to go home.

"How can I ever repay you for what you have done?" Françoise asked.

"Your Highness, I am anxious to see how my new home is coming along and I just want to get back to my position with the FBI once I am settled again. Your thanks and good wishes are all I want, and just keep me informed from time to time on what's happening," Harry responded.

Bob and Carlo thanked Harry for bringing them together. With all the good wishes, Harry bid farewell and asked for a ride to the airport for a seven o'clock flight to Paris. He would then take a direct flight to Boston the following day and expected to be back in Providence by July 9th.

An hour later, Kaleel approached Françoise and whispered in her ear. She looked up at him and immediately rose to her feet and excused herself to Bob, Carlo, and Ahmad. She hurried down the walk to the palace door and disappeared.

Moments later, she reappeared in the gardens leading Fr. Merrill toward the others.

"I believe the two of you have met, Robert, but not Carlo. Carlo, may I introduce you to Fr. Richard Merrill. Fr. Merrill is your natural father, Carlo."

Carlo rose to his feet and shook Fr. Merrill's hand as he was still amazed that his natural father was a priest.

"I am so happy to learn that you are alive and well, Carlo, and that you and Bob have found each other. I did not know I was the father of two sons until some months ago. Since I found out, I have done everything I could to find you both. Bob, I'm very sorry our first meeting went so badly, and I hope we can get to know more about each other."

"Fr. Merrill, I was the rude one the last time we met. I behaved badly, not you. I regret that, and realize you could not deal with this when you didn't even know I existed. I would like a chance to know you better as well," Bob replied.

"I would like that also," Carlo echoed.

CHAPTER 22

The trip back to Providence was uneventful for Harry, an unusually quiet end to roller coaster weeks from one country to another. His bus ride to Providence from Logan Airport in Boston took about an hour. The bus pulled into the downtown terminal around four o'clock in the afternoon, and he walked to the Bureau office nearby. Frank Cabral greeted him as he entered the office and immediately offered Harry his condolences on the death of Jim Howard. He told Harry he had attended the funeral in Lincoln at Fr. Merrill's church, and he noticed Laura Broadbent was there as well. Cabral told Harry she was very worried about his safety and was anxious for him to get back to the States.

"Something going on between you two, Harry?" Cabral asked.

"Sort of, Frank," Harry smiled. "She's brought me back to life. I can't bring back Lucy, and I'm certainly not ready to pack it in at my age. So, I think I've found someone I'd like to spend a lot of time with, and I think she feels the same way."

Harry was able to sign out a Bureau vehicle and decided to head for Narragansett. He knew that Laura would not be home yet, so he headed for his beach property to see how the new house was coming along. As he approached his street, he couldn't believe how beautiful the house looked. It was ready for occupancy. He peered through some of the windows on the first level, he could hear voices from inside the house. When he turned the door handle, the door was unlocked and he went in. He yelled out to see who was there and out came his contractor with one of the painting subcontractors.

"Harry, when did you get back? Am I glad to see you! That woman's been on my back every day now, and I can't move any faster," the contractor stated.

"By that woman, you aren't by any chance talking about Laura Broadbent, are you?" Harry asked.

"Yes, that's her. When she comes in here with her police uniform on, it's kind of intimidating. But, I must admit, she does get my attention."

The contractor told Harry that the house would be done in a week. He said he would have a punch list and the final bill to him then, and a certificate of occupancy would be issued by the town. Harry's insurance would pay for most of the house's construction costs, leaving Harry with about a $100,000 mortgage. He was pleased to hear this, and before he headed for Laura's house at Bonnet Shores, he decided to take a short walk on the beach. He wanted to see the view of the house from the beach. There were people on the beach. Suddenly he realized it was July, and beachcombing was in full season.

He absolutely loved what he saw. In the next moment, he turned toward the ocean, sat himself down in the sand, and just gazed at the horizon in front of him.

"Hello, stranger," the voice came from behind him. It was Laura. As the contractor was leaving, Laura had appeared, and was told by him that Harry was back and was down at the beach.

"Boy, am I glad to see you. This has been one hell of a week. It felt like a year," Harry said as he turned, rose to his feet, and kissed Laura as hard as he could before hugging and squeezing her tightly.

"I know, Harry, your boss kept us informed every time he had more news. I'm so sorry about Jim," Laura said.

"Yes, me too. I heard you represented me at the funeral, thanks. I really wanted to be back for that."

"How did it finally turn out? Did the boys go to meet their mother?"

"Yes, that's finally over, and Fr. Merrill was there too," Harry answered.

"I know, Harry. He called me to tell me he was going to Khatamori a few days ago. It was kind of a strange conversation though. He wanted to know who you were dealing with for the house, the name of the bank you were using. I don't know what that was all about, but I told him anyway. Maybe he wanted to see if you were using the same bank his church uses or, if you didn't have one yet, he might have had somebody to recommend."

A week later, Harry walked into the Washington Trust Bank in Narragansett for the closing on the house. The

mortgage lender had a pile of documents for Harry to sign
involving title insurance, property restrictions and regula-
tions from the town, release forms for all the subcontractors, and other such documents. When the process was
nearly complete, the lender grabbed an inked stamp pad
and pressed down on the closing document "Paid in Full".

"What's this all about?" Harry asked. "The balance due
at the closing was $102,545, which was automatically going
to be converted into a twenty-year mortgage. We agreed on
this earlier."

The lender handed Harry an envelope which he had
been instructed to give to him that day. Harry opened the
envelope.

My Dear Mr. Esten,

*You have brought joy to our home for which we shall be eter-
nally grateful. I have brought you nothing but pain and grief during this time. I can never erase the sorrow of losing a friend, but I
can at least try to bring joy into your new home in the future. My
sons are alive today because of you, and for this, no sum of money
is enough. Ahmad and I have paid this debt on your home as a
small token of our appreciation to you. We hope you will return to
Khatamori someday.*

Françoise and Ahmad

Laura and Harry met at the new house at noon, and
Harry had bought lobster rolls at George's in Galilee, and
a bottle of white wine. They sat on two lawn chairs on the
second level deck overlooking the ocean. Harry told Laura
about the gift from the king and queen, and she now understood why Fr. Merrill had asked questions about the bank.

Harry looked at Laura, put his wine glass down, and
said, "Laura, this house is much bigger than my old one, I
can't live here alone. I don't want to live here alone."

"What are you saying, Harry?" she looked at him seriously.

"I'm saying I'm falling in love with you, Laura, and I want to spend much more time with you, here in this house. And, if it goes the way I think it's headed after a few months, maybe we can talk about what's next for us.

"Harry Esten, you are the nicest man I have ever met, and I've met a lot of men. I will move in with you on one condition, no more hunting for lost sons in Africa," Laura replied as she lifted him to her with a smile on her face and tears flowing down her cheeks.

CHAPTER 23

In November, 1988, Carlo had decided to end his stay at Mekelle Hospital and return to his home in Orvieto. He had not been home for three years and he missed the vineyards and the town dearly.

His Aunt Lucia had arranged for Carlo to join her at her practice near Orvieto Hospital. Carlo would perform surgeries at the hospital after Lucia had arranged for him to be added to the hospital staff. Lucia was a member of the hospital's board of trustees and the respect she commanded made Carlo's appointment easier.

The World Health Organization had assigned a new AIDS doctor from the United States to relieve Rachel of her duties in Ethiopia as well. The widespread increase of AIDS required a larger staff in Ethiopia, and Rachel was burned out after three years of dodging other illnesses in the villages, avoiding the continued threats posed by rebels as she rode from village to village, and the drudgery of a seven-day schedule.

Carlo and Rachel had discussed their future plans, and although marriage had been talked about, she wasn't ready to live in Italy when her family lived quite well in South Africa. She too had been offered a position as a resident at the Dr. Yusuf Dadoo Hospital in Krugersdorp, and had not decided whether she should accept the position or not. The residency wasn't until January, so she had time to decide. Carlo was not pleased with her decision and invited her to at least consider visiting him in Italy at the end of the year. She told him she would think about it. It was typical Rachel, an independent thinker and decision-maker. She would go to visit Carlo in Italy only if she really wanted to. No amount of pressure from Carlo would convince her otherwise.

Their farewell in early December was very tearful and neither wanted to admit their relationship was coming to an end. Ironically, on her flight back to Johannesburg, all Rachel could think about was Carlo, not her parents in Krugersdorp, not her upcoming position at the hospital, not even the thought of spending time at the family beach house, something she always cherished when in Ethiopia.

She needed time to think things through before deciding to visit Carlo in Orvieto. What had started out three years earlier as nothing more than a good friendship between two doctors, had gradually turned into an on-again, off-again intimate relationship. Rachel had never seriously been involved with another man before. She was always content to focus on her career and the joy it brought to her.

As her plane landed in Johannesburg late that day, her parents were there to greet her and were very pleased she was in good health and away from an area which still was awash with danger and rampant disease. While AIDS was still very much a part of her practice, she found herself leaning more toward pediatrics after having attended to so many afflicted children while in the Tigray region. Much of her work at Dr. Yusuf Dadoo Hospital would be in that field.

The holidays came quickly, and Rachel's mood was quiet and reserved as New Year's Eve arrived. Her parents noticed the change in her from a very bubbly and energetic person to one taking walks by herself on weekends along the shore near the family beach house in Richards Bay. The family always spent the holidays there, but this year her parents noticed that something was definitely troubling her.

"I think I love him, Dad. I didn't think I'd miss Carlo as much as I do. I miss his smile, his constant wise-cracks, the way I felt when I was with him, and how I felt when he was not there. The reunion with his long lost brother last June was unbelievable. I need to know if this is real, if he is the one I want to be with, wherever it is. I need to go to Italy, Dad. I don't want to go on like this, and I can't start at the hospital here until I know that it's really over between us."

"Rachel, your mother and I have been married now for nearly forty years and we've never been apart, not even for a day. It just never happened. So, being apart from Carlo the last few weeks might be telling you something. We've tried to raise you to think for yourself, and I think you do exactly that. What I say to you doesn't mean anywhere near as much as what you say to yourself. Either be done with Carlo or become one with Carlo, I don't think there are other options for the two of you. When will you leave for Italy?"

"Tomorrow, Dad, if I can get a flight to Rome. I don't know when I'll be back, maybe sooner than I think."

* * *

Carlo had just attended Mass with his parents in town, and was looking forward to their holiday dinner with his aunts. He, too, was not the same when he returned home several weeks earlier. It was not how he had expected or planned it to be. He had hoped to introduce Rachel to his parents with a grand announcement that they were to be married and she would go into practice in Orvieto too. He would also announce they planned to build a home on the vineyard property where Vito and Camille had been married years before, but there was no announcement because there was no Rachel by his side.

Carlo was sullen, always by himself, wandering about the vineyards, never quite focusing on the beauty before him. Camille could see the unhappiness in his heart, and she felt nothing but sorrow for her son's disappointment. Carlo had written to Rachel several times in the weeks since he had returned to Orvieto, but Rachel had not responded. Was it truly over? Were they destined to go their separate ways? Camille did not know.

Lucia had rented additional office space alongside her own and carpenters were busy constructing a connection between the two offices. Carlo had met with the head of the surgical department at the Orvieto Hospital and they seemed to hit it off well.

On January 5, 1989, Rachel's flight from South Africa landed in Rome at one-thirty in the afternoon. She rented a car, and after getting a road map from the attendant, began the drive south to Orvieto, about an hour away.

She entered the town, stopped at a gas station, and asked for directions to the Melucci Vineyard. Ten minutes later, she drove past the tree-lined entrance to the vineyard, passed the rows and rows of vines ahead, and arrived at the villa. She parked her car on the graveled area near the entrance and rang the doorbell.

Camille opened the door, stared at Rachel for a moment, then smiled.

"Hello, Rachel, I am so happy to finally meet you."

Rachel was stunned by the gracious welcome. "How do you know my name, I don't think we have ever met?"

"Oh, yes we have, in every letter we received from Carlo, every time he telephoned us, and all the pictures of you he sent us. We, Carlo's father and I, have known you for nearly three years, Rachel. We've just never spoken to each other before."

Camille extended her hand in welcome. "Come in, please, you must be tired from your journey."

Rachel shook Camille's hand, and the two of them entered the house and proceeded to the family room at the rear of the house. When Rachel entered and saw the view from the glass windows and Orvieto high up in the distance, all she could do was sigh.

"Oh, my, now I understand why Carlo always talks of his precious vineyards. What a magnificent view you have. That is Orvieto up there isn't it?" she asked.

"Yes, it is. That is where Carlo is today, getting ready to start his practice. And Vito, his father, is where he always is, somewhere out there in the vineyard."

"Perhaps I should come back when Carlo is here?"

"Nonsense. Let's have a cup of coffee or tea for now. Carlo will be back soon, I'm certain. You didn't come all this way to come back later. My son has told us so much about you, the work you do, and how much you care for people. He has also told me about your life in South Africa and how you helped him find his twin brother, someone we even haven't met yet. You lead a very busy life, Rachel, don't let it slip by too fast.

"Would you like to take a walk through the grounds of the vineyards by yourself before Carlo returns? I'm preparing dinner right now, and unless you like to cook, you might find the walk refreshing."

"I would like that." Rachel stepped out the back sliders to the patio which led to several paths in the vineyards. She made her way to the grotto where the wines were stored, and into a building where there were several vats for wine-making. The vastness of the property was overwhelming to her.

Twenty minutes later, Carlo arrived home, and asked his mother, as he entered, whose car was parked out front. Camille just smiled.

"There is someone here to see you. She is somewhere out there in the vineyard. I told her you would be home soon. She is very nice, Carlo."

Carlo dropped his shoulder bag to the floor, threw his car keys on the kitchen counter, and bolted for the rear of the house. His heart was beating so fast as he trotted down the vineyard path that he became out of breath.

Suddenly, about a hundred feet in front of him, Rachel appeared as she turned a corner walking back to the villa. When she spotted him coming, she began to run, she didn't know why, she just couldn't help herself. Carlo began to run faster, smiled and waved as she approached. Their bodies locked together as she wrapped her arms around him and cried.

"I thought I didn't want anything to complicate my life, Carlo, but I was wrong. I don't want to be without you, I don't care where it is. I love you, Carlo, please complicate my life."

Camille smiled as she watched the reunion from the glass window. Rachel would not be going home this day, and perhaps she finally was home. At dinner that night, Rachel met Vito and noticed how similar he and Carlo were, and how much love there was in the family.

They were to be married in June.

CHAPTER 24

On May 2, 1989, the Associated Press announcement appeared in the Boston Globe, the Corriere della Sera in Italy, and other major newspapers throughout the world.

Khatamori Has a New Ruler

King Ahmad Maurier, the ruler of the tiny oil-rich country of Khatamori, north of Saudi Arabia, died on May 1, at the age of 72. The late king's health had been failing in recent years and he underwent a kidney transplant in 1987 at Massachusetts General Hospital in Boston. Earlier this year, Maurier's transplant started to exhibit chronic rejection when the kidney became resistant to treatment. He is survived by his beloved wife, Queen Farah, the former Françoise Dupont of Paris, France. The royal couple had been married for thirty-one years and had no children. The new monarch is Jamal Talon, a second cousin to the

late king. Talon had been the guardian of the nation's oil industry and is highly respected by leaders of surrounding Arab nations. His brother, Nabil Talon, will now become the head of the oil operations. Queen Farah will continue in her role of promoting women's rights in the country but will be succeeded as the first lady by Talon's wife, Malika.

Bob and Carlo had each decided that, although they were pleased at knowing that Françoise was their mother, they wanted no part in being considered an heir to the throne, and preferred their connection to Françoise not be revealed to anyone else. As a result, Ahmad had discussed who should succeed him with Françoise and a tribunal of his most trusted advisors. He then put his selection in writing, to be opened only upon his death.

Her well-being would not be a problem as Ahmad's entire fortune would go to her, several hundred million dollars in assets held in various banks throughout the world. But he had decided that the royal palace should remain as such, and therefore, would become the home of his successor, should he desire it to be so. Jamal had made the choice to occupy the palace with the understanding that Françoise could remain there as well, for the rest of her life if she chose to stay.

This was a difficult decision for her, especially when she would go out to her terrace overlooking the gardens where Ahmad spent so much time, and where his body had been found the morning of May 1st. Françoise could not bear to continually remember that fateful day, every time she was there, and she decided to vacate her suite for another residence nearby. She also bought a large suite in a prestigious residential building in Paris, near her beloved Louvre.

Now that Ahmad had passed on, she was no longer restricted from travelling outside the country on her own, and since her two sons were outside of Khatamori, she planned to do exactly that.

Following a huge funeral procession throughout the streets of Banra, the coronation of Jamal as king was to take place on the steps of the palace grounds. There were thousands of well-wishers who were allowed entry onto the grounds, although security forces prevented anyone from entering the palace itself. Françoise had been asked by Jamal if she would do the honor of coronating him that day. His wife, Malika, had such high regard for Françoise that she had relinquished the honor to her rather than performing the coronation herself.

When she began to do the honors onto Jamal that day, the throngs of people attending applauded Françoise so loudly, it took ten minutes before the roar subsided enough for her to proceed with the coronation. Françoise, their beloved Queen Farah, was in tears as she waved and smiled faintly to her people. She would never forget the day.

CHAPTER 25

August in Orvieto is oppressively hot. Carlo's medical practice with his aunt, Lucia, was very busy and Carlo was even performing several operations per week either as the lead surgeon or assisting on other procedures. The upcoming wedding in Krugersdorp was scheduled for the tenth of the month and all preparations had been made. Rachel's parents had scheduled the reception after the wedding ceremony in Our Lady of the Holy Rosary Church at the Misty Hills Country Hotel, the largest banquet facility in the area.

Carlo's parents were flying with him to Johannesburg on August 1st and were staying at the Owens' residence at their insistence. His two aunts would arrive on the sixth and had reservations at The Westcliff Hotel in Johannesburg, about thirty miles away.

The Elliotts were scheduled to arrive in Johannesburg on Thursday, the seventh. Bob and Julie and their newborn baby daughter had reserved a two-room suite at the same hotel where Carlo's aunts were staying. Adjacent to their suite, Bob's parents and his brother Ben had their own two-bedroom setup. Lastly, Fr. Merrill, who was on the same flight with the Elliotts, had a room nearby. The Owens had reserved almost an entire floor for wedding guests.

Vito had asked his son if the Owens would be upset if he shipped twenty cases of the Melucci wine to Krugersdorp for the reception. Carlo told his father that Rachel's dad would be honored to serve the fine wine from the Melucci Vineyard. Carlo had sent them a case earlier in the year to make sure they liked it.

There were nearly three hundred guests expected to show up for the wedding, most of them from South Africa.

Harry and Laura had moved to the new beach house in Narragansett. Harry had received his invitation to Carlo's wedding in late June and replied that two people would be attending. He told Laura it was time that she finally met the cast of characters in all the recent events and they could extend their stay in South Africa after the wedding as a mini vacation.. Laura couldn't wait. They were the last to arrive, and they too occupied space in the hotel set aside for the wedding guests.

A small rehearsal dinner had been arranged for the night before, which not only included members of the wedding party, but also included all the guests and relatives who had travelled from the United States and Italy. Missing from the group, and noticeably so, was Françoise. Everyone was certain the wedding was much too soon after Ahmad's death for her to attend. No one at the rehearsal dinner talked about it, nor was there any message from her to Carlo on this festive night.

Clearly, the buzz in the room was on Bob Elliott, and his uncanny resemblance to Carlo. Everyone there, however, already had been told the story about the adoption and how they eventually had found each other earlier that year. Carlo and Rachel believed it was better for everyone there to know who Bob really was, and what connection he had at the wedding. It still made for quite the side conversation at many tables at dinner.

On Sunday morning, August 10, the wedding ceremony was scheduled for ten o'clock with the reception immediately afterwards. Rachel acted like any bride, her hair wouldn't cooperate, her dress didn't look right, her shoes hurt, and on and on. Carlo was much more subdued, but still nonetheless showed signs of anxiety. He constantly looked down at his watch, paced the floor in the sacristy in the front of the church, and could be seen by guests peeking out toward the rear of the church on more than one occasion.

Our Lady of the Holy Rosary Church, a Catholic church, was first opened in Krugersdorp in 1891 and subsequently rebuilt in 1956. It was not an exceptionally big church, but easily could accommodate the estimated attendees at the ceremony.

The organ music in the background suddenly stopped, and immediately following a few seconds of silence, started up again with the wedding procession. Rachel looked beautiful as she began her long walk up the aisle, holding her father's arm as he proudly escorted her toward the altar. Carlo beamed. Rachel's father kissed her, handed her off to Carlo, who led her to the altar where the priest awaited them. Before the ceremony began, the maid of honor whispered in Rachel's ear,

"She is here, Rachel, it must be her. She is with a man in a turban, and they are sitting in the back of the church."

Rachel leaned over to Carlo and said, "The queen is here, Carlo, but she is sitting in the back by herself."

Carlo looked up at the priest and said, "Please, Father, just one more minute."

Carlo rose from his kneeling position and began walking down the center aisle of the church. This created a buzz throughout the guests who wondered what was happening. He spotted Françoise who tried not to focus on him, but she could not take her eyes off of him.

He approached her pew and extended his hand to her. "A mother should sit with her family when her son gets married."

Françoise, dressed in an elegant blue dress, blushed at Carlo's gesture, but took his hand as he escorted her to the row where Bob and Julie were seated. Bob smiled broadly, as did Julie, when she entered their pew. Bob leaned over to her, held her hands in his, and gently kissed her on the cheek. Carlo made his way back to the altar and told the priest they were now ready to begin. Rachel grabbed his hand and gave it a squeeze to convey her approval.

Following the ceremony, all the guests went immediately to the reception hall except Bob and Julie. They told Françoise that they would meet her at the reception in a short while, but needed to first make a stop along the way. They drove back to their hotel in Johannesburg and went directly to their suite where a hotel babysitter was watching over their infant daughter. Julie dressed her in a pink dress with a matching pink headband. They then returned to the reception hall.

The festivities had already begun, and guests were toasting the newlyweds when they entered the hall. On a table nearby, matchbooks were laid out with guests' names and table assignments. When Bob and Julie picked up their seating assignment, they were pleased to see they were seated with Bob's parents, his brother, and Françoise and her guest. Her guest was Kaleel, Ahmad's trusted advisor for over thirty years. He had asked Françoise if she wanted him to now serve her going forward. Françoise was shocked by his gesture. Kaleel himself was nearly as old as Ahmad had been. She realized he had served a member of the royal family for all these years, and gladly accepted his service. She now felt obligated to care for someone who had dedicated his life to her late husband. Harry and Laura completed the table and Harry was pleased to be in their company under such happy circumstances for a change.

Julie lifted her young daughter from the child seat the hotel had provided. The hotel had offered to care for the infant in a separate area away from the music and noise of the reception, assigning a nanny during that time.

Françoise spotted the child and her eyes lit up immediately.

"Robert, this is your child, your daughter?"

"Yes, Your Highness, this is our first child which, I guess, now makes you a grandmother, doesn't it?" Bob gave her a grin.

"And what is the name of your child, my granddaughter?"

Julie looked at her with a very sincere and loving look and simply said.

"Her name is Farrah, Your Highness, as in Queen Farah, but with two Rs. Bob and I hope you get to see her grow up over the years."

As Françoise held the baby, she beamed.

Later during the reception, Carlo could be seen dancing with Camille on the dance floor. Camille was then seen whispering in Carlo's ear and he nodded. He broke away from Camille, and Vito took over while Carlo walked directly to Françoise.

He then took her hand and led her to the dance floor despite her insistence that she had not danced in years. Carlo ignored her laments and put her clearly at ease as they moved about the floor.

She cried on Carlo's shoulder and then looked at him and said.

"I believe God has finally forgiven me, my son, I only wish Ahmad was here to see this."

"He is here, mia madre. He is looking down on us right now and smiling. He would not have missed this for the world."

ACKNOWLEDGEMENTS

I'd like to give special thanks to the following people, without whose help, *Dangerous Bloodlines* would have taken a lot longer to complete.

To Jennifer Givner at Acapella Book Cover Design for the incredible cover design; to my son, David Ayotte, for coming up with a captivating book title; and to my wife, Pauline Ayotte, for her vision for the cover of a spilled glass of red wine that fit nicely with the plot for *Dangerous Bloodlines* and the vineyard depicted in the book.

To my daughter, Barbara Ayotte, and to Christina Paul, for the fantastic copyediting and proofreading work. Your keen eyes make me look good.

To my daughter, Julie Ayotte, and her husband, Michael Healey, for providing me with voice recognition software to make my word processing of the manuscript easier.

And lastly, to Glenn Ruga, creative director and owner of Visual Communications and founder of www. SocialDocumentary.net, for his incessant critiques of the design and the presentation of the contents, and for his magnificent work on my new website, www.julienayotte. com. I am forever grateful.